I blushed very prettily as I curtseyed to young Mr Cl—t. And as I led him upstairs I prattled gaily, like the innocent he took me for. I told him I had no idea what we were going to do but Madame had assured me he was a kind, considerate young gentleman who would be a humane and generous guide to the arts of Venus — whatever they might be.

The second flight of stairs was narrower and I tripped demurely ahead of him so that his eyes were level with my derrière. I gave my buttocks a little squeeze at each tread to impart an extra shiver to my bustle which, in turn, made the flounces of my dress quiver delightfully. I have always found that a girl who makes proper use of the staircase in a House of Pleasure has half her work done before she even reaches her room . . .

The Ffrench House

Faye Rossignol

HEADLINE

First published in 1992
by HEADLINE BOOK PUBLISHING PLC

10 9 8 7 6 5 4 3 2 1

ISBN 0 7472 3732 8

Typeset by Medcalf Type Ltd, Bicester, Oxon

Printed and bound by
HarperCollins Manufacturing, Glasgow

HEADLINE BOOK PUBLISHING PLC
Headline House
79 Great Titchfield Street
London W1P 7FN

The Ffrench House

INTRODUCTION

[*The following is an abridgement of Charlotte ffrench's own introduction to the second volume of her memoirs — 3rd Edition, private press, Paris, 1913.*]

Volume Two already! And when I first set out to write this little memoir, I hardly thought I should fill *one* with what I had to say! My intention then was quite simple. When my fame as the proprietress and Madame of the Maison ffrench began to spread, people kept asking me the same questions over and over again until I grew weary with answering them: What is it like to work in a House of Pleasure? What sort of girls take up our ancient and honourable profession of harlot? What happens in a House when you close your doors for the night and all the patrons have gone home? What do you look for in a girl who applies to work for you? What advice do you give her about the business? What are the patrons *really* looking for? Tell me some of the dreadful (or funny, or bizarre) things that have happened at the Maison ffrench . . . And so on.

I thought if I could set down the answers in a little book, I could tell people where to buy it and I wouldn't be wasting my breath repeating the same tales, time after time. It started well enough, but I hadn't written more than a dozen pages before I realized that the bare answers would make no sense to people who knew nothing of my background and history. In other words, behind those superficial questions lay others of a deeper nature: Why, for instance, did I take up my profession in the first place? After all, I was the daughter of an Anglican bishop; I had been left a wealthy widow at the age of seventeen; I was surely the last sort of woman who would either desire or need to sell her favours for money. So why did I do it? And how did I form my ambition to build, own, and manage the finest House of Pleasure in the world — the Maison ffrench? How did I set about it? What experiences did I deliberately seek upon the way, which I might then apply in the management of my own House? And so forth.

The answers to those questions filled all of Volume One and are about to spill over into the first few chapters of this Volume Two, I fear. But be patient with me, Gentle Reader; I *shall* get to it anon!

If you have read Volume One you will know what an earnest and pious little girl I was until the age of sixteen or so. Superficially it must seem I have turned my back on all that, but I do not think I have; I do not even think I have forsaken my faith. Rather, I believe I have deepened my understanding of our human nature to the point where I comprehend our Creator's purpose a great deal better than many a dried-up old cleric. In *my* faith there are but two Commandments: Bring happiness to others. Enjoy yourself. To do either, or both, is to complete Life's purpose. And to complete Life's purpose is itself an act of worship.

You will know, too, how I was first awakened to these notions by my darling husband, Jack ffrench, the randiest colonel in the Indian army, who died on active service (very actively servicing me, in fact) in India. He left me his considerable fortune outright, which was a rare thing in those days, when the Married Women's Property Act had only just come into being and the average husband still considered a wife's property to be morally his, no matter what the law decreed. But Jack was cunning; he knew that the two great and unashamèd loves of my life are carnal pleasure and money. By leaving me rich, he made me a target for every fortune hunter in the kingdom; but he knew I would never marry again if it meant yielding, even in part, my control over my wealth. Yet nor could I return to the vestal life I had known as a spinster. I like to think he has been sitting up there in paradise all this while, with his seven well-satisfied houris at his side, watching my erotic progress and beaming down with approval.

Be that as it may, let me recall the early stages of that progress as swiftly as possible so that we may get on with the rest of it:

Jack no longer being around to assuage my desires, I had to resort to volunteers, of whom there was suddenly an inexhaustible supply; gentlemen who would consider a spinster maiden's virtue as sacred as their own honour would attack a widow's modesty with all the dashing élan that gave us Balaclava — especially if she were only seventeen years old and (though I say it myself) excessively pretty. For my part, I found these casual embraces utterly delightful.

Oddly enough, it was the first of my paramours — out in India, soon after Jack's death — who unwittingly pointed me along the path I was to follow. He was a captain in one of the irregular cavalry

3

regiments and we spent a delightful afternoon in bed together at a government rest house. Out of conscience, perhaps, he left a small pile of sovereigns in my holey of holeys, claiming it to be an excellent Malthusian remedy [*a contraceptive*]! I have never forgotten the deep, visceral rapture it gave me to turn those coins over in my hand, still hot and sticky with the libations of Eros with which he had anointed me. It forged an unbreakable link in my heart between men and the spending of the gold and the spending of their milt. To this day, after tens of thousands of such encounters, it is still a thrill to me to receive money from the hands of a man and then yield myself to that ultimate adoration of his body.

On my return to my parental home, the bishop's palace in Melchester, I became involved with good works — to wit, the rescue of "fallen women." Seventeen-year-old spinster-Charlotte had not even been allowed to know of their existence; seventeen-year-old widow-Charlotte was expected to play her part in such good works as a matter of course! Strange, indeed, are the ways of men!

One of those fallen women, Miss Lily de Mauny (or Sapphire, as I call her, because she is the sapphic jewel in my life), became my maid, companion, confidante, and lover — for I can love both men and women with equal abandon.

It was not long before the cloying, cloistered life of a small cathedral town palled on both of us. So, with Sapphire to assist and guide me, I took rooms in London and embarked upon the most ancient and noblest profession of all. She herself claimed to hate men too much (and not without cause) to join me on the sacrificial bed, where, four or five times a day, I enjoyed a fate worse than death and, thanks to my delicacy of manner, breeding, and beauty, earned another small fortune − all of which went into the safest of government stock. (I encountered many young females who were quite unsuited to The Life and sent them down to Melchester − which satisfied everyone there that I still trod the paths of Virtue!)

I enjoyed The Life mightily for several months. Among my lovers I had the good fortune to know Professor O'Brien, the world-famous anatomist, who taught me more about the intimate portions of the female body than most men would think it wise for a woman to know. Scarce a week has gone by since then without my blessing him for that instruction.

Even at that early date I knew I should one day create a House of my own, just as I knew that I had always been intended for this Life of mine and would die in misery if I did not die a harlot. So, when my darling Sapphire had to go and nurse a dying aunt, I seized the opportunity to work anonymously abroad − in Hamburg, in fact − in a variety of Houses, just to gain experience. My first was Plutos, a cheap house for sailors and working men, where I stayed for several months and "did" over a hundred customers each day.

It must sound like a living hell, but, apart from the appalling drudgery of satisfying so many men, I was actually quite happy there; certainly, I learned a great deal. I learned, above all, that if you keep the girls warm and comfy, feed them well, and treat them firmly but not as children − and give them the chance to earn lots of money − you'll hold on to them without any trouble and the House will be a happy one.

My second place of work (I will not call it House

of Pleasure) was Le Moulin, a "posher" establishment where we did *only* fifty-odd customers a day. There I learned that if you treat the girls as children and constantly pickpocket them with spurious "fines" and humiliate them with parades in front of the men and canings on the bare posteriors, you will have a miserable house full of lying, catfighting females who will cheat the customers and let you down at every opportunity. In short, it was a living hell, that place. However, all was not dark for it was there that I met my dear friend Gisela Fromm, who taught me so many things about our business and about whom you will hear much in the pages to come. She and I left Le Moulin together and went on to my third House, the Doves' Nest.

The clientèle there was very high tone — but not as rich as it liked to pretend. We girls still had to do more than a dozen men a day to make any sort of a living from our charms. There I learned that, for a girl to stay fresh and lively at this trade, and to enjoy it as much as her customers, though perhaps in a different way, she really ought not to be asked to gratify more than four gentlemen a day; but oh, what gratification each of those four would receive! I also learned that Sapphire was not the only woman whom I could love intimately and passionately — a discovery that led to the instant dismissal of Gisela and me from the Doves' Nest, where the proprietor turned out to be a surprising prude.

I being then unsure how Sapphire might take to the idea of a ménage à trois — her, me, and Gisela — we parted company, I to return to London, Gisela to continue her professional studies in Paris. By sheer chance (except that I believe we are always guided by

6

a wise Providence in such matters) my path crossed that of the Prince of Wales, or Bertie, as I soon had the privilege of calling him in intimate circumstances. In fact, it was a year before I became his kept mistress because, having tried me out once, he was convinced I was the lass to wean his eldest son, Eddie, away from his predilection for his own sex. (That doomed young prince later became Duke of Clarence and died tragically of the clap — though, I repeat, it was certainly not I who clapped him.)

Eddie put me up in a charming villa in Maida Vale, where most of the aristocracy keep their mistresses. There Sapphire learned that she was not as hostile to *all* men as her earlier dreadful experiences had led her to believe. And in Sapphire's arms (not mine) Eddie learned he was not so hostile to *all* females as his upbringing and natural bent had made him feel. Meanwhile, I entertained Eddie's circle of men friends right royally, and with such personal happiness that I became absolutely confirmed in my Four-Men-a-Day rule.

While at Maida Vale I also made friends of — though not in any carnal sense — a Miss Cynthia Morgan, mistress to a Scotch peer. She intrigued me because she behaved as if we girls were all as chaste as vestals. No indelicate word ever fell from her lips, no hint of how we earned our keep ever sullied her conversation. It was as if she simply could not face the truth about us and our way of life. And yet I sensed, beneath her frigid surface, a smouldering passion, an ardour that would be truly stupefying in its power and strength — if only I could find the key to unlock it. I knew direct assault would be hopeless but I found the secret at last, and quite by accident.

7

By then I was Bertie's mistress, Eddie having transferred his patronage to Sapphire, from whom I was, as a consequence, briefly estranged. With Bertie there was no question of pleasuring all his friends as well; that would have been lèse majesté of the worst kind – which everyone knew but me. So when I spent a wild and wonderful night with Clifford K—n, Lord K—n's son, HRH conferred upon me the Grand Order of the Boot. He was very decent about it, but utterly unyielding.

Clifford (about whom you will also be hearing a great deal) is really rather an awful fellow – as he himself admits. He's cocksure (in any sense you care to give the word), vain, idle, indolent, arrogant . . . also devilishly handsome, articulate, and simply magnificent in bed. He understands a woman's body better than any man I know apart from Professor O'Brien. He also knows all about men's lusts, however strange, and has the gift of making me understand them in ways that would be impossible without his help. Many of the best features of the Maison ffrench are, I gratefully admit, his ideas, taken up and acted upon by me (for, of course, *he* wouldn't lift a finger if he could find someone else to do it for him).

Anyway, with Clifford's help I wrote a letter of application to Mme de Marly, the châtelaine of the famous Numéro Douze, which was then considered (by its customers) to be the finest House of Pleasure in Paris, which is the same as saying it was the best in the world. And with Bertie's recommendation to back it, Madam could hardly refuse me. The same could not be said of Cynthia, who got wind of my intention, wrote an application to Mme de Marly off her own bat, and got accepted, too, without a hint of patronage.

We were both to begin our life of pleasure and pleasing at Numéro Douze on Monday the 1st of January, 1886. I was then almost twenty-one years old and I was going to pursue the profession I loved in what everyone told me was the finest House in all the world. I felt as if, indeed, I had all the world at my feet.

I suggested we should go to Paris in mid-December and have the most wonderful and extravagant Christmas ever before we went to work. Cynthia fell in at once with the notion, but I thought there was something odd and secretive in her manner — a feeling that strengthened as our departure drew near. Imagine my surprise when, on arriving at the Gare du Nord, I was greeted by none other than my own darling Sapphire, from whom I was still estranged! It was at once obvious to me that dear Cynthia had engineered this reconciliation. But more was to follow. Sapphire, in her turn, had heard of my brief attachment to Gisela Fromm, had sought her out in Paris, and had brought *her* to this rendezvous as well!

It now transpired that both of them, Sapphire and Gisela, had lately taken up with the Chevalier de St-X—, who always had his mistresses in pairs. He, it so happened, was down at his family estates in Périgord until well into January, so the four of us had the run of his magnificent apartments in the Faubourg St-Honoré until it was time for Cyn and me to go to work.

It was the most memorable two weeks of my life. We were surely four of the randiest girls who ever lived. And, unlike men, who, with few exceptions, have but two shots in their lockers and then must recover for twenty-four hours or die, we had a capacity for erotic pleasure that was as good as infinite. Also, as I pointed out in the concluding paragraphs of Volume I, those two weeks were the salvation of dear Cynthia. To quote my conclusion:

"The girl who stepped off the train with me at the Gare du Nord on that first evening was lamentably equipped to deal with life at Numéro Douze. A woman's emotional interior is like a garden. Leave it to Nature and all you get in the end is an impenetrable mess of thickets, thorns, and nettles. It is one of my profoundest convictions that the girl who has not explored her own nature, her feelings, her attitudes — and, indeed, cultivated them as the gardener cultivates his chosen plot — will find nothing but a bed of nails in a House of Pleasure. By contrast, the woman who has drawn out all the weeds, blunted the thorns, made straight all her paths — who *knows* herself up and down and through and through — will find there a life as rich and rewarding to her emotions as it surely will be to her purse.

"And during the last two weeks of that year of grace, 1885, we three experienced girls transformed Cynthia from the first sort of woman into the second. As we settled into the fiacre on New Year's Eve and gaily directed the driver, 'To Numéro Douze, Monsieur! To laughter and prosperity!' Cynthia knew her own carnal nature, its strengths and weaknesses, its pleasures and pitfalls, as well as she knew the lines in her own hand — as well as I knew mine. We could not wait to begin deploying that hard-won knowledge — in what all agreed was the finest House of Pleasure in the world."

It was the best of Houses; it was the worst of Houses.

However, its defects as "the finest House of Pleasure in Paris" did not become apparent to me for some weeks. I was young and giddy; I was in the gayest, most erotic city on earth; and Madame de Marly, knowing my connection with the Prince of Wales, was respectful and wary toward me to begin with. Also, the faults were not of the glaring kind I had experienced at Le Moulin in Hamburg, which any fool of a girl straight off a mountain farm would spot inside the first hour. No, the defects of Numéro Douze were deep and subtle.

There was no intimation of our future disquiet as Cynthia and I stepped down from our fiacre outside that stylish front door; our boxes had been sent on earlier that day, so we carried no baggage at all. To the world we must have seemed like two elegant young ladies who had innocently made an unfortunate choice of locations before which to alight. We stood a moment in silence and stared up at its gaslit exterior, trying to imagine what sort of life awaited us within.

Cynthia took one brief step toward the side entrance when I touched her arm and stopped her. "Just look at it a moment," I said.

"Why?" She was shivering with nervous anticipation and was eager to get indoors.

"You've never worked in a House before," I replied. "And here is the most glorious establishment in Paris. Look at it. Imagine you are a young man, absolutely burning with hunger for a woman. You're walking up the street and you pause here, just like us. You look up at the House, just like us. You see all those windows filled with soft, seductive candlelight. What pictures does it conjure up in your mind? What are you hoping to find when you get inside?"

She giggled. "A hundred young girls in a state of nature?"

"I don't think so. That picture in their minds, Cynthia, is all-important to us. It's what we've got to give them in reality when we open our own establishment one day."

"What d'you think they're hoping to find, then?" she asked.

"A sweet disorder," I murmured. "A confusion of shadows and lights, of rich furnishings, heavy drapes, and dimly lighted pools of mystery. And, here and there, glimpses of something almost unattainable — a sense of femininity that is, at one and the same time, both demure and erotic. Something secret and mysterious, tender and overpowering. Something they all sense every time they visit — but which they never can take away with them. All they carry away is a memory, a fading memory, which they must constantly return and renew between our thighs."

"Yes!" she whispered ecstatically. "Oh, Charlotte! You make it seem so . . ." The precise word escaped her.

We stood in silence awhile, contemplating the great mysteries of The Life we were about to assume.

Numéro Douze stood at the bend in the Chaussée d'Antin, just off the Boul' des Italiens in the Ninth Arondissement, conveniently near the Opéra. As its name implies, it was Number 12 in that street. The numerals stood out almost two feet high in the stained-glass fanlight over the front door. (Houses of Pleasure in Paris at that time were called "Big Number Houses" because they were always emblazoned with such large figures.) It had a tall, narrow, but extremely elegant façade which gave little hint of the size of the establishment behind it. In fact, it had once been a small town house with a large garden; now it was a large House of the Town with no garden at all.

What with the thoughts and imaginings that were now whirling through our minds, it was a thrilling sight to the pair of us, as we stood on the foot pavement, well wrapped up against the gently falling snow, clutching each other's arms like a pair of waifs, bathed in the warm, discreet illumination that seeped out from its curtained windows and struggled through the evening mist. It was New Year's Eve and the whole of Paris was bent on enjoyment of one kind or another − mostly of one kind, of course. The snow hushed the fall of feet and the rumble of carriages, so that even in our small byway of the city we could, from where we stood enraptured, hear the strains of at least three bands.

Loudest, of course, was the quartet which played nightly at Numéro Douze itself − waltzes, polkas, mazurkas, and gavottes . . . the gay melodies of Strauss, Offenbach, and Bizet filled the House while it was open for business.

Two laughing gentlemen, hot from some dancing establishment in the Boul' Montmartre, passed us at that moment, eyeing us curiously but not quite daring to speak. They trotted jauntily up the stairs of Numéro Douze, rang the bell, and were at once admitted by a maid in a black dress and starched apron.

Cynthia sighed. "How easy it is for men!"

"Oh, no!" I protested. "Do not envy them! Just think what it must be like to be such a wretched creature! Somewhere out there in Paris, at this very moment, there are a dozen gentlemen who are going to wake up tomorrow with the invincible compulsion to enjoy a girl. And all through the day, as the weary hours drag on, that itch, that craving, will plague them fiercely and yet more fiercely, until at last it almost drives them to distraction. And one by one they'll give in to it. They'll join a hundred others and make their way here to Numéro Douze."

As if to underline my words, three more gentlemen came down the street at that moment, from the direction of the Opéra. One of them, a tall young fellow with curly golden hair, cleared his throat and started to speak to us, but his companions pulled him away. They, too, rang the bell and were admitted immediately.

"See!" I said. "Seventy . . . eighty . . . a hundred! Who knows? But I'm just talking about one particular dozen or so — the gentlemen who will walk through that door tomorrow night and pick either you or me to take upstairs for a frolic in bed. Think of it, Cyn — they're out there now somewhere. And the dozen who'll follow them the day after tomorrow. And the dozen after that. Why, it's almost as if that soft, warm little paradise between our legs were sending out magnetic rays to them now! I often think of that, don't you? We don't need to do anything. We just sit there and send out the rays to attract them. Just the fact that we're there and available for their pleasure is enough. Like whipped curs they troop in and hand over their gold! Just think of that when one of them turns to you and says, 'Mademoiselle?' with that half-fearful lift of his eyebrows. Just think of the fever he's been in all day, tormented by that devil beneath his belly who has whipped him up those steps and through that door. It's a devil that will give him no peace until he has spent himself into us and his gold upon us! And then think how easy it truly is for us! All we need do is sit there, bathed in warmth and good music, while they troop in and volunteer to pleasure us by the dozen!"

"It's no pleasure if we don't like them," she said.

"Well, what's half an hour out of our lives — especially when compared with the hour we can take with the ones we do like!"

At that moment the golden-haired youth threw up one of the windows and called out to us. I blew him a kiss and we hastened to the side entrance of the establishment; it would never do to begin our careers in that illustrious institution by swapping banter from the foot pavement like a pair of common *putains!*

We had to knock twice before anyone answered — a cheeky young commis chef (for Numéro Douze served excellent meals, too). He said, "Oh, two more saucy little *filets mignons*, eh? Are you expected?"

I replied that we were.

He directed us down the passage, which was but dimly lighted, to the third door on our left round the corner. La Marly would come to us when she had a moment — if we were still there, he added enigmatically.

The waiting room was where Madame interviewed all hopeful candidates for a horizontal position in the boudoirs above, for even the meanest House has three or four times as many applicants in a week as it has beds to fill. La Marly always left them ten minutes to cool their heels. We were no exception, even though our places were already secured.

There was a fair-sized mirror facing the door and we spent some time preening ourselves and prinking out our dresses to best advantage with its help. Then Cynthia discovered a number of bound leather volumes in a bookshelf near the door. The shelf bore the label: *Duplicate Copies of Suggestions for Gentlemen Visitors*.

She gave a little cry of pleasure. "Come, this will surely be amusing," she said.

She pulled one out, opened it at random, stared at the page in amazement, cried, "Oh, goodness gracious me!" and snapped it shut again.

As I crossed the room to join her I recalled that curious last comment of the commis chef — "*if* you're still there." I wouldn't claim to have worked it all out to the last detail in those three or four paces, but some sixth sense warned me that those particular books hadn't just been left there by accident. In the lowest possible tones I murmured to Cynthia, "Stay calm. I think we may be overheard." Then, more loudly, "What's all this?"

I opened her book, again at random, and, if it had not been for her earlier response, it would then have been my turn to exclaim in dismay. Yet all it showed was a gentleman's spermspouter spouting sperm all over a girl's face; her eyes were closed and she was smiling seraphically. The photographer had retouched his negative to make the most of the jellylike quality of the fluid and the scintillating highlights upon it. It is something I must have had done to me at least two dozen times during my months in Hamburg; yet I have to confess that the *sight* of it, photographed with such loving care for detail, was nonetheless a shock.

It was the same with all the other pictures, too. None of them showed couples engaging in what one might call normal activities — the stock-in-trade of the harlot's repertoire. They were all pictures of things I myself had done with gentlemen at various times; but doing them is one thing, seeing them frozen in lascivious detail is quite another. It was not easy to contain my shock, but I managed it without being too-too-obviously blasé, either.

By now I was certain they were left there for a purpose. I even began to suspect that conveniently placed mirror. Did Madame even now sit grimly behind it, assessing our value to her trade?

I found the spermspouter picture again and turned the book toward Cynthia. "Did no man ever do that to you?" I asked calmly.

"No," she replied, almost calm herself by now — taking her cue from me.

"It's not nearly as bad as it looks," I assured her. "These photos are all taken with the gentlemen in mind, remember. And for most of these privileges they'd have to pay extra, too. Quite a lot extra for *this* one, I'd imagine." I showed her a picture of two girls putting on a "show" for a customer.

A moment later Madame de Marly confirmed my suspicion by entering and showing no surprise at catching us with one of the books open. "Ah, Mrs ffrench!" She saluted me on both cheeks. I did not shrink from her embrace, though I never saw a woman who more closely resembled a toad. "And you, Mademoiselle, are Miss Morgan." Cynthia was brave about it, too. I gained the feeling we had just passed a further test.

"So you have found our *source d'inspiration!*" she exclaimed, taking the book from my hands and riffling its pages with pride. "A girl at Numéro Douze is strong and resourceful, you know. The higher the price, the more liberties she permits. You understand?"

"Perfectly, Madame," I assured her.

"Sit!" She gestured expansively toward a group of arm chairs.

We waited for her and then seated ourselves, facing her, side by side.

"Your French is excellent," she assured us, "as one would expect from two English ladies of breeding. However, while you are in the salon or with our gentlemen, you will speak English, please? It has great cachet, I assure you. You will not lose by it." Her flytrap mouth stretched in a brief, grim smile.

Paradoxically both Cynthia and I felt sorry for her, because of her looks, and felt greater warmth toward her than her somewhat cool and formal attitude commanded. We told her that was perfectly agreeable.

"About how many gentlemen shall we be expected to accommodate each day, Madame?" I asked.

"We have no daytime business, Mrs ffrench," she replied. Now she spoke in English, too. "We open at six in the evening for ten hours. During that time you are either upstairs with a gentleman or down in the salon, waiting to be chosen. On a slow day, it might be two men. When business is brisk . . . ten? Normally it's in between. Each gentleman is entitled to at least forty-five minutes of your . . ." She broke off and smiled. "But it's too much detail now. The other girls, they will tell you. Come!" She rose and we followed suit. "I'll show you to your room. I've put you together — you don't object, I trust?"

Cynthia and I smiled at each other and assured her we didn't mind. The meaning of our smile was not lost on her. "Good," she said firmly. "I like such arrangements."

As we went out into the corridor again she turned to me and said, not very convincingly, "Oh, I almost forgot. There is a young scoundrel up there who witnessed your arrival. And he insists he wants you, Mrs ffrench. He must have you or he'll go away and never return and tell all his friends what a miserable place this is!" She raised her shoulders, arms, and finally her hands in hugely expressive shrug.

"Is he important?" I asked.

She smiled broadly. "I like you already, Mrs ffrench," she said. "You ask the right question always. He is not important — but his father is. His father is in the present government — Monsieur de Cl—t. You've heard of him?"

By chance Cynthia had. His name had been in yesterday's *Figaro*, which I had bought to discover how my stocks were doing after the Christmas lull. She had read it to practise her French. "The Minister of the Interior!" she exclaimed. "*The* most important member of the government from our point of view, I imagine."

"Quite, Miss Morgan. You — how d'you say? — *vous cachez votre jeu?*"

19

"She is a dark horse," I translated.

The expression did not seem very poetic to Madame. "You don't say much, but when you do, it's of substance. I like that, too." Surprisingly, she took our arms and led us upstairs. "I am very pleased with the two new ornaments to my House this New Year."

"And I, Madame de Marly, will be honoured to gratify the importunate son of the Minister of the Interior. In . . . fifteen minutes, shall we tell him?"

She chuckled. "I don't know why it is . . . it may have been some careless word of mine . . . but for some reason he supposes you are a young English rose, straight out of school, who has never lain with a gentleman before."

I smiled at her. "Then pray assure him, Madame, that his instinct is unerring. I shall, indeed, be all he supposes."

⑩

He desired an English rose, straight out of school and never been touched, and so I made sure he got one. Hilaire was his name, Hilaire de Cl—t, son of the Minister of the Interior. He was as gorgeous a specimen of young manhood as any poor girl could hope to find, but, alas, he proved solid ivory from the neck up.

On my way downstairs to meet him I said on a sudden whim, "Madame de Marly, you know so little of me you have no cause to grant my request, yet I ask it nonetheless — as to the matter of my price, will you trust me to negotiate it with the young gentleman?"

She replied, slightly huffily, that he'd been such a confounded nuisance she intended asking five hundred francs [worth some £1400 at the turn of this present century!]; if I thought I could do better, I was welcome to try.

I blushed very prettily as I curtseyed to young M. de Cl—t. (I can do it to order, merely by thinking of a dreadful gaffe I made at the age of sixteen, which I shan't go into here − except to say that nothing in life is wasted!) And as I led him upstairs I prattled gaily, like the innocent he took me for. I told him I had no idea what we were going to do but Madame had assured me he was a kind, considerate young gentleman who would be a humane and generous guide to the arts of Venus − whatever they might be.

He turned a little pale at the responsibility; all Madame had said was, "She is very inexperienced, Monsieur. Be good to her, eh?" However, he promised me I was about to enter a wonderland of beautiful feelings.

The second flight of stairs was narrower and I tripped demurely ahead of him so that his eyes were level with my derrière. I gave my buttocks a little squeeze at each tread to impart an extra shiver to my bustle, which, in turn, made the flounces of my dress quiver delightfully. I have always found that a girl who makes proper use of the staircase in a House of Pleasure has half her work done before she even reaches her room. Certainly young Hilaire was gasping a little and making massive rearrangements of his trouser cloth by the time we gained the landing.

Madame had shown me on our way down which room to choose − an opulent boudoir in pale shades, full of chintz and little bows. "Our room for virgins and corpses," she said laconically. "We have others more suggestive of sin, of course. All crimson and scarlet.'' The virginal boudoir was the perfect background to my masquerade.

I indicated the door and he opened it to let me in. As I passed him he said, ''Confound it! I forgot to make any arrangements with Madame.''

''You mean money?'' I asked, guilelessly catching his arm and dragging him in after me. ''Never mind that. Pay me what you think I'm worth afterwards. I don't know at all what I'm to do, but Madame said it'll be all right and I'll be well rewarded. Well now!'' I gave a few little skips in front of him, making my breasts shake. ''What's first?''

''Aiee!'' He put both hands to his temples. ''Are you sure Madame told you nothing?''

I shook my head and grinned. ''Are we going to kiss? I think you're one of the best-looking men I've ever seen. I'd love to kiss you.''

He obliged.

For all his simplicity in the top floor, he was a smooth and experienced lover; I had little trouble producing sighs of pleasure when his lips worked on mine. Then a hand closed on my left breast.

''Mmm!'' I murmured.

He drew away from me. ''You permit, Mam'selle?''

I bit my lip naughtily. ''No man ever touched me there before. But it's . . . it feels . . .''

''Yes-yes! Tell me how it feels?''

I offered him my lips once more. ''I'm not sure. Do it again.''

A minute or so later I was able to tell him it was wonderful — but my other breast was feeling neglected. ''Also . . .'' I added hesitantly and paused.

''Yes? Don't be afraid to tell me anything, my dove.''

"Well" — another naughty lip-bite — "it gives me ever such a strange tickly sensation . . . you know . . . lower down."

"In your belly?"

"Lower."

He swallowed heavily.

"Can you explain that?" I asked.

He ran a finger round inside his cravat. "Look here — we're both rather overdressed for . . . what we're about to do. May I relieve you of some clothing?"

I glanced nervously at the door. "You're sure Madame won't catch us?"

He laughed and assured me all would be well on that score.

And so it went on. I bit my lip and grinned like a naughty gamine at every fresh liberty he took with my body — and then gave little sighs and moans of pleasure as I told him I'd never experienced anything so sweet and beautiful as . . . whatever it was he'd just done to me. It was an exaggeration, of course, but not by much; I was having real fun with him in every sense of the word.

But then, when we were at last lying full stretch on the bed, me reduced to my chemise, drawers, and stockings, and he in nothing but his pantaloons, I suddenly drew away from him in alarm and cried, "Oh! You've got something . . . some . . . it's a *growth* of some kind."

"Where?" he asked in a mixture of annoyance and alarm.

With no trace of coyness, as if I truly had no idea what fire I was playing with, I grabbed his rapier through the material of his pantaloons and gave it a little shake. "That!"

He lay on his back and roared with laughter. "Oh, Mademoiselle! Oh, my dear Miss Rosie! Have you truly no idea what that *growth* may be?"

"No," I assured him stoutly. "But I know it can't be right for I have no such thing down there."

"Ah! We'll come to that anon. Let's deal with this growth, first. Undo my pantaloons and open them out."

I did as he bade me. His laughter had temporarily overcome his lust so that the column of his organ was now half flaccid and its knob somewhat small and pale. I tried to stare at it as if I were truly seeing such a thing for the first time.

"Well?" he prompted. "Does it look like a growth?"

"No!" I scarcely breathed the word as I touched my breast. "It gives me the strangest feeling in here, Monsieur. And . . . lower down — where I said before. I feel . . . don't laugh at me now, but I feel I *want* it in some strange fashion. It is beautiful. I want to kiss it. May I?"

He nodded, not trusting his voice suddenly.

It swelled magnificently under my innocent attention until it grew so hard and tight it seemed ready to burst its skin; and how fiery red the knob turned, too! I was beginning to grow impatient of my charade and longed simply to couple with him in full, hearty fettle.

"Now let me do the same," he said, easing my lips away from his splendid organ, in case I brought our festivities to a premature conclusion. A moment later I was lying on my back, knees bent and thighs spread, while he slowly parted the folds of my drawers.

"Hallo!" he cried in a voice laden with suspicion. To be sure, he could see that no maidenhead was there to guard the gates of paradise. I thought this was my chance to confess my prank and begin a full and lusty engagement with him. But I could not come out with it crudely, just like that; I decided instead to tell him something so preposterous he'd see the joke at last and we'd both have a good laugh about it.

So I told him that at the age of fifteen I'd been stolen by gypsies who were in cahoots with a famous London surgeon. "And he," I went on, ". . . now I don't quite understand this but apparently there are girls in London who somehow lose this veil of skin you're talking about. And they'll pay well to have it replaced. So the gypsies sold him mine, which he cut out very carefully with those very sharp knives they use. Lancets, is it? Anyway, after he'd gone the gypsies used to rub a special salve to heal me – though there wasn't any wound to speak of. And then, within a month or so, my veil grew back again. They rubbed the salve in every day, so perhaps that's what made it regrow?"

Do you know – the fool believed every idiotic word!

He lay there between my thighs, hands propping his chin (or his jaw would have dropped off), drinking in this preposterous tale! *Aiee!* to borrow his phrase. What was I to do now? Why didn't the surgeon simply buy the salve and rub it into those London girls? Why didn't the gypsies do it, come to that? The surgeon wasn't needed at all! There were a dozen damaging questions he could have asked, but all he said was, "My poor Rose! How many times did it happen?"

"Fifteen," I replied at once.

"Oh! My poor angel! Let me kiss it well again!"

And he bent to my wide-open fork and began to

apply his beautifully chiselled lips to my own dumb grin, and then to follow it with his extremely cunning tongue.

I gave up at that. I simply yielded myself to his skill, while he broke off from time to time to chortle with delight at the thought of it. "Just think! You've lost your maidenhead *fifteen* times and yet I shall be the first man inside you! Just wait till I tell those others!"

That really put the wind up my sails! I could just see him scampering back to his chums and breaking the news to them like a merry wee puppy. How cruelly their laughter would cut! He would never forgive me. Come to that, I should never forgive myself. I obviously had to do something but no remedy occurred to me. Apart from anything else, he was so good with his tongue down there it was becoming quite impossible to think about anything at all. The thrills he sent through me were so gripping and powerful it was all I could do to exclaim *oh!* and *ah!* like a virgin rather than like the experienced harlot I was.

At last, when I had come, quite genuinely, for about the fourth time, he judged it right to mount me properly. And that was well done, too. His golden-curly head suddenly hung over mine, his eyes gleaming, his lips all cherry red and wet with my come; and then, as he lowered himself to kiss my neck and breasts, *in* he went, as smooth and creamy as a girl could hope for.

I had not had a real man inside me since my last night with Bertie, more than a month ago. I had almost forgotten what an exquisite feeling it is to a girl, to have that most perfect erection of flesh and gristle sliding smoothly in and out of her. I came again, immediately, and then remained on that plateau, coming time after time until — much too soon for my liking — he gave out a mighty cry of satisfaction and spent himself like a firehose, rammed to the hilt of him inside me. I felt every spurt of it and almost swooned with the pleasure.

He fell sleep at once. There was a time when I thought men were brutes for doing that but I have come to realize it is something they cannot help — the one in five who fall asleep immediately. In fact, I came to prefer them in time; they're never any trouble, the sleepers. But of the ones who stay awake about one in four become difficult after they've shot their bolts. They get disgruntled, somehow, and behave in a surly, belligerent manner that is highly insulting to a girl who has just given of her professional best.

But I digress.

He woke up a minute or so later, smiled sweetly at me, and said, "Wasn't I right now? Isn't it fun?"

Suddenly I saw the way out of my dilemma. "Fun?" I echoed. "Fun! Why it's the most . . . the uttermost . . . how is so much pleasure possible? I thought I would die of it."

"Oh! I say!" He preened himself.

"But you are marvellous!" I assured him. "Why do our parents strive so hard to keep us young gentlemen and ladies apart. Just think of the pleasure we could have!"

He laughed indulgently. "Well, I mean to say . . . rather obvious, what?"

I frowned. "I don't understand."

"Well, it leads to . . . I mean it *can* lead to . . . oh dear! Do you honestly not know anything about it?"

"All I know is I never want to do anything else. It's

a revelation!'' I caressed him suggestively. "Let's do it again, now!''

"Ah, well, that might be just a little difficult. But see here − this place is full of chaps who'd simply love to come up here and take my place. Especially when I tell them all about you.''

"I only want you,'' I murmured. By now I had him stiff as a poker again; he stared at it in a mixture of pride and annoyance.

Judging from the speed of his recovery, I guessed he was good for at least two more goes, by which time, with any luck, his chums would have had their fun and gone.

"And just think how your friends will envy you,'' I added, stepping completely out of character − not that he noticed.

"By Jove, yes!'' His eyes gleamed at the prospect. Why dash down now to boast of a single conquest when he could regale them with two!

Around eleven o'clock we pulled on our nightshirts and dressing gowns and sent down to the restaurant for a meal. And what a meal! It took us two hours to consume; the cuisine at Numéro Douze was said to rival that of the Grand Véfour and the Café d'Orléans. Actually, it took us two and a half hours to consume but that was because, between the Tournedos Rossini and the Marmite Maison, young Hilaire felt an urge to dash downstairs and tell his companions all about me. To save the situation I went down instead − but only as far as one particular button on his nightshirt, the one that allowed me to ventilate, and then osculate, and then aspirate, his proud manhood yet again.

And so back to bed and our carnal capering. I freely

admit it was one of the most satisfying nights I have ever passed with a man. I came and came until I ran dry. By that time — around three in the morning, I believe — he had been dry for at least three goes. And he had made the most amazing discovery, which was also new to me.

"The third go really hurt me," he confessed. "I was squirting away and I could feel just one or two little drops popping out the tip of the poor old fellow. But after that — it's like getting your second wind when you go running, you know — after that the pain drops away. Now I think I could go on rogering away all night."

I didn't actually count but we must have had a go at least once an hour — twice in the first few hours. So when he poked me for the last time, at around six the following morning, it must have been our tenth coupling at least, and *twelfth*, more likely.

We rose and bathed at noon, after which we breakfasted *à deux*. Then came the delicate matter of payment. I broached the topic as I led him to the door. He opened it, took my hands between his, and stared at me with eyes suddenly large and soulful. "Dearest Rose," he murmured, "I came to this House for an hour with a whore. Instead I passed an eternal night with an angel! Yes! In the space of one night you have passed from merest ingénue to the very top of your new profession. All Paris will soon be at your feet — this I promise! And you have given me a blessèd and holy memory. I would no more dream of desecrating it with filthy lucre than I would dance on my mother's grave. Adieu!"

I was too astonished to reply.

When he had gone, I returned to the bed, threw

myself upon it, and laughed until the tears would roll no more. Then I was spent out and dry at both ends!

§

La Marly was beside herself with fury, of course. Never before in the history of the House — or of any other House she'd ever managed, come to that — had a gentleman enjoyed the favours of one of her girls for a whole night without paying a sou. It no longer mattered that HRH was my patron, I had transgressed the most fundamental rule of the House — indeed, of the Noble Profession, itself — and nothing could mitigate the crime. She went on and on and on at me, putting her ugly toad face an inch from mine and screaming abuse at the top of her voice.

She would have stopped if I'd broken down and flooded the place with my tears, but I wasn't going to give her that satisfaction. I just sat there, icy calm (on the outside, at least) and repeated that the story wasn't finished yet and she would see. Of course, I had no idea what I was talking about. What would she see? She'd see a young buffoon roaming about Paris, boasting he'd plugged a girl all night at Numéro Douze — a virgin, too, for whose favours they could have charged the earth — and he'd tricked her into letting him have it all for nothing! And he'd got out past that old Cerberus, Madame de Marly! And, to be sure, every gentleman in town would rib her with it — turning the blade in the wound.

No matter. All that lay in the future. For the moment I just sat there, staring coldly at her and telling her it would all turn out well. At last she saw she wasn't going to break me, so she gave up. She told me I was

30

not to go down to the salon that night but stay in my room while she decided what to do with me. I would pay for our meal, which came to fifty francs, and if I were permitted to stay, she would dock another five hundred out of my earnings.

I knew then that she had, in fact, decided I should stay on, but she was too proud to admit it. I suppose some tiny cautionary memory of Bertie's interest in me had at last managed to penetrate that white-hot fury. Also there was the rather legalistic fact that I did not officially start at Numéro Douze until the evening after my Great Transgression.

So I sat in my room and kept up my spirits by doodling sketches of the grand House I would one day build. Looking back now, I must confess I feel a little more sympathy for La Marly than I was able to muster at the time. She was such an odious, ill-tempered old harridan. Yet, I confess, the right was more on her side than on mine. I must have been a terrible trial to her, certainly during my first few months. If the Charlotte ffrench of that time came to *me* today and applied for a position, I doubt I'd take her on!

My trouble is that although I'm a born harlot, I really ought to work alone. I should never have gone to gain experience in those Houses in Hamburg; for, though the work itself was the most awful drudgery, I found I adored the company of the other girls. I loved it when the doors closed and we relaxed together and talked about the extraordinary encounters we'd had that day, the weird things men had asked us to do. I loved to hear us talking about men — those vain, irrational, mysterious, babyish creatures whom we both adored and despised. I loved the way we were always more impressed by a man's position in the community than his positions in the boudoir. I loved to hear us trying not to admit that this or that gentleman had truly lit a fire in us that day − yet long to talk of it, too, like a different scalp to hang on our trophy pole. I loved the way we could hold the most offhand conversations about things that would make other women's eyes pop and all their hair fall out. In short, I was the sort of harlot who was born to work in a House − except for one small drawback: I could never abide rules!

Show me a rule and the first thing I want to do is break it. Admittedly, I had neither wished nor intended to break that most fundamental rule of all with young M. de Cl—t, but, having done so unwittingly, part of me was really rather glad of it − but only part of me; the rest was as furious as Madame herself that the young whippersnapper had cheated me out of what ought to have been a great deal of money.

At about eight o'clock that evening Cynthia came up to see me. I asked her if she had done any business yet. "Two," she replied nonchalantly and then gave me her gamine smile. "You'll never guess who the first one was. Monsieur A—n D—n!" She named one of the leading actors of the day, a man famous for his Quasimodo; he was certainly not love's young dream! "And he chose me!" she went on. "I was so thrilled."

"And your second gentleman?" I asked.

"Oh," she replied in a dismissive tone, "he was quite nice, a youngish fellow, good looking and very considerate. He promised to return next week and choose me again."

I said that would put her in Madame's good books.

"Talking of Madame," she said warily, "the other girls are wondering if you couldn't possibly see your way to eating humble pie? La Marly is being quite insufferable and we're all feeling the lash of her tongue.''

I said it was out of the question. She looked as if she would argue the matter, but then thought better of it. "Try, anyway," she said as she left.

Half an hour later came a knock at the door. I called out to come in, whoever it was, and − to my utter amazement − La Marly herself opened the door. "May I come in, Mrs ffrench?" she asked politely.

I had never felt so wary in my life as I rose to usher her in. "Madame, don't embarrass me," I begged. "My right to this room hangs by a thread and we both know it.''

"No, Mrs ffrench," she said with some dignity, "it is I who have wronged you. In all my years in this business I have never encountered anything quite like this.''

She would not sit down before I did; in the end we both took our seats simultaneously.

"Tell me frankly," she said, "what is your real purpose in taking up this profession? You are as different from the ordinary cocotte as it's possible to be.''

I wasn't falling into that trap, of course. "To earn enough money by the time I'm thirty to keep me in luxury for the rest of my life, Madame.''

She did not believe me but nor did she press the point.

"May I most respectfully ask what has wrought this change?" I continued.

"Circumstances," she replied with a slightly baffled smile. "M. de Cl—t is here and is asking for you.''

"Again?" My heart both rose and fell − rose at

the thought of deliverance from my transgression, but fell at the prospect of another night with him so soon. I would have been thrilled to gratify him again in about ten days time, but there is quite enough repetition in our work without duplicating whole nights of it in immediate succession.

"I mean M. de Cl——t *père*," she said. "The Minister of the Interior himself! He is here and he wishes to see you. It is without precedent. I cannot understand it."

These last words meant little to me, of course. I asked what there was to understand.

"You know nothing of his reputation?"

When I shook my head she explained that his hatred of Houses of Pleasure — even of a grand establishment like ours — was notorious. He had tried to persuade his government to close them all down but his colleagues had laughed him to silence. However, that didn't stop him from doing all he could to make life difficult for us. So to have him turn up out of the blue like this was astonishing, to say the least.

I rose. "Perhaps I should see him at once, Madame?" I had no idea what I should say, of course, but it was my sole hope of reversing my disgrace.

She appeared not to hear me. Talking as much to herself as to me she said, "He even paid me for last night. It was the first thing he did. He had the money in his hand."

"As much as we'd hoped?" I ventured.

She stared blankly at me before replying, "One thousand francs!"

I was careful to let no surprise — and certainly no jubilation — show in my face.

She frowned. "Don't tell me that's what you expected!"

I decided to make what capital I could out of this baffling affair. "I thought the son was a sprat to catch a whale — I mean his father, of course."

"Mon Dieu, you took a risk!"

"Not yet, Madame. The risk is now. Do I go to him or not?"

"Of course you do!" she exploded. Vitriol was never too far beneath her unlovely surface. "The very idea!"

"Then tell me quickly what sort of man he is. Why does he detest Houses of Pleasure? I must know such things. Is he a puritan of some kind?"

"Not at all. He has two mistresses that I know of, both with fine houses on the Bois. He is one of the richest men in Paris. And he is a notorious collector of erotic literature. Oh no, he is certainly no puritan!"

"And why has he paid such an absurd amount for his son's pleasures last night?" [*Around £3000 in modern terms!*]

I could see that the question had been bothering her, too. "A matter of pride, I suppose. Family honour . . . paying one's debts . . . that sort of thing."

I felt that was only part of it, but I gave up trying to fathom the man before I met him. I told her I was ready to be conducted to him — if she would just give me time to bathe and change.

She rose and went to the door. "He is in the same boudoir as you occupied last night. He says you are not to wash anywhere except your face."

I thought she had gone, but a moment later she was again at my side. "He is a most powerful man in this

35

country," she said, touching my arm nervously. "Please remember that."

I said I was most unlikely to forget it.

"Whatever he wants . . . let him do it. Give him your best, Madame ffrench. Give him your all!"

"Of course, Madame," I assured her. "I never do less."

"No matter what, mind. I will make it up to you later, I promise. Anything he wants! No matter how . . .'

Apparently she could not find a word that was both honest and soothing. It was hardly a conversation calculated to reassure a girl! I put on my most enticing lingerie and a dress with extreme décolletage and set out to join my unknown — and seemingly unknowable — paramour.

The girls' bedrooms were all on the top floor (the fifth in the French system, which calls our "ground" floor the first); we never slept in the boudoirs except with a client. The next three floors, going down, held six, five, and four boudoirs respectively; the sumptuousness of their decor increased as you approached the first, or ground, floor, which held the salon and restaurant. The virginal boudoir, where the Minister awaited me, was one of the four most sumptuous. I began a leisurely, but by no means tranquil descent of the intervening stairs.

There were hydraulic lifts to all floors, mainly for elderly clients; younger ones — for reasons already given — preferred a stimulating walk upstairs, a yard or so behind the girl of their choice. As I traversed the fourth-floor corridor, Vera, a tall, dark-haired beauty with something Spanish-Mauresque about her, was leading a cavalry captain to one of the middling boudoirs. She smiled at me and whispered something to the captain. I heard him give an incredulous whistle as I began the descent of the next flight.

A similar thing happened on the floor below. Alexandrine, a pert little blonde girl with an elfin sort of face and generous breasts and derrière, was just coming out of the lift ahead of me with an old dotard. "Well done!" she called out to me, for which I thanked her. She, too, spoke to her lover-of-the-moment in a low tone and, as I passed, he touched me reverently and murmured "Yes! Yes, indeed!"

It was superficially flattering of course; but at a more thoughtful level it was disconcerting, too. I was being turned into the stuff of which legends are made, and for no good reason at all.

I entered the virginal boudoir without knocking.

He was standing with his back to the fire, fully dressed. I could hardly see his features, for he had turned down all the lamps, but I would have known him for Hilaire's father from his silhouette alone — the same panther-lithe figure, the same curly locks (not quite so golden, as I soon discovered). Yet somehow these features, which were so fetching in the son, were merely sinister in the father. A man approaching fifty, which would be the youngest he could possibly be, should bear more signs of age, I felt.

"Good evening, Mam'selle," he said. There was a family timbre in the voice as well, though his was deeper and more resonant.

"Madame," I informed him. "Madame ffrench. Good evening, M'sieu."

"You will not correct me in anything I may say or do," he snapped.

I made no response to this. I was close enough now

to make out his features; he was beyond doubt Hilaire's father.

"I thought as much," he said, running an appreciative eye over my charms before he gestured me to be seated. He, however, remained standing where he was.

Trying to appear relaxed, I settled into a comfortable arm chair and looked him up and down as frankly as he had just quizzed me. I don't know why a man who was superficially so healthy and good looking should have radiated such menace; but he did. My heart fell and I hoped our interview would soon be over. Even an hour with him would be most disagreeable.

He grinned as if I had spoken the words aloud — which, I suppose, my eyes had as good as done for me. Plainly he enjoyed being disliked and even feared. "I simply had to meet the young lady who was bold enough to tell my son the most outrageous story I've ever heard . . ." I drew breath to explain but he raised a finger. ". . . and who was alluring enough to make him believe it, and who was then tactful enough to keep him all night so he couldn't make an idiot of himself in front of his friends. That last quality, young lady, especially interested me: tact and understanding. I now intend to put it to the test."

And before I could stammer out my modest reply he pulled something out of his pocket and said, "You will now cover your face with this." Then, without so much as a by-your-leave, he crammed what proved to be an empty flour bag down over my head. It was quite clean and freshly laundered — I could still smell the soap, in fact — but its tight weave prevented my seeing anything except my own décolletage.

I adjusted it for comfort, leaving a V-shaped opening in which I could see the toes of his court shoes, too . . . and his hands fiddling with the buttons of his fly. A moment later I saw him pull it out — a good, stiff organ of respectable length and more than usual girth. For once I saw no family resemblance. The son's had been attractive and enticing; the father's was neither. I had felt flattered to see Hilaire's tool paying me the compliment of standing so rigidly to attention and so often. But this gnarled old warrior of who knows how many thousand encounters radiated the same menace as the man himself only even more concentrated.

"I shall now remove your clothing," he told me, starting on my hooks and buttons without waiting for my reply.

What was his pleasure, I wondered? Why did he not wish me to see his face, which a thousand passers-by could see in the street every day? And why had he no objection to my staring at that part of him which no passer-by could possibly expect to see?

He removed my clothing, item by item, without a word. He folded each one as fussily as a good lady's maid and made a neat pile of them on a chair. And his cock grew fatter and fatter, the more of my flesh he revealed.

A harlot's view of men is quite unique. We pass through the streets, of course, like other women. We go to church, the opera, the races . . . we see men there just as other women do. But there is an extra little picture in our minds. We see them by the hundred, stark naked and grinning happily with their cocks all hot and swollen, eager to get inside us with the minimum of preliminaries. So I never meet a man on any social occasion, nor see a priest mount his pulpit steps, nor watch a tenor brace himself for a top note, without some part of me picturing his cock in that desperate state of urgency.

All the same, it is not good practice for a harlot to stand and stare at her paramour's pride; a brief appreciative glance, an admiring lift of the eyebrow, a murmured "Mmm!" — these are all the situation demands. So it was disquieting to me to have to stare at the thing for the best part of twenty minutes.

For ten of them he undressed me slowly, taking care to touch no part of my flesh, no caresses or embraces, though I could feel the weight of his gaze upon me like a heavy mantle. He removed every stitch, even my stockings — which is something only one man in a hundred will do with a harlot, whatever may be their way with their wives.

"And now, young nymph," he said, "you will walk up and down on the carpet. Stay between the bed, this chair where I shall be sitting, and the fire. Just keep moving around, slowly and gracefully."

He was sitting facing the bed with the fire to his left. The space he had indicated was only about three paces by four, so I never moved very far from him; also, by a judicious tilt of my head every now and then, I could keep an eye on what he was doing.

As I suspected, he was playing with himself. I like to watch men at that game — not that I find it particularly stimulating but I can always learn something new to aid their pleasure. M. de Cl—t was not one of those who go all the way; he was merely toying with himself to increase the pleasure of watching my naked body in motion. With the back of his left hand he held his rod still while he stroked upward, all along its underside, with three fingertips of his right hand. When he reached the point where the knob is fiery red and swollen he placed the tips of all four fingers vertically along the tube where the sperm comes spouting up and made it tremble and shiver. Long, gentle, upward caress; brief ecstatic shiver. I had done both to various men in my time but had never thought of combining them in a repeated cycle like that. I stored it away for future use.

Then, just when I was thinking this wasn't too bad after all, he suddenly asked, quite sharply, "What is your opinion of men, Mam'selle?"

"Madame," I said. I drew breath to say something flattering when he leaped at me, grabbed my wrist very hard, and hissed in my ear, "You will not correct me in anything! Do you understand, Mam'selle?"

"Madame," I said quietly. I don't know why. It was most unlike me not to give a lover what he demanded and paid for; but something told me to hold my ground with this one. Something told me it was what he really wanted of me. He gave me a stinging slap across my bottom. "How does that please you, Mam'selle?"

"Madame."

Another slap, in precisely the same place. I made no attempt to evade his hand, though I saw it coming. It was the same when I refused to cry for La Marly, earlier — I would not give him the satisfaction of cringing and whining.

"You will not defeat me that way," I told him, using the familiar *tu* to show my contempt.

He struck me really hard after that — but only once. And then, surprisingly, he gave up hitting me altogether. I suppose he felt that my provoking him

41

to *genuine* anger and to hitting out with a genuine intention to hurt represented a distorted sort of victory to me. But he obviously found it highly stimulating, too, for his cock was now so hard and stiff that it moved with the rest of his torso rather than a fraction of a second after, as is usual in most men of his age. It also looked as if it wanted to plug his own navel, which, again, is a feature of a much younger man in that state of excitement.

I was by now beginning to form one or two ideas about this fellow. I had put him down as a cold fish; I thought he had no heart at all. But now I began to suspect he had — though it simply wasn't in this present business.

But I had no time to develop the thought for he uttered an oath and said he was going to come. "Kneel down, quick!" he added.

Before my knees sank into the carpet he had whipped the flower bag off my head and was pointing his spermspouter straight at my brow. Squirt! Squirt! Squirt! I felt the jets of warm, glutinous fluid splatter over the bridge of my nose and one on either cheek. Between the third and the fourth I opened my mouth, sucked it inside, got the knob of it well down my throat, and swallowed as hard as I could. It startled him into coming again — three good, large ejaculations.

The first man who ever came on my face like that was a sea captain in Hamburg; afterwards he told me that when a man comes in the open air, he doesn't ejaculate half as much as when there's something warm, firm, and alive around his knob; it is then much easier for him to get it hard for a second go. Since then I've often used the trick with men who pay for two goes but who are not, by my guess, up to it physically. I suck them off the first time and when they come I remove all contact between them and my mouth, except a little touch now and then with the tip of my tongue, just so they don't feel cheated. Then they're fit for their second go.

With de Cl—t, of course, my purpose was quite the opposite. I *wanted* him to have difficulty getting it hard for another go. But I might as well have saved myself the trouble. A man whose erect phallus is high enough to peer in his own navel isn't going to have much trouble taking two bites of the cherry. And, as I was to discover, three . . . and more.

It didn't even go limp! To punish me he grabbed hold of my hair, quite ferociously, and kept my throat rammed down tight on that iron-hard knob until I almost choked. When at last he pulled out, I half staggered to my feet, coughing and spluttering. But he gave me no time to recover. He grasped my left arm, just below the shoulder, and propelled me so violently toward the *chaise longue* that I collided with its sloping headrest and plunged headlong forward over it.

Such was his intention, of course, for it left my *derrière* just where a man would like to see it and at just the perfect height for him to mount and ride to his cock's content. Monsieur wasted no time on finesse. Still spluttering I tried to straighten myself but he put both hands just above the small of my back and thrust me down even harder. His knees pinned mine to the *chaise longue*, so I was now bent very nearly double, and wide open to whatever assault he now chose to make on me.

With none of the usual cries or gurgles of pleasure, he grasped the base of that fat *würstchen* of his and ploughed it up and down my furrow several times, pushing hard and oiling himself well in my tenderest regions, where the flesh is so dainty a feather can make it sing. Then, without warning, he rammed himself to the very hilt in me. If he'd been a fraction of an inch bigger, he'd have hurt. I decided to pretend it had, anyway — not by crying out in pain but by gritting my teeth and making it appear I was accepting the distress rather than give him the satisfaction of calling out.

He gave me a couple of dozen extremely vigorous pokes in that position and then suddenly whipped it out and thrust it straight into my bumhole, where he again rammed himself in as deep as he'd go. Fortunately Cynthia and I had been working on each other's bums with larger and larger candles over the past two weeks, not so much for the pleasure of it as in preparation for the ordinary traffic at Numéro Douze — for it is a rule among all Houses of Pleasure that the higher its fees, the more tricks its fillies must know and the more prepared they must be to let men do strange and out-of-the-way things to them.

Again I made it appear I was accepting some considerable pain rather than cry out. He gorged his vanity for almost ten minutes on the sight of my screwed-up face in several mirrors around us. All the while my dislike of him was growing until it was something close to pure hatred; and the thing I hated most of all was that, against all my will and finer feeling, he was starting to give me a carnal thrill. The pain in my features was genuine once that started to happen, for I fought myself with all my powers to stop it from happening.

And, of course, the struggle only made it worse. I

held my breath. By a superhuman effort of muscle control I stopped my body from trembling with obvious pleasure. But I needed Svengali himself to prevent my skin from blushing in those unsightly patches of bright strawberry which always give us poor girls away. The sight of it made him brim over, too, and I felt him spouting away vigorously but with little actual come in my bumhole.

My body — my damned and damnable body! My flesh, which craves men and the touch of men and the tricks of men and the pleasures and pleasuring of men — my body turned traitor on me at last and, like some pauper-glutton taking leftovers from Savarin's slop pails, snatched her pleasure from this filth at my back.

He dragged me to the washstand then and got me to wash his tool — which *still* did not go flaccid! I took especial care with it, guessing what might soon follow. And, indeed, I was not wrong for he lifted me in his powerful arms and carried me to the bed, where he dropped me unceremoniously on the sheets. "What do you think of men Mam'selle?" he asked as he walked. "Are you enjoying this? No, of course not. But then, *you're* not supposed to enjoy it, are you! You're just here to do anything I want. Anything. I'll bet that's what Madame de Marly told you, isn't it? Give the Minister whatever he wants. Deny him nothing."

He threw himself beside me, head toward my feet, and went on, "Well, you can part your thighs and give me your fig to start with. And you can take my fellow inside where you seemed so eager to have him twenty minutes ago."

I did as he commanded. I have pleasured some fairly unpleasant gentlemen in my time but never one as consistently and determinedly unpleasant as M. de Cl—t. I lay there, sucking at him with all my skill and loathing him with all my might — and wishing there was some way of commanding that dumb glutton down there between my thighs to sit this dance out. But the man was as skilled in his arts as I was in mine and, having got me going, knew an infinity of ways to prevent me from ever stopping. I regret to say he soon had me on the boil again, and this time no amount of self-control could stop me from writhing and quivering with my ecstasy. I wept with frustration even as those darling spasms went through me in wave upon wave. When he was sure I wasn't simply counterfeiting my extremity, he came, too. Five or six tiny shots from a cock that leaped like an electric eel between my lips.

At last he had the decency to go limp. But then, just when I was looking forward to some brief respite, he leaped from the bed, threw a couple of logs on the fire, and gestured me to lie down on the rug before it, gazing into the flames. He lay behind me and clasped my waist with both hands. What he did with them I'm not quite sure, but they were suddenly alive with subtle movements and powers. And the most amazing sensation of sweetness began to flow through me. It was not a question of *wanting* to surrender to him; the plain fact is, there was no independent *me* left, either to want or to resist. I was not simply a creature in his hands, I had become the creation of his hands.

His poignard swelled and hardened again, but, since even in its slackest position it had lingered at the portals of bliss, every swelling heart beat made it grow longer and thicker *inside* me! The moment he had me well and truly impaled he rolled onto his back, lifting

46

me on top of him, both of us looking at our reflections in the mirror on the ceiling. I watched his left hand go to my breasts and felt an ineffable joy radiating from my nipples into every part of my body. I saw his right hand go down to my cleft and a moment later I was fed with silent screams of bliss from my loins.

"Are you enjoying this?" he asked again. "No, of course not. But then you aren't supposed to, are you, Mam'selle! Dear me! You're not supposed to be enjoying this at all!" And he gave out a great laugh of triumph.

And I suddenly realized what this man's secret was: He, too, could not abide rules. He only had to see a rule to want to break it! And I only just managed to prevent myself from laughing aloud in my delight.

The rule among gentlemen was that they satisfied their lust at Houses of Pleasure — so he wished them all closed. The rule among gentlemen was to keep a mistress, with whom one maintained a fiction of some romantic attachment to prettify the naked lust; so he kept two — and I'll wager there was no romance in either liaison. The rule on taking a harlot to bed was to indulge in mutual rather than one-sided pleasure — something which the harlot supplied by artifice if the genuine feeling were absent; so the great M. de Cl—t makes it impossible for the girl to find any pleasure in him at all. And *then*, the supreme bit of rule breaking, this — having made it impossible for her, he uses his enormous skill to compel her body into breaking its own rule!

I laughed. But I also shuddered to realize that this man was in charge of the police, the prisons, the entire system of justice in France!

And so he went on all night. We broke off around

midnight for another sumptuous meal, during which he was quite charming to me, asking me a great many questions about my home and background, my previous experience. I told him the exact and literal truth in answer to each of his questions, but never volunteered a fact for which he did not specifically ask. For instance, he would ask, "What does your father do?" And I would reply, "He is well established in his profession." He got nothing of any substance out of me but he enjoyed the game.

And so we returned to bed, he to his mockery and insults and me to . . . well, no, I had changed my whole attitude toward him now. I lay there more than half encouraging him, thinking to myself, *Go on, go on! If I were a man, I think I would be very like you!*

If I were a man I would detest my slavery to that hole, that emptiness, that *nothing* between a woman's legs. I would despise the urges in me that drove my body to come to houses like this and hand over more money than a kitchen maid can earn in a year for a pleasure that rarely lasts an hour. But what I would hate most of all, I think, would be to go back downstairs with that lank, damp, exhausted fellow sticking to my thighs, unable to rise again that night, and to see my lover of not five minutes since going straight back to her boudoir with another quivering, lust-plagued man — and to know there will be half a dozen more at least . . . and again tomorrow . . . and on and on and on. No wonder men sometimes hate us! We lead in reality the life they can only taste in the most absurd flights of fancy, where they join Hercules and impregnate the fifty daughters of the king of . . . wherever it was . . . in a single night.

But, as in so many other ways, M. de Cl—t was surely immune to that kind of hatred? He and his son were that rare kind of man (I have met no more than two dozen or so in a most promiscuous life) who can go at it time after time without flagging. So in this as in almost everything else no ordinary explanation would do for our contrary minister. From being an object of my hatred and contempt, he was turning into a most interesting bedfellow.

§

As the reader might by now have guessed, I would not have spent so much time describing my none-too-pleasant encounter with M. de Cl—t père if he were of no later importance in my story. Indeed, he was to prove of the utmost importance to me; had it not been for that encounter, and what followed it, I doubt whether the Maison ffrench would ever have been more than a gleam in my eye.

What immediately followed my first night with him was that he paid La Marly a further thousand francs, of which my share was four hundred [*around £1000 today*]. What followed in the longer term was that the Minister of the Interior, so famous for his detestation of Houses of Pleasure (Houses of Infamy, as he called them), visited Numéro Douze once each month and spent the entire night with me − never with any other girl, only me. He would send a *pneumatique* in the morning and I was not permitted to take any other man upstairs on that day − nor to wash any part of me but my face. One time I forgot these instructions and got round it by smearing a little Gentleman's Relish in my Valley of Joys and wearing underthings

I had put aside for the laundry. After that I did it every time, for I detest any girl who goes about unwashed.

His son Hilaire spent an hour or so with me, usually on Tuesdays, during the other two weeks of the month — never during the week when his father saw me. Hilaire used to turn up between midnight and two and didn't care how many other gentlemen had preceded him that evening.

(I should perhaps explain that the arrangement at Numéro Douze was no different from that at other Houses of Pleasure. A girl worked for twenty-one days without a break, 6 pm to am [though Sunday was only until midnight], and then took a week off for obvious feminine reasons. It may seem odd that those "obvious feminine reasons" came around regularly for most girls every month, especially when you think that, during those twenty-one days, something between one hundred and fifty and two hundred gentlemen would have laboured mightily to ensure the opposite! Indeed, they would have ejaculated into her the equivalent of two full wine bottles of their quickening sap; but I believe that very quantity is self-defeating, for it creates a milieu in which the poor little sperm-homunculi can barely survive. But I digress.)

Gentlemen adore turning a girl into a *cause célèbre* — a legend in her own lifetime. In one century it's Nell Gwynne, in another it's the Duchess of Richmond or La Pompadour; and in our own century . . . well, we could all name dozens, from Harriet Wilson on! She is a girl with carnal favours so astonishing, with amatory skills so rare, and a capacity to gratify so profound, that any gentleman who wishes to remain in society and count himself a man of the world simply *must* have her, and boast discreetly that he has enjoyed the current "sensation." In our own century, as I say, they have been legion — girls like "Skittles" and Cora Pearl, La Mousseline and the Comtesse de C (and her equally illustrious grand-daughter) — all have been treated in their time as if they were the earthly incarnation of Venus herself. And in 1886, it seemed, the bubble of reputation fell upon me. And so, for all that year and most of 1887, I, too, was hailed and fêted as the latest sensation.

What made my situation so rare — indeed, unique, I think — was that I lived and worked in a brothel. If you wanted to experience the delights of an hour between the thighs of Cora Pearl, you had first to be elected into her unofficial club and then you had to gain her preference. It helped if you were a duke and very rich, of course, but even then you were not absolutely guaranteed your reward. But I was there for any who wanted me — *quicunque vult*, a truly Athanasian wench!

Within a week of starting work at Numéro Douze, there was no point in my going down to the salon at all; no sooner had my slipper touched the topmost step of the grand staircase than I was bombarded with offers and requests from below — like bidders in the ring. It was most degrading. So I stayed in one of the boudoirs and the gentlemen came to me in an unbroken succession.

I hated it. To me it was like returning to Plutos in Hamburg, where I stayed in my little room for fourteen hours every day and the Frau Chefin sent the men up to me in an unending stream. The great difference was that at Plutos it had been eight to ten men every hour; at Numéro Douze it was never more than twelve in our eleven-hour working night — but

51

that was almost twice as many as the other girls entertained. How I envied Cynthia and the rest of them, who spent almost as much time down in the salon as up in the boudoirs. There they could gossip with each other, dance and dine with the gentlemen sing, play the piano — in short, enjoy a full social whirl in and around that one carnal activity which governed all our lives.

Perhaps I should explain a little of the ways of the House — to make the dire nature of my own position plain.

There were thirty of us girls at work on any given day. Our ages ranged from nineteen (me) to around forty, but most were in their early to mid-twenties. Monsieur de Marly, who saw all the applicants (and tried out many of them, too) would not take a girl under nineteen, though there were plenty of Houses where they went as low as twelve, which is much too young in my opinion and ought to be forbidden by law. On any given day the girls who were working were all in the salon, washed, powdered, and perfumed, all sweet and ready for service, at ten minutes to six. La Marly would inspect them minutely, telling this girl her hair was unkempt, that one not to wear pearls with opals, and so on. They were all dressed as if to join a fashionable crowd at the opera, with nothing more salacious or suggestive than would be worn by any lady of the haute monde (though the lingerie and underthings were quite a different matter!).

At six the doors were opened and the gentlemen streamed in to make their choice. After that the traffic was fairly regular; Numéro Douze was a long-established House with a good core of regular clients who had learned that some hours are less crowded than others and timed their visits accordingly. In general a girl could expect to be taken up to bed by between six and eight gentlemen each night. Half of those experiences would be in the boudoirs, the rest in one of the speciality chambers at the back of the building. These included a cubicle from a girls' school, a maid's garret, a ladies' gymnasium, a morgue, a harem chamber, a prison cell in a female house of correction, a medieval torturer's dungeon . . . all the usual stock-in-trade of any high-class house. A lark with a girl in one of the speciality rooms cost at least half as much again as a caper in all but the best boudoirs.

So in an ordinary working night a girl could expect to spend between three and five hours not on her back with a gentleman but down in the salon or restaurant, enjoying a meal and the ordinary society of her colleagues and admirers. But there were no such pleasures for me; apart from an hour or so in the restaurant, I was a prisoner in my boudoir, trying to gratify three times as many gentlemen as I would like to entertain in a single night. I even began to look forward to the visits of M. de Cl—t, which shows how desperate I grew!

(I should also explain about the restaurant, whose cuisine was compared favourably with Durand and the Maison Dorée. It was all carved and gilded plaster and glass, something like the Café Royal in London, and it was situated at the back of the building, below the speciality rooms. I often used to sit there, toying with a Suprême de Volaille St Petersburg or a Poulet à la Forestière, and wondering what strange little playlets were being enacted not fifteen feet above my head. The waitresses were big, solid women from the country, with fat faces and necks like bulls. Every now and then a gentleman would express a preference for one or other of them and she would be led away, giggling and blushing, to what the gentleman believed was the waitress's own bedroom. The girls in the salon would wheedle the gentlemen to take them in to dinner, promising that nothing made them feel randier than a good meal and two or three glasses of wine (not to mention the commission they earned on the meal!). The gentleman paid thirty francs for her company [*over £60 in modern terms*] and their meal could easily amount to another thirty. If a girl could not wheedle a meal out of an admirer, it not only put her in La Marly's bad books, it also cost her five francs for her own dinner and she had to bolt it down in solo disgrace in a little annexe near the kitchen.)

I, to be sure, had an admirer to buy me a meal every night − and a dozen more who would have filled the breach had he cried off. But I would have traded it all for the chance to lead the ordinary working life of the ordinary harlot at Numéro Douze. Matters came to a head after a couple of months when Madame de Marly − thinking no doubt to please and impress me − showed me a waiting list of gentlemen that covered several pages. "I can tell you, Madame ffrench," said she, "precisely which twelve gentlemen will go sporting between your thighs on Saturday the fifth of June!"

As the date was only Saturday the twenty-seventh of March, this was acutely depressing to me. "We will have to do something to shorten that list, Madame," I told her.

"Take on more?" she asked nervously.

"No!" I exclaimed. "Fewer."

"But I don't understand." She riffled the pages beneath my nose as if they might act like smelling salts on an hysterical woman. "You are earning almost five hundred francs a night here. That's more than any girl has ever earned — certainly night after night. And see how it goes on!" Again she riffled the pages close to my face.

"But it's no fun!" I complained.

"Fun?" The very word — on the lips of a woman — gave her difficulties. "What do you want with *fun* when you're earning money like that? Isn't that fun enough? Your friend, Miss Morgan, is only earning . . ." She consulted her book — though I would wager she knew it to the last sou. "Two hundred and eighty-eight was her best night last week."

That was around eleven pounds [*or some £700 in today's money*], which was more than Cynthia had received from her Scotch protector in a month in Maida Vale.

"I'd gladly give half my earnings to lead her life instead," I declared.

"Then you are the most stupid and ungrateful girl I ever met," she snapped.

"Fortunately," I went on with a smile, "I don't think it's necessary to do anything so drastic. All we need do is raise my price to the point where the custom falls off to only four a night — which is my ideal."

"Raise your price?" she echoed in alarm.

"Yes. I believe that at three hundred and fifty francs for an hour in bed with me we should find four takers a night — which would earn both of us more money than the present dozen at a hundred each."

"But a hundred is the price of a girl at Numéro Douze. It has always been so. And my God, the men complain enough about that! Three hundred and fifty would be impossible. That absurd thousand francs from M. de Cl—t has gone to your head, young Madame. No, no – put the whole idea from you. It's impossible."

"Just try it!' I pleaded.

"Out of the question!"

I left that interview saying to myself, *You are not here to earn money, nor to have fun. You are here to find out how a high-number house is managed. That means doing what you're told and causing no trouble and keeping your eyes and ears open. It does not mean making your own rules and conditions.*

All the same, that fear I had glimpsed in her eyes when I spoke of raising my price left me puzzled. And when M. de Cl—t and I next dined together I found myself talking about it.

He was still as obnoxious as ever. He did all he could to humiliate and hurt me (short of leaving a mark on my skin, of course), and he still spoke of me and all other harlots with contempt and loathing. Yet in some odd way I'd grown almost to like him. It had nothing to do with his uncanny ability to seduce my body into pleasures I would rather have enjoyed with any other man but him. I used to face him at the start of each of his nights with a dreadful sinking feeling in my stomach, for I knew he was going to give me the wildest pleasures – and he knew it, too – and I loathed him with all my heart, no, with all my *mind* for it. But when we broke off to dine, he became, as on that first night, a different person. He was urbane, witty, charming, and attentive to all my desires.

To be sure, that was no more the *real* M. de Cl—t than the irascible boor who occupied me and my time during the rest of the night; perhaps even he himself no longer knew who the real man was.

And so, at the flood tide of his *diner-à-deux* charm, I found myself telling him how dreadful life had become since *he* had made me the talk of the town. And then I went on to speak of La Marly's puzzling refusal to raise my price.

"Puzzling?" he said, looking puzzled himself.

"Yes, I would have thought it one of the basic rules of commerce. If a commodity is scarce, the vendor raises his price until demand tails off to meet supply. Yet she won't even consider it."

He stared at me what seemed like a year and then said simply, "You disappoint me."

It was so unlike him to be harsh while we dined that I took his words to heart. "There is something I have not understood, you mean?"

"What are you? One girl among thirty. Madame does not make her profit from you alone. She has twenty-nine other girls sitting on their under-employed *commodities* down there."

I saw it at once then – and kicked myself for not having worked it out without any help. To rub it in he added, "If she thought she'd get away with it, she'd hang a sign round your neck saying *Free!* That would really bring them running to Numéro Douze! Every girl would be doing a dozen a night then!"

I said, "I don't know why it disappoints you, Monsieur, that I think like a harlot. That's all I am and all I ever wish to be."

He merely shook his head and smiled at that.

⑃

If Madame de Marly was the weather of the House, her husband was its climate; she did nothing important that was not first sanctioned by him. However, we saw very little of him in our day-to-day life — and I, stuck away in my boudoir, saw nothing at all (until one particular day, which I shall come to in a moment). But even I, without the gossip of the other girls to assist me, except what filtered to me through Cynthia, soon grasped how important his influence was on all our lives. And, though I had not exchanged more than half a dozen words with him, I soon perceived that his one most important attribute was his hatred of women.

Perhaps hatred is too strong a word. He certainly despised us. And that disdain coloured Madame's attitude toward us and became, as I say, the "weather" of Numéro Douze — the steady drizzle of dissatisfaction and contempt in which we had to enjoy, or pretend to enjoy, our intercourse with gentlemen. He considered us to be vain, egotistical, shallow, temperamental, disloyal, fraudulent, mercenary, and conniving. And so — on the principle that if you give a dog a bad name, he'll bite you — I have no doubt we were, at least to him and his odious wife.

I have a particular reason for loathing her, which I had better explain at once. In the early weeks of my popularity, just after she had rejected my suggestion about raising my price, she decided I needed taking down a peg or two. Actually, the decision was probably his; he had always resented the fact that I had got in on HRH's say-so. He liked to try out every girl who worked at Numéro Douze — and a great many others who applied but did not get in, as well. In my third week there he decided to exercise this unofficial *droit de seigneur* on me. He had exercised it the day before on Cynthia and left her in tears. I simply refused. He didn't like it, but he realized he couldn't throw me out — nor risk mistreating me so much that I left of my own accord. But from that moment on he hated me.

I was already puzzle enough to the pair of them. They knew I was daily receiving offers that would have turned most other girls' heads and they couldn't really understand why I was rejecting them. I wasn't that sort of "nymphomaniac" who adored the work; indeed, I wished to reduce my number of lovers to four a day at most. So why did I stay? Not for money — despite the handsome sums I was earning, I could do far better as *une grande horizontale*. Not for carnal pleasure . . . and certainly not out of loyalty to them! I was a bone of contention between them, I'm sure — a bone that stuck in their throat, and they could neither swallow me nor spit me out.

Madame tried next. Part of her compensation for her husband's professional "tasting" of all applicants was that she got her pick of them *after* they began working at the House. (Once a girl started at Numéro Douze, he would never so much as touch her — that, too, was part of the strange bargain between them.) After lunch every day, which was, of course, our breakfast and which we all ate together in our dressing gowns and negligées, she would bark out one of our names — "Arlette! . . . Madeleine! . . . Garence! . . . Claudine! . . ." — and the unfortunate girl would have to go upstairs and kiss and cuddle the old harridan, and finger her, and play with her breasts, and finally submit to being poked by a dildo that La Marly strapped round her loins.

She had her favourites, of course, strange (and I think deranged) women who, out of natural inclination or a sense of their own insecurity, would go willingly to those bouts in Madame's bed. Usually it was their names she called, but once or twice a week she'd pick another at random. Few girls went more than six months at Numéro Douze without being chosen once. Two days after I had rejected her husband, she called out my name. Her triumphant tone told me the two incidents were connected.

A silence fell and everyone stared at me, expecting me to reject her, too. But I decided to comply — partly because I genuinely did not wish to acquire a reputation for being "difficult," and partly because it seemed to me that this was one aspect of managing a successful House and I could not afford to miss it; at the very least I should learn what not to do when I had a place of my own.

I shall not dwell upon the horrors of her bed, the squalor of her body, the brutality with which she gripped my hair in both hands and forced my face down into her muff. Professional stubbornness alone prevented me from retching on the spot. Indeed, I began to pleasure her with all my skill — with such success that she, no doubt thinking she had another acolyte in me, let go my hair and stretched herself out luxuriously. Then, like quicksilver, I leaped upon her and plastered her mouth with kisses, giving her an enforced taste of what she had forced on me.

She flung me from the bed and told me to get out of her sight. As I reached the door her husband came in to inquire what was wrong. I kissed him fervently, too — which he accepted with delight until his taste buds woke up to what I was offering.

The incident was never mentioned between us again but our relations thereafter were never more than cooly civil — for which, indeed, I was heartily grateful. She never dared call out my name again after lunch.

§

I said earlier that my absurd popularity lasted some eighteen months; in fact, it began to wane after only nine — though it was a long time dying back to the level where I became no more and no less desirable than any other girl in the House. I prolonged its death — unintentionally — by my behaviour in the boudoir.

Most harlots have a regular "patter" with their gentlemen, that is, an assortment of conversational commonplaces to pass the time in a congenial manner. I include an example or two in my *Guide for Girls at the Maison ffrench*, which is printed as part of this volume, so I shall say nothing more here. At the simplest level they comprise carefully worded comments on his physical attractions and personal magnetism. Above that they branch out into his profession . . . the part of the country or world from which he comes . . . his views on the latest exhibitions, plays, books, and so on . . . social chitchat in general . . . in short, anything but politics, religion, and marital fidelity.

This latter *tabu*, as it is now the fashion to call it, makes it difficult to have a frank discussion of the only real topic of immediate interest to the gentleman: his own carnal desires. To be sure, one can talk of them at the most trivial level — "Shall I lie like this? . . . Do you enjoy it like that?" But to plumb his motives at any deeper level calls for considerable tact.

Looking back now, I doubt whether such tact was, in fact, mine to command; I suppose I made up for it by my youth and vivacity, for which men will forgive a young girl much — especially when she has put at their disposal a supple and voluptuous body and is using it to please them in every possible way. Instead of approaching the topic from twelve miles off, I would ask, straight out, what they were really looking for when they visited a House like Numéro Douze. And if they answered with a bucketful of platitudes, I'd say, "Yes, yes! Every man tells me that, Monsieur. But you're different. Don't try to deny it, now! You have a rare discrimination. I can always tell . . ."

What man would deny such an accusation!

And then, in desperation to impress me, they'd delve deep into their souls and return with some real gem of truth. Often, the more ordinary the man seemed on the surface, the more remarkable was his revelation. One I remember, an extremely ordinary person and a rather dull lover, blurted out that he didn't really come to Numéro Douze looking for carnal pleasure at all! He poked away because it was what the girl expected and she felt she oughtn't to take the money if he didn't have his fling with her. But really he liked to get it over quickly (I'd already noticed that!) and then spend the rest of his agreed time just talking with her.

"What about?" I asked.

"Not necessarily about *that*. Anything will do. You are the only girls in Paris with whom I feel thoroughly comfortable and relaxed — and that's because you're relaxed, too. Once our little carnal transaction is over, you know you can't go back to the salon too quickly or Madame will reprimand you for not giving value. So there's nothing to do but lie back happily and chatter away like a little bird. I love that. And that's what I really come here for."

I asked why he chose the Numéro Douze, which was, after all, the most expensive House in Paris. He said that in most other places they thought half an hour quite adequate and the girls began to twitch after that. "Of course, you can't blame them," he allowed. "If they're earning less they must take more men up to bed. But for me, it's the chance to meet charming young ladies and feel completely at ease with them and talk without restriction or inhibition — as I can with you. And Numéro Douze is the *only* place in Paris where that's possible!"

Silently I promised him that the monopoly would one day be broken.

§

Another gentleman, a famous essayist and a member of the Académie Francaise, told me he had been cheeseparing for two months in order to afford my favours. A statement like that is a cue to tickle him archly and ask, "And shall I see you again two months from now?"

"I fear not," he said merrily. "You are much too beautiful."

Of course I asked him what he could possibly mean by that!

"A beautiful woman arouses fear as well as lust in a man," he replied. "Fear . . . and something . . . *other*. A feeling of sadness — yes, that's it. A tristesse. I look at this perfect brow of yours, so untrammelled by the marks of care . . . and these great, limpid eyes, behind which who knows what is going on? No — don't even try to tell me. I prefer them so, two pools of unfathomable mystery. And these generous cheekbones, which tell me you are great of soul. And these lips, which Canova himself would have sacrificed his ten best sculptures to have carved. And these shoulders, these adorable breasts . . . but why go on?"

I was embarrassed (and delighted) enough to burst out laughing. "Because it would make a delightful anonymous piece in *La Vie Parisienne*, Monsieur!" I chided.

He pressed my nose, like an electrical button. "And, yes, the ready wit that lurks in ambush behind so much perfection. Oh – perfection! That's what I was talking about, wasn't I – why your kind of perfection frightens me even as it stimulates my desire. I *feel* that such perfection should somehow be immortal, yet I *know* only too well how transitory it is. Your beauty rouses in me the intimations of human mortality, and specifically my own. So, *chère Madame*, grateful though I am to the gods for this rare privilege, next time I shall be wiser and choose a more ordinary beauty."

§

Cynthia and I, sharing the same bed, soon came to share the same monthly cycle, so we enjoyed our week off together. I believe that a seven-day break after twenty-one days non-stop is a perfect arrangement – like the one season of winter against the three of spring, summer, and autumn. In winter the leaves are off the trees just long enough for us to forget the shape they impose upon a landscape; we grow familiar enough with the skeletal branches to welcome their new bursting into leaf. By autumn we have tired of the dark, heavy canopy and long for the free vistas of winter. So, too, in my life as a harlot, I am never more ready to forswear the company of men for ever than when I have been opening my legs to ten or more of them a day for the past three weeks; and I am never happier to feel that thrilling rod of gristle thrusting and bursting inside me than after seven days of chaste separation from it.

For Cynthia and me, however, those days were hardly idle. We would usually meet with Gisela and Sapphire and drive out into the environs of Paris, seeking a suitable site for the Maison ffrench. We were all agreed that, apart from the fact that it was *my* name, it was a very good name for such an establishment, especially as the Parisians would pronounce it "franche." Thousands of English gentlemen come to Paris each year in search of erotic pleasure of one kind or another — shows like the Folies Bergères, spicy books, naughty postcards, and, of course, the big-number Houses. Their usual comment on anything of that nature was that it was "very French," or, if they wished to make some slight concession to the natives: "très French." And so the word *French*, pronounced "franche," had passed into the argot as meaning naughty-but-nice, erotic, stimulating . . . and so on. A perfect name, indeed, for a House that would be all those things and more!

But where should we build it? That was the question that impelled us to take those glorious summer and autumn drives into the outer suburbs and rural fringes of the city. We soon ruled out all the land to the north, east, and south of Paris — that is, between twelve o'clock and six if you think of a clock face being superimposed on a map (which personally I find much easier than trying to remember east from west). It was too industrial or simply unfashionable. The country between six and eight, roughly from Villejuif to Sèvres, looked slightly more promising but in the end we decided that the way to it through the poorer southern districts of the city would deter too many potential customers.

Really a gentleman would only consider leaving Paris (for his pleasure) by the Versailles road or through the Bois de Boulogne – and that narrowed our choice to the rather small expanse of country between Ville d'Avray and Puteaux, or eight and ten o'clock. By the time the leaves started falling from the trees we had selected possible sites in St Cloud, La Celle, Vaucresson, and Suresnes – half a dozen in all.

"And shall we start building as soon as the spring comes?" Sapphire asked eagerly.

"Spring, eighteen-ninety, perhaps," I replied guardedly.

"Four years!" The three of them were aghast at the prospect of having to wait that long. "But surely you've got enough money now?"

"I can chip in thirty thousand francs," Sapphire said.

"And me," Gisela added. "More if you want."

"I could if we started next year," Cynthia put in.

I threw my arms round them and hugged them to me. "Darlings! Dear, sweet darlings. That is your own hard-earned money for your own well-earned old age. Besides, money isn't the thing. I've got oodles of money."

"What is it then?"

"Politics. Mostly politics. The men who run this country are quite happy for women to *work* in brothels. They may not be so sanguine when a woman tries to own one. It's not one of the positions they like to see us adopt! So I shall need protection, high up in the government. And, since French governments have been known to fall, I'll need protection-in-waiting, as it were, among the present opposition, too. Also the police. But it isn't just politics. It's also my ambition. Listen — do you really want to help me? Far more than you could with your money."

Eagerly they expressed their willingness to do anything . . . yes, anything. Even so I felt I had to prepare them a bit. "When Cynthia and I came to Paris," I explained, "my idea of building my own House of Pleasure — and making it the best ever — was really just a pipedream. If I'd taken so much as one single step in that direction then, I'd have fallen flat on my face immediately. And they'd probably never have let me rise again. Now? Yes, I could probably manage it now — with a great deal of luck and by spending a lot more money than I really should . . . and making a lot of mistakes and enemies. But, with M. de Cl—t on my side, I probably could. However, if I hold my hand for just another two or three years (maybe four *is* a bit much!) and really work at it behind the scenes, then we can do it without wearing our nerves to a frazzle and risking my entire fortune."

"But how can we help?" Cynthia asked.

"The one thing I cannot do — without revealing something of my hand — is find out about all the other high-class houses in Paris. What are their specialities? What sort of gentlemen frequent them? What rules do they impose on the girls? What value do they give for the money they charge? How do they handle the authorities? Who protects them? What do they have to pay for that protection? Oh, and millions of everyday little things like what laundries do they use and how much do they charge per sheet or pillowslip?"

"You want us to strike up friendships with girls in these establishments and quiz them?" Cynthia asked uneasily.

I merely smiled.

Gisela was the first to see it. "She wants you to leave Numéro Douze and she wants Sapphire and me to chuck the Chevalier so that we can all go and work in these places ourselves!"

I nodded, rather gravely, for I knew what a sacrifice I was asking of them. To be one of the girls at Numéro Douze or the mistress of the Chevalier was to be *somebody* in the demimonde — and there is no other branch of society where one's position counts for more. To work at any one of thirty-odd Houses, though all were of some calibre, was a marked downward plunge. "If you take ten a piece," I hastened on, "and move on every two months or so, you can cover all of them between you before the next two years are up."

"You mean we can't even stay together?" Gisela took Sapphire's arm.

"It's only for eighteen months or so, dearest. Then we can all be together for the rest of our lives, if you want. But don't you see the beauty of it? Nobody's going to connect what you're doing with what I'm playing. And if I can rely on you to gather all that sort of information, I'll be free to concentrate on the political side of things — which is just as important and which is something only I can do."

The logic was inescapable but we were a sombre party who returned to Paris that evening.

Cynthia left Numéro Douze in September, much to La Marly's mystification not to say annoyance, for she was one of the stars of the House by then and very popular with our patrons. To lose her to private service with one of the gentlemen would be bad enough, though understandable; but to lose her to a vulgar establishment like the *Jeunesse Dorée* in Montmartre was quite insupportable. Naturally enough the suspicion fell on me. But I was still too much a favourite with M. de Cl—t to be touched. Madame gritted her teeth and bided her time.

And so did I.

On two or three occasions that autumn I tied my courage to the sticking place and prepared to divulge all my plans to my dear Minister; but always at the last minute something (my guardian angel, as I later realized) held me back. Of course, with the wisdom of hindsight, you could say that Christmas wasn't too far away and at the back of my mind I must have remembered that the Prince of Wales had promised to visit Paris sometime around then — and he would certainly never do so without spending at least one night with me — and that, in my usual reckless manner, I expected it might impress M. de Cl—t into taking me more seriously.

Well, that may be so, but I could never have guessed that on the very day the Minister sent me his usual terse *pneumatique* about rubbing Gentlemen's Relish in my crevice — oops! I mean about not washing that day — as I say, I could never have guessed that on the very afternoon of that same day, HRH would send word that he had just arrived in Paris and desired to spend the night with me!

The Minister was out of town and could not be reached in time to put him off. Fortunately, Bertie arrived a few minutes before M. de Cl—t. What a delight it was to see that dear, rotund figure again! To feel those big, powerful arms enfold me! To hear his beautifully modulated tones murmuring in my ear how much he had missed me! And to feel the importunate bulge in his trousers swelling to prove it! So, after some heartfelt kisses and equally heartfelt tears of happiness, I was swift to explain something of the situation to him. Bertie was the most perfect gentleman who ever came out of England. "What d'you wish me to do, my dearest Lottie?" he asked as he dabbed my cheeks dry.

"Invite him to dine with us, sir," I suggested at once. "He's every inch a gentleman, so he won't take advantage of it and linger on. But it would salvage his *amour propre*."

Of course, I knew Bertie would do so anyway. European diplomacy was in his bones, and M. de Cl—t knew the dirt on everyone in Paris — and dirt is the very meat and drink of diplomacy, as everyone knows. But it looked much better that the suggestion came from me; and Bertie was delighted to have a chivalrous excuse to issue the invitation. When I broke the first part of the news to the Minister his face went black as thunder; when I added the sweetener of the second part, he almost went down on his knees to thank me.

It was a most fascinating dinner. One of the many advantages of being a harlot is that gentlemen lose that desperate urge to protect one from the real world at all costs — as they would a "decent" woman. I don't mean they become unchivalrous — though, of course, some of them do — but they feel able to talk away without those stupid inhibitions that render ordinary intercourse between the sexes so tepid. I heard things about members of the government, members of the opposition, foreign ambassadors, and the royal courts of Europe and Russia that would have lifted the scalp off many a fine lady of their acquaintance.

And then, over the dessert, Bertie dropped a bombshell. "Tell me, Monsieur," he said, "you've known Madame ffrench for some time now, and you're obviously a shrewd observer of life, so what d'you suppose her real business in Paris might be, eh?"

I, of course, turned scarlet and tried desperately to think of some outlandish project with which to fob him off . . . and then I noticed that de Cl—t was staring uncertainly at me and the Prince in turn.

He knows! I thought at once. *And now he's torn between revealing that he knows or appearing ignorant.* Fortunately he noticed my panic, or he might later have decided that I had put Bertie up to all this.

Since Bertie had made it a sort of challenge, I could hardly interrupt. The best I could do was to smile encouragingly at the poor Minister.

"We have never discussed it," he replied guardedly — directing the words at the prince but aiming the thought behind them at me.

At once I said, "But surely you know I was very close to consulting you on the entire project, Monsieur?"

He smiled thinly, reasserting his usual self. "I've been waiting for it. Tell me, though, do you wish to buy out this House, or build one of your own?"

I laughed. "Really, M. de Cl—t! You know me far

better than that. The standards of this wretched place would never satisfy me.''

"What is your capital?" he asked tersely.

I looked at him askance but in the corner of my eye I saw Bertie nod. I took the biggest chance of my life and told him at least half the truth. "Just over a million francs."

It was around forty thousand pounds [*or two and a half million today!*] but he didn't bat an eyelid. Bertie, by contrast, almost dropped out of his chair. De Cl—t glanced at his watch and uttered a mild oath. There was a tedious ministerial chore that had to be performed tonight – an execution on the guillotine – and if he were not there as a witness, that tripehound from the Quai d'Orsay would collar all the limelight. He trusted HRH understood.

HRH understood perfectly, had *so* enjoyed their discussion . . . looked forward to a speedy renewal of their acquaintance, either under this same roof or (here a smile at me) one that will be even grander!

At the door, de Cl—t turned. "We have spoken of many futures tonight, sir – of countries, institutions, and people. But I know of no person whose future seems more assured than the one who has been closest to us both all evening – and no institution more secure than the one that is, I feel sure, closest to the hearts of all three who are here!" And with a slight bow he was gone.

I expected Bertie to enthuse about de Cl—t and say how much he had learned this evening and how grateful he was to me for the introduction . . . Not a bit of it! His first words to me were, "I say, Lottie – is it true you've really got forty thou' stowed away?

You couldn't possibly lend me one of them till Friday, could you?''

The fact that men tend to lose their chivalrous inhibitions with harlots is not, I then discovered, an unalloyed blessing! ''Why only till Friday?'' I asked foolishly.

''Figure of speech, my dear. I mean, I'll certainly pay you back before you need it for this grand House of yours.''

I thought rapidly and said I'd give him *two* thousand if I could put three ostrich feathers and the motto *Ich dien* over the entrance. ''And I mean give, not lend,'' I concluded.

He told me *he* was being serious — and anyway, biologically speaking, it is the male that *serves* the female in the carnal act.

Well, it had been worth a try, I suppose. I lowered my sights a bit and said I'd still give him one thousand for his assurance that if I ever got in a tight corner, I could count on his using his considerable influence behind the scenes to assist me.

God bless him! He said he couldn't possibly accept payment for something he'd freely have given, anyway.

So a loan it had to be.

''Huzzah!'' he cried. ''Now at least I can afford this night with you!''

And he rushed me to the bed, where, as after our very first dinner together — in Holborn more than two years previously — he bent me forward over the mattress and pillows, threw up my negligée, and got his hot, throbbing rantallion inside me at once; and then we were off in a whirl on the old familiar dance of life.

He claimed his powers were fading, though he was only in his mid-forties then. All I know is he managed four mighty pleasurings of himself, and me, before rosy Aurora painted the windows pink. The fourth was actually during the dawn, when for a long, sweet, and gentle hour we rolled slowly over and over in the bed, him on top, me on top, and side by side, and he poked me slowly, all the way in until I could feel the swelling of his knob deep in my belly, then all the way out until the one eye of his Polyphemus could see the portals of heaven . . . again and again and again, as slow as any man has ever poked me.

And when, finally, we favoured each other with the last drops of our juices of ecstasy, he murmured in my ear that I was the finest bedmate he had ever known. And I wept a little more and told him nothing would induce me to compare him with any other man. And so I fell asleep wondering if there could possibly be a finer, nobler profession for a woman than the one I had chosen. Surely there were millions of women, indeed tens of millions, who would have given all they possessed to pass such a night as the Prince and I had just enjoyed!

§

De Cl—t returned the very next night, of course.

"How did your execution go off?" I asked with a laugh, thinking it had all been invented.

"The bugger got an erection on the scaffold," he said. "It was most distasteful. There were ladies present."

"Was he naked?"

"No, but he had a bulge in his culottes the size of a siege gun. I wanted to have him flogged for his impudence but they said it couldn't be done.''

It was an amusing sidelight on my dear Minister — that he would take it as a personal affront that a man about to be executed should appear in a state of carnal stimulation. "I would hardly have thought that *ladies* would attend such a dismal ceremony," I commented drily.

He laughed. "Don't you believe it! They're the ones who want all the front-row seats!"

"Ah then," I said, "who can tell what waves of desire they send flooding over your poor victim! Can you wonder at his state of excitement?"

He knew I was jesting yet he shot me a curious glance, as if I had unwittingly said something quite profound. "D'you think you might understand what moves such ladies?" he asked — then waved the question away. "Another time. Another time. It is too big a matter to go into now. Besides, we have unfinished business, you and I.''

I smiled and toyed delicately with a button of my negligée.

"Oh no!" He plucked my hand away and waved a finger under my nose. "No more of that. If we are to be partners in this project of yours, there can be no more of that!"

"Partners?" I said warily.

"Your money and talents . . . my influence and power . . . an even match, wouldn't you say?"

It was the hardest *no* I ever said in my life, but I said it nonetheless.

He grinned. "Oh, did I forget the land? And the château? Well, actually, it's more of a palace than a château but you know how absurdly modest we French are." He laughed at my consternation.

"Are you saying you already have the land . . ."

"Listen, Madame ffrench." It was the first time he had used my proper name – though last night with Bertie he had gone as far as to call me Madame. "Come over here and sit down. Let me send for some wine."

The footman brought us a bottle of Château Lafitte – something to celebrate all on its own; and he poked up a cheerful blaze before he withdrew.

"To be quite serious," de Cl—t said as he clinked his glass to mine, "it has been my ambition since boyhood to own – or part-own – a really grand House of Pleasure."

"But I thought you detested them."

"And the fox leaped a third time to snap up the grapes in his jaws. And for the third time he missed. 'Bah!' said he. 'They are sure to be sour, anyway!' And the amazing thing about that fable is that Monsieur Æsop never even met me!"

Here was yet another de Cl—t, and one I had never met before! If there was a real personality there after so many years of striking poses and attitudes, I suspected this was closer to the man than any I had yet seen.

"To be sure," he continued, "I realized I could not manage such an establishment myself. I could not sit at the *guichet* and take the clients' money! I could not go out and trawl the villages of France for fresh wenches – or however it is you get them. In short, I realized from very early on that I needed a partner – a woman, and one who either was or had been in the trade."

He took another sip of wine and stared into the fire; I thought his expression rather melancholy. "In twenty years of searching I had many false dawns — enough to make me a thousand times too wary when I met you. And for that I owe you an apology, Madame ffrench. I have treated you abominably.''

"Get on with it," I said, not in a very insulting way.

He looked daggers at me and then burst out laughing. ''That night I first met you, I was so sure I had found my partner at long last that I frightened myself. I think all absolute conviction is frightening, don't you? Religious, political, artistic . . . if there's no room for doubt, it's ominous, somehow. Anyway, I put you to the test that night.''

"And many nights after!"

"And *every* night after! Oh, I admit it. I wanted to find out if you were gold or base metal. I found you transcended both. You are fine as gold. You are brilliant as diamond. You are as sharp as the finest Toledo steel. Then your very perfection began to frighten me. You will run circles round me, I thought. I shall never be a match for you. And that continued to be my fear right up until last night.''

"And what happened to change your mind last night?''

"Your unbelievable generosity. Look at the situation you found yourself in: The Prince of Wales has paid only this one visit to Paris all year; he can spend only ten or twelve hours with you. And yet you sacrifice two of them for me! To save my face you give up something so precious. What a monster of churlishness I should be to continue to hold back!''

I saw precisely what he was seeking to do, of course — he was trying to hammer my emotions on the anvil of his cunning until they were welded fast to his will. For a fleeting moment I toyed with the idea of letting him think he'd succeeded — but the sheer ennui of having to keep up the pretence for God knows how long soon killed the impulse.

"Poppycock!" I said briskly. "Even if you had not already arranged to visit me last night, I should still have tried to persuade the Prince to invite you to dine with us. I *need* you, Monsieur. I know you are still trying to test me — and probably will never stop trying." I put that in to allow him a face-saver, if he wanted to take it. "I need you — and now I'm delighted to discover that you need me, too. I'm even more delighted to be told of this château-cum-palace and the park that surrounds it. When can I see it?"

"Tomorrow?" he suggested. "It's the Château Bougival, near Malmaison."

As it happened, my twenty-one days were up that night. I said tomorrow would suit me admirably.

⚜

It is a pleasant drive out of Paris, past the racecourse at Longchamps in the Bois de Boulogne, past the Rothschild château and demesne, over the Seine to St Cloud, then straight out for four or five miles to Malmaison, where the Empress Josephine lived between her divorce from Napoleon in 1809 and her death in 1814. The entrance to the Château Bougival is to your left, about half a mile before the even more imposing gates to Malmaison; the château itself — or, as de Cl—t more correctly described it, the palace — stands in wooded grounds, about half a mile in from the road.

I never saw a palace that more obviously cried out to become a House of Pleasure. Even as we approached it up the winding driveway, I determined that, one way or another, the name *Château* Bougival would vanish from everyone's lips, to be replaced by "the *Maison* ffrench." We English can be absurdly modest, too.

It was modelled on Versailles, though a great deal smaller — in fact, it had no more than a hundred and twenty rooms, not counting servants' quarters, kitchens, pantries, and other domestic offices; I seem to remember that we once counted up every walled-in space with light and a door and it came to over three hundred. It was not only adequate for its purpose, it even matched my most vaunting ambition! My hardest task, on that first visit, was to curb my enthusiasm and maintain a mildly critical, somewhat dubious air — lest de Cl—t should raise his claim to sixty-forty; for in my enthusiasm I might well have capitulated.

As we wandered from one splendid chamber to another, each the size of a ballroom, both on the ground floor and up on the first, I became aware that we had so far seen nothing you could call a domestic bedroom. Everything was on too grand a scale. I finally asked de Cl—t where the bedrooms were and he laughed. There were only three — one for Monsieur, one for Madame, and the state bedroom for visiting royalty. Everyone else curled up where they could in one of the grand salons. In the Winter Palace in Leningrad, he added, you could find archdukes being obliged to "kipper down" in quarters that an English clerk would not dream of asking a scullery maid to sleep in.

I said that was all very well, but I wasn't going to pay for coals to heat those vast rooms in winter to a temperature that would allow girls and gentlemen to cavort together naked for an hour or more. He replied that a clever architect could no doubt divide them and reduce their scale. I made a number of outrageous suggestions for practically gutting the place and starting afresh inside its shell — and he didn't turn a hair. Plainly he was not in love with the building as some kind of family heirloom.

It was impossible to see it all in one visit so I arranged to come back with the other girls and make our plans in more detail, which, indeed, we did. On our third visit we discovered a number of smaller rooms at the back of the central section and at the far ends of both wings. They were still larger than the grandest salons at Numéro Douze, but they were small enough for a gentleman to sport his member without feeling dwarfed.

"Perhaps we can devise some other purpose for the larger chambers?" Sapphire suggested.

"Not us," I replied. "But I know someone who can."

§

Clifford K—n arrived in Paris within twenty-four hours of receiving my cable. I was flattered until I heard that Bertie had invited Clifford's father to lighten the tedium of Balmoral for Christmas and Papa had insisted on dragging him along. A "poor brother officer on his deathbed in Paris" had proved a godsend.

By now my seven days were up and I was back in service at Numéro Douze. He was feeling as randy as me but there was also a proud, stubborn streak in him. He said he was damned if he'd ever pay a sou to put *me* on my back. So, for the first time in my life, I was forced to pay a man to pleasure me; I thought it would quite ruin our first ten seconds together. I gave him the money to come visiting, like an ordinary client, and choose me for the night, but the tripehound had the gall to go to the Sphynx where Cynthia was then working, and pick her instead, leaving me to go up with an old goat in his seventies, who just wanted me to sit in countless positions on his face and let him, at long long last, poke his way to heaven between my breasts. There followed two or three other clients, not particularly memorable.

And then, when he finished cavorting with Cynthia and finally turned up at Numéro Douze to do what I'd paid him for, he had the audacity to say he'd spent so much money at the Sphynx that I'd have to lend him some more. I would have refused but, while he was speaking, he took out his rascal to give him an airing: ten throbbing inches of white and scarlet distress begging me to provide some snug, warm nest where he could hide and find relief; I should have been a heartless wretch indeed to spurn such pleading.

"D'you remember the first time I ever poked you?" he asked. "On a piano stool?"

"It was behind a curtain in the music room," I told him, already shivering with my longing for him to stop talking and poke me anyway and anywhere he desired.

"It was on a piano stool," he insisted, coming to stand behind me and push me down upon a chair. "You sat so and let my hands wander at will inside your décolletage . . . like this . . ."

Webs of fire spun themselves inside me, radiating out from my breasts to fill every corner of my being. I could feel my nipples bidding to burst their skin as his fingers toyed with them. So sweetly did they ache, they shone like burnished pears as he freed them of their lacy coverings. And when he raked their swollen undersides with the gentlest caresses of his nails, I almost swooned with my ecstasy.

"Don't delay," I begged, for I could feel the insides of my thighs already soaked with the juices of my passion.

He slid himself beneath me, lifting my skirts and petticoats in the same easy motion. And when he eased me down again I was all around that riotous randipole, which swelled in my hungry *canal d'amour* and filled me to perfection.

Unless I moved up and down, little of that delicious friction which precipitates life's most frenzied pleasures was possible. But the moment I obliged him, as I thought, he slipped his hands under my skirt, wriggling his fingers in through that froth of lace and silk, until he could grip my bare hips firmly and hold me still.

Then, with his hands still clamped like two vices there, he began the slowest, most delicate undulations and gyrations of his pelvis. It was heavenly to me beyond words. Because of our situation and because of the most satisfying girth and length of his erection, the slightest movement caused me to experience a most delightful pressure against one or other side of my *concon* — and an equally delectable relief of pressure on the opposite side.

I find it hard to visualize that place inside me there. Anatomies are no help at all. They show an emptiness surrounded by a hollow tube of flesh. But to me it is no emptiness at all. A space, yes, but a space filled with ghosts, formless memories, whispers, and yearnings. When a skilful and well-made man fills it as Clifford filled it that evening, *then* I can picture it. It is still a space, but now its memories and desires have been moulded to the perfect negative of that darling rod, thrilling to his every move, begging more and yet more and *impossibly* more of his mastery.

"How can you?" he gasped in a voice close to drowning in the waves of our sensual extreme.

I was past all words by then. All I could do was gasp and cry out in my joy and beg with that hungry space for more.

Moments before he shot me full of the milk of human adoration he relaxed his grasp on my hips and, placing one hand flat on my belly to pull me tighter onto him, let his magical fingers wander down into the cataract between my legs and press the fleshy button which, in that condition, has the power to detonate every atom of my wanton body and stun me with its excess.

How we got from there to the bed, and with all seventy-four of my buttons, hooks, laces, and studs opened, and every last stitch off our backs, and all the candles slaked but one, I do not know. But when my senses revived I found myself lying on my back in his arms, both of us facing the ceiling, my legs forked over his right thigh, and his lank, damp *bougie* in my left hand. His fingers coyly shielded my breasts from the gaze of the gilded cupids that held up the tester above us.

"How can you?" he repeated.

Now I had breath and voice to ask him what he meant.

"All the way over the Channel I kept wondering how much you might have changed — what would a year's usage by several hundred Froggies have done to you? And I find you haven't changed at all. Think of all the fellows who must have poked you, in this very room, or another just like it, since we last met . . . all those hundreds of pricks that must have stabbed away at you down there . . . I felt sure it must have blunted your appetite, stilled your fever . . ."

I laughed. "Good heavens! D'you suppose I respond like this with *all* of them? How could I possibly do that? Though I'm sure they believe I do."

"If not all, then some?" he suggested.

I agreed.

"How many?"

"One or two a night — if I'm lucky."

"Each night! One or two! God, and I thought I was the most cunny-haunted creature in Europe! You beat me hollow."

"We're both cunny-haunted, my darling —if that's how you wish to express it. Don't you see it? The House of Pleasure is our only true home."

"And Cynthia's. She's a passionate little thing, too, you know — but, funnily enough, quite different from you."

"In what way?" I asked.

He lay there thinking for a while. I could tell he was thinking hard from the way his cracksman began to swell in my hand. "She's a very calm, deep sort of frig," he said at length. "She doesn't move much. It's almost as if any sort of movement would be too exquisite for her to bear. Have you ever felt a greyhound just before you slip him on a hare? All tense and trembling. Cynthia's like that. She lies very still while you're poking her and just gives out sighs and little shivers. She has the biggest repertoire of oohs and aahs I ever heard. Also I get the feeling she's ashamed of the strength and size of her carnal appetite. And shame is a powerful aphrodisiac to a man, you know."

"Obviously," I said, giving his bone a wag. "If the mere memory of it can do this! But what about me? Shame is one commodity I cannot offer, I'm afraid."

"Oh, you!" He chuckled and lifted me onto him again and he stretched my dumb glutton just as agreeably as before. "You're wild, and tender. You're firm and luscious. And energetic. And juicy. You and Cynthia would make a perfect duet as mistresses. The pagan wanton and the conscience-stricken jade."

I tried to stay as still as possible, copying what he had told me of Cynthia's manner. At once he understood what I wanted and began to caress my breasts and belly and down into my furrow with those outrageously cunning fingers of his. Then, without thinking or consciously duplicating anything I had heard, I felt my body become almost unbearably tense and begin to shiver as if I had a sudden fever — which, in away, I had. It was the fever of discovering (after how many thousand pokes with how many thousand men?) a new way of enjoying an orgasm. This one didn't start anywhere, nor did it reverberate back and forth all through me. It simply *was* me, all over, every atom, through and through, from the very beginning. I was as amazed at the discovery as I had been on my honeymoon, when my darling Jack introduced me to a pleasure equally intense but of a very different character — a lively, active delirium that went crashing through me like thunder and lightning, and which I had, until now, taken as the only kind, the kind all women enjoyed.

Thank heavens it was Clifford who helped me discover this other pleasure, lurking there within me!

If some other anonymous lover had uncaged it accidentally in the normal course of a night's business, I should have worn myself to a frazzle trying to recapture it all night with every subsequent lover — for fear it might vanish on me. But with Clifford there, and that marvellously *reliable* member of his, ready to drill me for hours, I could safely explore all the nuances and variations of my glorious new *plaisir* without fear of losing it.

And so we passed that night away in hours of merry copulation — and, like thousands of my gentlemen lovers (or so I trust), I could face myself at dawn and honestly say I never spent my money better.

⑪

Clifford soon got the measure of de Cl—t. "That man," he said, "hates women. Perhaps not *all* women. I believe he's taken quite a liking to you, Lottie. But he can't abide the species as a whole — and that is surely dangerous. I can't understand how you ever let him talk you into becoming your partner in such a venture as this."

I pointed out his three great advantages: the château, the land, and his political power, but Clifford would have none of it.

"As to the buildings and the land," said he, "that's just your greed and stinginess. You've got plenty of money — easily enough to build your House of Pleasure from nothing. By accepting de Cl—t's ready-made place, you're simply storing up trouble. As for his political influence, he's only one minister out of twenty-odd. I'm sure you could find another whose price will not be so ruinous. I tell you, this man will

86

enjoy humiliating and letting down your girls at the very time they need him most. You should certainly exclude him most rigorously from any say in the day-to-day management of the House.''

Very kindly he offered himself as my assistant in that department. Nor did his generosity stop there.

He went on to point out that my weekly reports from Sapphire, Gisela, and Cynthia were all very well, but I couldn't create the House to end all Houses out of reports from the girls who worked in them, no matter how intelligent and conscientious my three present reporters were. He didn't attack them on that score, nor did he claim their insights would be valueless. ''But you're acting like a wretched *communard* Lottie. You seem to think that Houses of Pleasure exist mainly for the benefit of the girls who work in 'em! That's yet another recipe for disaster. My God! It's beginning to look as if you sent for me just in time!''

I asked him what he proposed instead. His answer did not exactly cause me to jump out of my skin with surprise: ''Pretty obvious, isn't it, old girl? You need a man to visit all these places, too, and report to you with a man's perspective. Otherwise you're in danger of forgetting what the whole enterprise is *for*.''

For a long time I stared at the ceiling, desperate for an answer to this serpent's suggestion, desperate to avoid what was obviously coming next.

''If you suppose I'm going to lie here, letting gentlemen pay me for the privilege of plugging my tail, just so that you can take my hard-earned cash and spend it plugging the tails of girls in the thirty best Houses in Paris . . .''

''You're quite right,'' he interrupted. ''That would

be insupportable. In fact, I wasn't going to suggest any such thing.''

"Oh!'' It fair knocked the wind out of my sails. "What, then?''

"Twenty Houses would be quite sufficient. Twenty-five at the very outside.''

I thought I saw the answer then. "I'll agree to twenty,'' I said, "*if* you can tell me one thing you learned at the Sphynx tonight that I would be unlikely to learn from Cynthia.''

Clifford K—n is without doubt one of the idlest and most self-centred men who ever drew breath; but where his own pleasures and survival in a state of indolence is concerned, no man works harder or thinks more quickly. In short, he had anticipated my cunning and matched it with his own vastly superior brand.

"Why,'' he drawled. "Nothing could be easier. I chose Cynthia this evening a couple of seconds ahead of a priest, a Monsignor from Nôtre Dame. On our way to her boudoir, she opened a large wardrobe and took from it one of the filthiest sheets I had ever seen. She spread it briefly in the corridor before folding it and putting it back. Then, when we were in her boudoir, she asked me what I had thought of it. Well, what could I think? It was spattered with old semen stains and it gave off that cloying, gluepot reek of debauchery. I told her I thought it should be burned at once. She said that if I hadn't chosen her, she would now be spreading it for that old satyr of a Monsignor. It was the sheet he had used for his horizontal pleasures at the Sphynx for the past five years. He visits them every week – religiously, you might say. Also, she added, she would have to find some surreptitious occasion to smear her cleft with anchovy paste and spray a little dilute formaldehyde into her armpits, from a bottle the Sphynx keeps expressly for the Monsignor. Yet the man himself is as clean as could be . . .'''

I interrupted him then. "Actually," I said dismissively, "all this is in her last report to me. He makes the girl kneel on that sheet while he, like an old boar, snuffles around it and all over her body and into her exposed crevice, relishing the stink of ecstasies past and future. And then he hurls himself upon her with a maniacal laugh and pokes her like a beast. I already know all about it, you see."

"Including *why*?"

"What d'you mean, why?"

He grinned at me, lazily, full of self-satisfaction, as if to say, "Now you're beginning to grasp my point."

"You mean why the Monsignor has these strange preferences?" I went on. "Believe me, Clifford, if you'd been asked to do queer things by as many gentlemen as I have, you'd long ago have given up asking why!"

He nodded at the ceiling and yawned. "So, you're not interested in the reasons in this man's case?"

"Oh damn you!" I exclaimed. "Go on!"

"Well, it seems he was riding in his carriage through the Dordogne some years ago when he stopped to take up two pretty young girls who were walking by the roadside in some distress from the heat. They were girls of the most respectable class . . ."

"How d'you know all this?" I asked suspiciously.

"He told me, of course. We had quite a lengthy conversation, in fact. I was with Cynthia for less than half an hour." He grinned. "You could say I was already working for you, Lottie."

"Get on with it! I'm sorry I interrupted. These two young bourgeoises . . .?"

"Oh yes. They'd gone out walking with their parents on the morning of the previous day. The family hobby, apparently — long country rambles. Well this one proved too long. Their parents took an afternoon nap while the girls went off to collect mosses or something and got . . . lost. They had spent all night wandering in the forest. Well, the family drill in such cases was to return to base camp, in this case an auberge — which they named to my Monsignor. I'll tell you what followed in his own words:

Horrified, I pointed out it was thirty kilometres away.

"We know," they said ruefully. "It's only twelve as the crow flies, but somehow we've arrived at the wrong side of the mountain."

I invited them to enter my carriage and promised I would take them at least half way. But a moment after they joined me I knew I was lost, lost and damned into perdition for eternity. The aroma that arises off the body of a young girl is heady enough to most men. If she is the sort of slattern who hardly ever washes, it soon becomes so powerful as to be offensive. But if she is the kind who is usually fastidious yet who has been prevented from her normal ablutions by the force of circumstance, and who has, moreover, been labouring for hours though the heat of the day — or, in this case, the heat of *two* days — then I tell you, it is the aroma with which Circe turned men into swine. It is the very incense of the Court of Venus. They had not sat facing me for one minute before I knew, I absolutely knew, I must have them, both of them, before another hour had passed.

I was beside myself with the fire of my desires. It was as if both girls had already clamped around my nose those mysterious glands they carry between their thighs, whose sole purpose is to drive us poor males insane. They saw my distress and ordered my coachman to stop at the nearest inn. They were most prettily concerned for my parlous condition. I said it was nothing . . . would soon pass . . . all I needed was to lie down in a shady room. Perhaps if they would sing to me? And bathe my brow with a damp kerchief?

Of course, it did nothing to assuage my craving to posses them. They saw my condition worsen by the minute and grew quite alarmed. In the end, all I could do was murmur, "First Book of Kings, Chapter One . . ." again and again, scrabbling feebly for my Bible in my bag.

Eventually they decided I wished to have a comforting passage from the Scriptures read to me, so they opened the book and read the verses I had named.

Clifford broke off his narrative to ask me if I knew the chapter in question. I smiled, for it describes how when King David was old and stricken in years his courtiers sent throughout the land for a beautiful virgin to come and lie with him so that he might "get heat."

Clifford continued in the person of the Monsignor:

In King David's case it was of no avail, but my two pretty young she-goats debated earnestly with each other as to why:

"Perhaps if there had been two virgins rather than one . . .?"

"Like us.'

I nearly swooned with sheer delight to hear that, as you may imagine!

"And our Monsignor is not nearly so stricken in years."

"No. In fact, I never saw a man who looked so eminently revivable."

"And it would be a religious duty . . ."

"Yes — it's in the Bible, after all. King David was a good one, wasn't he? So . . ."

And thus they argued themselves into doing what they, by now, were as avid to accomplish as I myself. Believe me, my young friend, I have never found the coyness of females to be more than skin deep. Those two had planned the loss of their maidenheads in a thousand different and delightful ways before ever they clapped eyes on me. And they now tried to realize them all in one go, using my body as their canvas and my *membrum virile* as their brush.

They almost tore the clothes off their backs in their eagerness to get me in heat — which they did with the speed of a silver bullet. And while I drowned my senses in that unbelievably seductive reek, they jostled for the privilege of engorging my lance with the maiden tribute of their years of chastity.

"Actually," Clifford said with a grin, "I begin to embroider his tale now. If I am to be your faithful reporter, I must admit that what he really said was,

'I rogered them standing and sitting and kneeling and lying . . . and then swinging from the chandelier. After that we all got dressed and went to my presbytery, where they stayed the night, and I rogered them all over again.' And he added that he still has the bloodstained sheet and the seminal evidence of their initiation into womanhood.''

'' 'And that is why I now visit the Sphynx,'' he confided at last. 'Of course, I know very well that it's not the sheet on which my delectable young nymph has been so frequently and so ardently rodded for the last two days. I know it's only fish paste they smear in their secret ruts for my delectation — and some other substance they spray beneath their arms, but it is enough. The rest is in here.' And he tapped his forehead and grinned. So there you are, Lottie. How much of that was in Cynthia's last report? But don't you think that a House of Pleasure which could promise him a young nymph who truly had not washed for two days would gain a valuable paying customer, faithful down the years?''

He allowed a long silence to grow before he added, ''Well?''

I sighed. ''How much do you think you will be needing each week?'' I asked.

⚘

In the spring of 'eighty-seven Gisela went to work at a House called Les Dominiques, officially Number Six, Passage Ste Dominique, just off the Champ de Mars; of course, that was some years prior to the building of the Eiffel Tower; in those days the district was almost entirely a military one, what with the Invalides, the Magasin Militaire, and the colleges for junior officers and cadets – all within a kilometre or so. There were more than half a dozen good class Houses between the Rue de Grenelle and the Boulevard de Constantin (on the farther side of which there were at least a dozen more, but they were associated more with the Chamber of Deputies than the military).

Les Dominiques (the name applied to the girls as well as the House itself) had the distinction of being "cornered" by the junior officers and cadets – an ever-changing population of around four hundred. The French army had abolished the purchase of commissions long before the English; competition was fierce and began as early as the age of eighteen in the case of the two-hundred-odd cadets. To succeed, those young men had to be fit, alert, bright, resourceful, and positive; they worked hard and they relaxed with gusto. I looked forward to Gisela's first report from Les Dominiques with especial interest for, in its clientèle at least, it was unique among the Houses I had chosen to study.

Even had I not already known it, though, I could have guessed as much from Gisela's behaviour the moment we met – which was in a dining alcove at Savarin's. We always did ourselves proud when we met in public; I suppose we spent so many hours at the receiving end of orders for the pleasure of others – lie here, Mam'selle . . . now this position, my pretty . . . unbutton that chemise, little angel . . . show me your treasure, sweet nymph . . . caress me so, little dove . . . that we need the pampering of luxuries like the food and service at Savarin's to restore our *amour propre*.

"What a week!" she exclaimed as soon as we were seated. She fanned her face with her hand.

"Busy?" I asked. It was only March and I had not expected a "rush" until spring.

She took out a stout pocket book and consulted it. Her little silver pencil dashed up and down the pages and her lips made a silent tot — culminating in two arches of surprise in her eyebrows. "Only a hundred and twenty-three," she exclaimed, as if she could hardly believe she had pleasured a mere eighteen lovers each day!

"And how much have you earned?" It is the first thing any harlot asks another when they meet and talk business.

More totting led to the answer, "One thousand two hundred and thirty-four, including tips." [*Just under £3,500 in modern terms — or about £28 a client.*] She added with a little laugh of discovery, "One-two-three clients and one-two-three-four francs! I never noticed that." Then, businesslike again, "So the House made one thousand eight hundred and forty-one out of me." She pulled a face.

I smiled and patted her arm. "It won't seem nearly so unjust a year or two from now. How many girls are you there?"

"Only twelve. Oh, it's a lovely little House, Charlotte. I just wish you were there with me."

"I can tell that from the glow on your skin. You look as if you'd found *one* lover rather than a hundred or more."

"Well, it feels like that," she exclaimed. "One continuous lover! In fact, I'm beginning to think your ideas about life may be the right ones after all. D'you remember you told me in Hamburg once, you thought that having only one single lover was the ruin of most poor girls, but that three or four a day would keep

95

any girl happy and healthy for as long as she could manage it?''

When she said I had told her this notion of mine "in Hamburg once," she was being supremely tactful, for I'm sure I've bored all my acquaintances to death with the opinion on countless occasions since, Gisela included. However, I just smiled and said, "Oh, did I mention that to you, too? And why do you believe me only now?''

She coloured a little and looked around as if about to confess a grave but amusing sin and said, "Well, d'you know, I'm actually enjoying the work for once!''

"Don't you usually?" I asked, honestly surprised at what she'd said, for I had always thought of her as one of the naturals of our noble profession.

"Enough," she admitted grudgingly. "I mean enough to keep me at it. Most of it is pretty dull and repetitive, some of it is awful, but there's just enough real pleasure each day to make me think, oh well, it's not too bad, after all. But here — at Les Dominiques!'' She fanned her face again and darted me an embarrassed glance.

"Really?" I leaned forward in delight and made my eyes invite her to tell me all.

"Well, they're all so young! And clean. And eager and happy and admiring and grateful and . . . oh, I don't know . . . it all passes in such a whirl.''

I held my peace and let my eyes go on begging.

"They're like a regiment of fit and randy young stallions at stud, I tell you. I've never experienced anything like them. It's become a matter of honour among them, you know, to visit us at least three times a week. *Of* course, some visit us *every* night and some

96

not at all, but three is about what they average. And they only stay twenty or twenty-five minutes . . . although thirty minutes is the time allowed for their twenty-five francs.''

"None of those long, boring hours with old goats who just want to stare at bits of you or lie with their head in your lap!''

"No, it's all one quick whirl, as I said. It's a very nicely balanced day, too — about two and a half hours sitting around with the young fellows and girls in the salon downstairs and about seven and a half hours upstairs with one or other of them. The longest I ever waited between times was twenty minutes. Usually it's only between five and ten, so there's never time to sit around and get bored. But I didn't tell you the whole of it yet. It's also a matter of honour among them to come twice while they're upstairs with us. Quite a lot of them — the afternoon ones mostly — do it in real style. They take a brace of girls upstairs and give each of us a jolly good rogering. So there's a sort of unwritten code of honour among us girls, too, that we do everything we can to help them . . . how can I put it in these elegant surroundings?''

". . . keep their end up?'' I suggested.

She laughed — and I thought I heard a stifled snigger from the alcove next to ours. A female snigger. We couldn't see into it, of course, but I put a finger to my lips and silently cautioned Gisela to lower her voice still further.

The waiters brought our meal and withdrew. "Are all the other girls as enthusiastic about the place as you?'' I asked.

"I was wondering about that on my way here in the cab,'' she replied. "You know how reluctant girls are to admit they get any pleasure from the clients? You were the first one I ever met who was quite honest about it — apart from simpleminded little country girls who didn't know any better, and thought they were in paradise, and died of exhaustion after a few weeks. I still don't think they'd admit it at Les Dominiques, either. But I'll say this — I've worked in five or six dozen Houses in my life, good, bad, and indifferent, and I've never known one where there was less bickering and catfighting among us girls. I've even heard girls there singing at ten in the morning! I tell you, darling, you'd better find me a nice place to go on to after this, because it's going to be a bit of a wrench leaving Les Dominiques, I can tell you!''

She had some errands to run to the pharmacist and her milliner, so we did not dawdle after luncheon that day, as we usually did. Indeed, we sometimes went on tò Clifford K—n's chambers and pleasured each other for an hour or so in his bed — not with him but with nothing more than Big Daddy, our favourite dildo, between us. But on that day, as I say, she had errands to run; so I stayed behind writing up her report in my own journal. All my ''spies'' brought their reports to me in their heads; the danger of getting caught with a list of statistics was too great.

I was deep in my task when the head waiter brought me a note. I looked first at the writer's signature — a Baroness de Cresson — but it meant nothing to me; the man inclined his head toward the alcove to our right, from where I thought I had heard suppressed sniggers greet Gisela's tale. The note simply read: ''Dear Unknown Mademoiselle — If you will join me for coffee presently, I may have a proposal to your advantage.''

Naturally I rose and went round to her at once.

Rosina de Cresson was a beautiful, rather fragile young lady in her early twenties. Her skin was pale as milk and she had the most wondrous azure eyes, troubled on that day. Her lips were sensuous, they just begged to be kissed. Her long blonde hair, elaborately coiffed, was so fine that even the closest inspection hardly enabled you to discern its individual strands. The flesh at her temples was finely veined in blue. I thought at once of some delicate Meissen doll, but her first words disabused me of any thought that her character might be equally frail.

"I overheard what you and that other pretty young mademoiselle were talking about," she said. No apology, no excuses. Just a plain, bald statement that she had overheard.

I told her I was Madame, not Mlle, Charlotte ffrench and asked her if I could be of any service.

"How does one start?" she asked. There was a slight tremor in her voice and I noticed that beneath her cool, aristocratic exterior she was quite agitated.

Naturally the question took me aback. It is one I was occasionally asked by little runaway servant girls, or would-be runaways, who loitered outside the back door to Numéro Douze in the hope of being taken on there; but the pat answers one gave to those poor creatures would hardly serve for a baroness who dined at Savarin.

I thought rapidly and said, "One starts by examining oneself, Madame. One's reasons, one's hopes, one's inner suitability to the . . . calling — one's vocation, if you like."

She emitted a vast sigh of relief and settled back in

her chair. "Some guardian angel surely led me to write that note to you, Madame!" she said.

"Madame la Baronne is very kind in her opinion," I replied.

"I mean, I can see you are a woman of education and understanding, a lady of some refinement."

I have to confess that I have one or two snobbish corpuscles at large in my veins; I could not help telling her that I had been the mistress of the heir to one of the greatest imperial thrones in the world. Sharp as a guillotine she asked me at once why I was not still in that exalted rank. I took a chance and told her that the mistresses of kings and heirs apparent may not take other lovers, and thus find themselves *occupied* on only one or two nights a month.

"One might as well be the wife of a Baron," she commented tartly. "Why then are you not a *grande horizontale* — if I may presume to question you on such intimate matters, Madame?"

"Because a *grande horizontale*, although she may live under the patronage of a duke, is expected to please his associates, cronies, underlings, and hangers-on; she finds herself spreading her thighs for the same two or three dozen gentlemen, month in month out. May I ask what Madame la Baronne's interest in this topic may be?"

She glanced about us and leaned forward, bringing her lips within inches of my ear. "Your candour with me deserves an equally honest response," she murmured. "You may think me a scandal, but the fact is that I knew nothing of the existence of . . . of women . . . like you . . ."

"Harlots?" I offered.

Her eyebrows shot up in astonishment. I explained

that to me it was a term of the highest honour. She smiled like a schoolgirl who knows she's being naughty and said, "Good for you! Oh, I am so glad I plucked up the courage to write that note! As I was saying, Madame, I did not even know of the existence of harlots until a few months ago — shortly after my marriage to the Baron."

"He told you of them?" I guessed.

"Heavens, no! His sister did — when she explained why he was never at home of an evening — and why, when he finally did turn up, he was too exhausted to do his marital duties by me — though he was keen enough in Venice, I can tell you!"

"On your honeymoon?"

"Yes!" An ecstatic light filled her eyes. I began to suspect what had happened.

"He . . . er, awakened you to the joys and delights that lay in ambush in your body, all unsuspected, during your spinster years?" I asked.

She nodded and the skin of her neck and ears flushed red.

"And you did not hide it from him?"

"Hide it from him? How could I? I thought I was going insane sometimes, the pleasure was so intense."

"Ah!" I responded sadly.

"Did I do wrong?" she asked.

I nodded. "I'm afraid so."

"But why? How can it be wrong to express my love for my husband?"

"I agree with you, Madame la Baronne," I said. "But such is the way of the fashionable world. I meet dozens of men like your husband and I know it is so. They are brought up to believe that a wife's duty . . ."

"Oh, I know all that! To have children — *his*

children. And then, when I've given him an heir and a few to spare in case of accidents, then I may take a lover and enjoy myself. But why should I take a lover? I love my husband. However,'' she added hastily when she saw me draw breath to interrupt, ''it was something you said to your friend that really pricked my interest — when she reminded you that you once told her that lovers are the ruin of a young girl but four . . . what can one call them? Not lovers. Four stallions? Yes, to copulate with four stallion-men at stud each day . . . surely that is bliss?''

''*I* think it is,'' I confessed. ''Many harlots will tell you it is not so for them, that they copulate without the slightest feeling — though they pretend to the wildest ecstasies. All I can say is that I think they are missing one of the greatest privileges of being a woman.''

''And what is that?''

''Why, the fact that, whereas most men have only one shot in their lockers, we have as many as we may care to fire.''

''Yes!'' she exclaimed excitedly, as if I had just enunciated a truth she had half-suspected all her life but had never been able to put into words.

''You mean, on your honeymoon . . .'' I began hesitantly.

''Yes! I mean I used to lie there wondering why he didn't want to go on. And on and on and on! I could have gone on all night.'' She stared intently at me. ''Four a day, eh? How many a week is that?''

''Two dozen or so.''

''Oh!'' Her eyes raked the heavens as if I had just confessed to a huge win at Longchamps.

''Mind you, a dozen and a half of them will range

between fair to downright awful. But the remaining half-dozen make you realize what life is all about and why a wise and loving Creator gave Eve to Adam."

"Ah!" she gasped. "I grow weak at the very thought of it."

"And the rest help to keep one in silks and bonbons."

"Oh but I couldn't take money for it," she responded at once.

I smiled. "You could if you thought about it for a moment, Madame. But may I ask why . . ."

"If I thought about it?" she echoed, interrupting my question. "A lady cannot possibly accept payment for *anything*. Least of all that, I should have thought."

"Most of all that!" I assured her. "The payment is what preserves your self-respect, don't you see? The girl who lets any man she fancies lift her skirts, is a mere wanton, a trollop — as despicable as the glutton, the miser, and the opium fiend. And no one would despise her more than the gentleman who takes temporary advantage of her lust. But let her insist on seeing the colour of a hundred francs, and ah!"

"*How* much?" Her pretty little jaw had fallen almost to her even prettier chest.

"A hundred francs is the very smallest fee in a House of the kind your husband, I imagine, would patronize, Madame la Baronne."

"Why the . . ." A hard, steely glint flashed in her eyes and she obviously squared herself to some great decision. "Madame ffrench," she said with solemn urgency, laying her hand upon my arm, "would it be possible for you to smuggle me into your place of work? Not every night — just one night a week, say? And could you bring gentlemen up to me . . ." Her voice tailed off as she saw me shaking my head. "I would not ask you to bring me only the best — the half-dozen you spoke of. I'm perfectly willing to take my chance on . . ."

I was still shaking my head.

"Why not?" she asked. I truly thought she was about to burst into tears.

"Because I have an even better idea," I said simply.

And then I explained my whole scheme — which had popped into my head, ready made and complete in every little detail, the moment she began asking the impossible.

It was not only *her* guardian angel who was hard at work that day!

§

Clifford once told me that my whole life is an enigma. I am a creature of impulse, he maintains, yet the last thing anyone could call me is impulsive! By saying I am "a creature of impulse" he means I am driven by a passion that lies so deep within me that I am not even aware of its existence much less of its power. And yet when I face a truly great decision, I mull over it endlessly. I certainly mulled over the decision to found the Maison ffrench for *years* — almost from the day I opened my thighs for my first customer back in the summer of 1883 — before I looked at the first sample books for carpets, furniture, and curtains. And I believe I must have been thinking of leaving Numéro Douze long before the actual moment came. The Baroness Rosina de Cresson was simply the trigger that made it possible; the perfect coincidence of her needs and mine gave me the ideal way out. The fact that I left Numéro Douze immediately after meeting her made me seem impetuous; but those who accused me of that fault did not know what discontents had festered in my soul from the very first night I entered that self-proclaimed "Finest House of Pleasure in Paris"!

But it was more than mere discontent that drove me to leave. Clifford himself had lately begun warning me that the French were far more snobbish than I supposed – "ten million times more so than we English," were his actual words. It would not matter if I brought Venus and Aphrodite down from heaven and every houri in the Mussulman paradise, too, and set them all to work at the Maison ffrench, fashionable Paris would not patronize a House of Pleasure owned by a woman whose last position in life had been a horizontal one at Numéro Douze.

Of course I asked de Cl—t at once if that were so. He pooh-poohed the idea, saying that his reputation alone was enough to ensure the most distinguished patronage. But then he must have thought it over, for the following month he said it might not be a bad idea if I could put a little grandeur between my leaving Numéro Douze and opening the Maison ffrench. He suggested I should become the mistress of the Duc d'A—con for six months or so and even offered to arrange it. I asked for time to think it over, for I did not wish to spurn so generous an offer; but nor did I wish to become the duke's mistress, either. He was well up in his eighties and found it very hard to go all the way with a girl. True, I should be able to take other lovers, but for me it would be a return to the unsatisfactory life I had led as Prince Eddie's mistress in Maida Vale – spreading my thighs for the same two or three dozen gentlemen every month. It would be like being a harlot in a tiny provincial town.

So the idea that sprang to mind, almost fully formed, when Rosie de Cresson pleaded to share my work at Numéro Douze had a long gestation behind it and was not at all the wild impulse that malicious tongues have suggested. It ran as follows, if I may artificially paraphrase a long conversation into one much briefer. I should also explain that only the preliminary exchanges took place at Savarin's. The following more intimate conversation occurred at Clifford K—n's apartment, where we repaired immediately.

§

"You, Madame la Baronne, are more like me than you may suppose. My darling husband, the late Jack ffrench, left me with a fortune sufficient to buy a large estate and live there with a hundred or more servants for the rest of my life — and all without even touching the capital. Both of us are interested in gentlemen for what we can get out of them — but that something is most certainly not money!"

She agreed, by way of a very pretty little blush.

I continued: "Do you, perhaps, know of other ladies of your circle, that is, ladies of equal rank with you, whose desires are equally powerful — and equally unsatisfied?"

"Beyond the slightest doubt," she assured me. "I could name you a dozen this minute."

"And I, through my work at Numéro Douze, know of *several* dozen gentlemen — and I stress that they are gentlemen, even though they would hardly move

106

in your exalted circles — princes of commerce and industry . . .''

''Gentlemen who would never dine with us, though they might call after dinner?'' she asked, wishing to pin them down precisely.

''Precisely.'' I smiled. ''As I say, I know several dozen who would be happy to *serve* you . . .''

Her eyes opened wide in alarm.

''But it is exactly what you yourself were proposing — in joining me at Numéro Douze,'' I pointed out.

''Yes, but there I should be anonymous, of course.''

''Of course! Nothing I'm about to propose would hazard your reputation by revealing your identity. My idea is this. We, you and I, shall form a small circle of your unsatisfied friends. But what shall we call ourselves? I have it! *Les Amateuses!* Yes — three or four to begin with, and never more than eight or ten, I suspect. I shall canvass for lovers among my princes of commerce . . .''

''What will you tell them?'' she asked nervously. ''Of us, I mean.''

''A little white lie. Some of the gentlemen I have in mind would be too overawed at the thought of parting the legs of a baroness, much less a duchess . . . too overawed to perform at all well; the rest of them would be so vain that they'd boast of it all around the town. So I shall tell them that Madame de Marly — the Madame at Numéro Douze, you know — turns away several very pretty and accomplished young ladies of good family each week. And that I have formed a select group of them for the express purpose of gratifying the more discriminating sort of gentleman. We'll leave the question of your rank as vague as that, I think: 'of good family.' It can describe almost anybody who can read and write.''

''Is it true?'' she asked, rather shocked. ''Accomplished young ladies of good family? And she turns them away?''

''Yes. They lack the stamina to pleasure the customers day after day, for twenty-one days with no day off. It's a long time, you know — and two hundred, three hundred men . . . Mind you, if I had a House of my own, I'd take some of them and break them in slowly. I'm sure they'd give better service in the long run than the daughters of skilled artisans and the petty bourgeoisie, who are La Marly's preferred candidates.''

''Why don't you!'' she asked excitedly. ''Since you are certainly rich enough?''

I tapped the side of my nose and smiled.

She was as quick as anyone I ever met. ''Will you make room for me when you do?'' she asked at once, giving a wicked little laugh.

I raised that same finger to my temple. ''The cogs have already begun to whirr, Madame.''

She pressed me no further then but returned to our earlier train of thought. ''These gentlemen,'' she said, ''surely they'll realize very quickly that we are not daughters of the haute bourgeoisie, which is what your words will lead them to expect.''

''Of course. But by then they will understand the reason for my little deception. They will see that it was not *really* intended to deceive them — merely to cover your modesty with an elegant fiction, which it will be their duty as gentlemen now to sustain. People will always keep a secret if they feel they're on the inside of it — look at the Freemasons. I shall tell them that none of the ladies will know the gentlemen's real names, either — which, incidentally, will be the truth."

"Really?"

"Indeed. I think it is essential that neither party to any assignation can possibly discover the true name of his or her partner. The only people who will know are you and me. I will tell you the gentleman's true name and you will make sure he is not coupled with any lady whom he is likely to have met. And the ladies will wear veils and the . . ."

"Like nuns?" she asked incredulously.

"No. Like oriental ladies when they leave the hareem."

"Ah!" Her eyes glowed already at the prospect. "But how shall we meet? Where will these assignations take place? Hardly in our own houses!"

"Hardly!" I laughed. "No, I shall take a large apartment in the Palais Royal — because any lady could have a hundred innocent reasons for going there. Also because some of those apartments on the second floor have front doors into one arcade and back doors into another — in fact, they've two front doors, both equally grand. And . . . how many days a week do you and your friends wish to enjoy these assignations?"

"Every day of course! But no" — she smiled ruefully — "we'd be suspected at once. Nevertheless, we could claim to meet for cards on . . . two afternoons a week, shall we say? Let's not be greedy."

"Two afternoons a week would be admirable. And the arrangement will be as follows. Suppose we are to meet on Tuesdays and Fridays. On Tuesday you will tell me how many ladies wish to come on Friday and how many gentlemen each of them wishes to enjoy . . ."

"Good heavens! I had not thought of more than one!"

"Well, in three hours you could easily enjoy the best attentions of four gentlemen. So think of it now!"

Her tongue darted rapidly across her lips. "I am!"

"I will procure the gentlemen . . ." I laughed. "*That* makes a change! I will procure the gentlemen and, when you have told me which, if any, must not be coupled with one or other of our Noble Amateuses, I will arrange their hour for calling upon us at the Palais Royal."

She nodded vaguely. "Three or four!" she murmured ecstatically, staring off into space.

"There is one other point I must make, Madame la Baronne," I said. "I would look a fool if I arranged an assignation for one of the gentlemen and the lady in the case turned out to be a blundering incompetent, all desire and no skill. So each would-be Amateuse will have to undergo a test to show that at least she has the basic skills needed to play the world's most enjoyable game."

"Test?" she echoed warily. "But who would test her?"

"A devilishly handsome young Englishman of my acquaintance – Lord K—n. In fact, this is his apartment."

"A lord!" she exclaimed in delight.

"Or if the lady preferred it," I added carelessly, "I myself could conduct the test."

She laughed, thinking I was joking.

"Oh yes," I assured her.

"But how?"

I rose and went to the drawer where we kept Big Daddy. Her eyes were large as saucers; her jaw fell almost to her breastbone. I let her touch the old warrior, which she did with tender reverence. The sight of her pale, aristocratic fingers closing round that magnificent pleasuring engine made me wet at once and I could feel my impatient *bouton d'amour* swelling and parting the veils that usually shield her from a prurient world.

"Is it possible?" she whispered.

I nodded. I could see she was excited, too. Her heart was throbbing in her neck and the pupils of her eyes were suddenly huge and dark. "You . . . I mean, how? Do I hold it in my hand?"

I shook my head, not daring to trust my voice.

"You?" she asked, gulping heavily.

I nodded.

"In *your* hand."

I shook my head and showed her the simpler, less ornamented end I should anchor within myself — and the ribbons that would secure it to me.

"Oh . . . I don't know . . ." she murmured fearfully.

"Not until you try it," I whispered.

"No!" she exclaimed suddenly, rushing for the door.

I was about to follow and plead with her when I noticed a momentary hesitation between one fleeing footstep and the next; so I held my ground and smiled. When she reached the door she realized I was doing nothing to prevent her from leaving. She paused, one hand on the doorknob, and then turned to face me, her bosom heaving wildly. Our eyes met; hers fell to Big Daddy, still in my hand; she nodded, almost imperceptibly. I tossed him lightly onto the bed, where he lay beckoning us silently to let him unite us in our revels.

I walked swiftly to her and, taking her head between my hands, began caressing the hair behind her ears with the tips of my fingers. A shiver ran through her as she closed her eyes and raised her lips toward me. I brushed them lightly with my knuckles and wiped a few stray wisps of hair from her perfect brow.

Then, with just the tips of my fingers, I traced the line of her neck down to the front and base of her throat. She opened her eyes at last, heavy lidded with desire, and gave the smile of one trapped in the toils of a lust so great it threatened to overwhelm her senses. My fingertips unbuttoned her bodice, like shelling peas out of a pod. They slipped inside, to her right, and began exploring the exquisite softness of her bosom, right down to her nipple, which I gathered up into the fold of my little finger and began to squeeze with a delicate and reliable rhythm. She gasped and began to struggle with the rest of her clothing.

I leaned into her and brushed my lips against hers. She stopped struggling at once and half collapsed against the door, reaching her lips hungrily toward mine. I began to tease her then, darting a hundred little kisses and licks all over her face, never lingering.

"I can't wait!" she cried, struggling once more with her clothing, this time managing to slip out of it with remarkable ease. "Don't torment me any longer. You would take such pity on me if only you knew how I feel at this moment."

While I shed my own clothing she walked with a naturally seductive grace toward the bed. She had a beautiful willowy figure with a slender waist that swelled to the most gloriously fleshed hips and buttocks. And when she turned toward me, holding Big Daddy like a gift from the gods, the soft beauty of her breasts took my breath away; her nipples were so engorged with lustful blood they seemed ripe to the point of bursting. She gasped at the sight of me and her breathing became so shallow and rapid I feared she might faint from that cause alone.

I realized there was no time for a long, lingering passage of arms before making my final assault on the citadel of her innermost joys. I took Big Daddy from her and thrust him swiftly into his anchorage within me. That delightful little pad touched my rosebud and I exploded at once in a thrill that left me breathless and shivering. "Hold him," I gasped, "while I tie . . . Oo-ooh!" I could not complete the sentence because she, guessing what was happening within me, twisted Big Daddy ever so slightly and made him tremble.

The sight and sounds of my rapture made her so eager to join me she lifted her thigh and tried to ease herself down on Big Daddy before my twittering fingers had quite tied the ribbons. "Wait!" I half-laughed, half-panted. "Get in between the sheets."

"No!" she cried. "Out here, standing up."

I got him tied securely at that minute and she fairly launched herself upon me, without the slightest finesse. I realized suddenly how jaded the other girls and I had become in our romps together — not with one another so much as with the whole business of pleasuring our bodies. We spent so many hours each day in vigorous coupling with so many partners that, when we had our own choice of the matter, we wanted nothing more than to lie down together and enjoy the most languorous copulation. We, with all our skill, could find the most exquisite sensations in movements of only a few millimetres either way, taking almost a minute to make one delicious circuit of a stupefied nipple with a maddening fingernail. It was a long time since I had been devoured with such passionate craving, such carnal vigour as this.

She began coming the moment I entered her, and it was such an astonishing display of the female at the very limit of lascivious rapture that I quite forgot my own desire. Humbled and awestruck, my instincts as a harlot took over and I found myself exerting all my skills and sympathies to multiply *her* joys, just as if she were a man who had paid me for the service.

But she wasn't a man, of course — and the fact that she was still coming a minute later, and a minute after that, was proof of it. I grew curious to see how long she could maintain that extremity of delight. At the height of her next great wave I withdrew brutally and, even as she began to fight her way through her drugged and drowned senses, back to the everyday world, I turned her round, thrust her two paces toward an elegant chair whose well-padded back was just the height of a woman's fork (and not by accident, either!), and, bending her forward over it, fed her Big Daddy from behind, to the very hilt of him.

She was especially delicious from that angle because the beautiful pearly rille of her crevice was more than half visible; its fine fleshy lips clung to Big Daddy, moving in and out with each thrust I made. I realized I had been too long in the company of other harlots — the only girls whose quims I had seen for the past three years. The quim of a girl who entertains, say, ten lovers a day will have to withstand the friction of ten excited tickletails, rock-hard in their ardour, thrusting in and out of her some four to five thousand times. It would take more than a fingerful of cocoa-butter and her own natural juices to prevent that most dainty flesh of all from showing the results of such incessant chafing. Her gasp of relish as Big Daddy nosed importunately in and out of Love Lane was ear-splitting; how she maintained consciousness I do not know, especially once my arms encircled her and my nimble fingers found her swollen nipples and the pearly little rosebud of all her joys.

And so it continued, on and on, in whatever position I, like the imperious male I was impersonating, chose to pleasure her – sitting, kneeling, lying with her straddling me and flailing like a marionette on invisible wires, or me straddling her, grasping her glorious hips between my parted thighs as a huntsman clamps his mount between his knees . . . no matter how we lay together, she rose to one ecstasy after another, for a full hour if not longer, until, at last, I felt her go lifeless and still beneath me. I was by then bathed with perspiration and quite breathless.

For a moment I feared that she had, indeed, died of sheer pleasure. Not even Sapphire and I in the earliest days of our mutual love had achieved anything quite like it, though we had run it a close second at times. However, as I fell from on top of her I perceived she was breathing deeply and easily and was suffering nothing worse than the well-earned slumber of profound exhaustion – a reward I shared with her as soon as I had wriggled myself and Big Daddy apart.

§

The afternoon was well advanced by the time I awoke. Even as I surfaced a voice in my mind told me I ought to be at Numéro Douze . . . whereupon another little voice in my mind, equally insistent, assured me I was never going to return to that odious House again . . . whereupon another little voice — most decidedly *not* in my mind — asked, "Is this the right way to tie it on me?"

I opened my eyes to see the familiar and well beloved shape of Big Daddy inches above my face, with Rosina de Cresson towering beyond it, caressing her nipples with her fingertips, already half abandoned to a new round of passion, this time with our roles reversed.

I leaped from the bed, desperate to pay a call of nature. She lay on her back and caressed Big Daddy with both hands, wondering, I supposed, what it must be like to be a man and to possess such an organ, outside of her body, down there.

"If you were a man," I murmured, sitting down beside her, "and that were really your *flageolet* you'd be howling with pain by now."

"Really?" she asked in surprise.

"Yes, you can't squeeze it and try to roll the tip of it like that."

"I was thinking, it feels something like one of my nipples."

"It may do, but you can't treat it like that. Here, do this. This is what they love." I ran the knuckle of my thumb gently up and down the underside of him. "And this." I teased the loose skin beneath his glans with gentle fingertips.

"God!" she exclaimed in a tone that sounded almost like fear.

"What?"

"When you do that, when I watch your fingers doing that . . . I — don't laugh now — I can almost feel it. I mean *feel* it, you know. As if that thing were real, and really part of me. It's uncanny."

I showed her all the other things men like us to do to that proud warrior of theirs, including taking him into my mouth and half-swallowing him so that my throat closed round him and squeezed with a force that will make them come so fiercely it can hurt for days after (or so several of them have told me). That fascinated her.

"What would a man do next?" she asked. "I want to see what it's like to do this from a man's point of view."

"You'd suck my nipples and then kiss your way down to that little mossy swelling which I will be coyly keeping tightly secret between my legs. And then with maddening and delicious little darts of your tongue you'd force me to yield, first the merest glimpse of paradise, then, when your tongue has pleaded your cause to such distressing effect on my poor, weak senses, I'll spread before you the dumb, gluttonous lips of my *centre de délices* all hot and engorged with their craving."

"And then," she said excitedly, "I push this fellow into you!"

"No. Because you are a supremely understanding lover, who knows the ways and wiles of a woman's flesh better almost than she knows them herself, you will postpone that moment until I am quite mad with the frenzy of my lust."

And so it proved. Like fine wine, the nectar that flows from between a woman's thighs when she is roused to that passion she cannot deny, is an acquired taste. Even girls who are naturally drawn to the enjoyment of their own sex do not take to that aspect of it all at once — and I think Rosina had never even contemplated such a thing before that evening; but she took to it like the most experienced Sapphic I ever knew.

And when at last she played the man and got inside me, she seemed to know instinctively the way I liked it — not all vigorous and athletic like her, but full of languor, stupefying and soporific, relishing every little twitch and shiver to the utmost. Of course I rewarded her by pretending to come before I was quite ready; but the pretence soon shaded over into the real thing and she, not knowing any better, kept me up there for almost an hour, until she, too came again in a shattering spasm that hit her out of nowhere and exploded in her belly, leaving her limp and exhausted.

And then came the most pleasant little episode of all between us, when we next awoke, which was sometime just before seven that evening. We rose, washed all over, changed the sheets, and, all passion spent, climbed back into bed and simply lay in each other's arms, talking.

"Your quim is very different from mine," she commented.

"Is it? In what way?" I asked, though I knew very well what she meant, of course, having myself noticed it earlier.

"The lips of mine are so thin and flimsy, and yours are so generous."

I chuckled. "You mean swollen and leathery! Compare the hands of a labouring man with those of a gentleman. Mine is the quim of a labouring woman, my darling."

"Oh, you are so lucky! When I heard you and your friend, back at the restaurant, when I heard her tell you about the young officers — like a regiment of fit, randy young stallions at stud . . ."

"You have a good memory, Rosina. May I call you Rosina?"

She laughed and hugged me. "What else? Oh, but I'll remember that phrase until the day I die. I . . . you know how you go wet down there? That's what happened to me, and − don't laugh now, but I got a sudden feeling, a conviction, that unless I myself experienced the life of . . . your way of life, dear Charlotte, I should never be happy. D'you think I'm awful?"

I kissed her and confessed it was precisely how I had felt before taking up our Noble Profession. Then I told her my life story − the nameless officer who had rogered me senseless in the Government Bungalow at Nowshere in India, at the age of seventeen, and left a pile of golden sovereigns behind in my quim; my return to England and my meeting with my darling Sapphire and how she helped me enter The Life in Mayfair when I was eighteen; my months in the brothels of Hamburg − from Plutos, the seamen's House, where I "did" more than a hundred men a day for a hundred days, to the Doves' Nest, where I did "only" a dozen or two of Germany's finest gentlemen a day; my return to London, to a year as the mistress, first of Prince Eddie, the heir presumptive, then his royal father, Bertie . . . and so to my present misery at Numéro Douze, despite all my great hopes of finding happiness there. And so finally to my hopes of founding what would truly be "the finest House of Pleasure in the world."

"If Les Amateuses are successful," Rosie said, "we could easily form part of the Maison ffrench when it opens."

Oh, she was *so* like me!

119

"I don't suppose you still have day dreams," she said with a wistful sort of sigh. "You hardly need them, do you."

I said that indeed I did, but I had done enough talking for a bit and it was her turn to tell me hers — for I could see that was what she really wanted.

"Well" — she licked her lips like a naughty schoolgirl — "it will also explain why Gisela's story so excited me. My favourite daydream — or, rather, last-thing-at-night dream — is where I'm left stranded up on our farm in Picardy when war breaks out and the whole countryside round there is overrun by the Boche. And I rush out into the haybarn and hide deep between two of the stacks, but it's no use. A young Boche subaltern — devilishly handsome but an absolute brute — oh, such a brute! — he finds me and hauls me out and . . ." She paused to draw breath.

"Ravishes you," I suggested.

"No! Far worse. He throws me over his shoulder and carries me back to their mess, which is in the ruins of our little church, in the sacristy. And he throws me on the altar and tears the clothes off me and then they *all* ravish me — all twelve of them, one after the other. For a whole hour I have them on me, ramming their huge cocks into me with never a moment's pause, until I faint from exhaustion. And so it goes on all the week, except that they begin to change subtly. One of them brings me a bunch of flowers, another has a gift of pretty lingerie, another finds a cushion to make my position easier. And then they kick the priest out of his house and install me in his bedroom. And before long I've made it into an exceedingly pretty little boudoir. And now they're not just coming in and brutally ravishing me one after the other. They're taking longer and longer and being much more gentle and considerate with me. And now I'm allowed to dine with them. Indeed, they seat me in a place of honour. And I sit there, the only woman among twelve men – twelve fit, randy young stallions! – and I steal shy glances around the table and think to myself all twelve of these men are going to roger my tail off tonight! And I feel so thrilled by it I can hardly eat a morsel. But I force myself to because I know I'm going to need all my strength!''

She paused and blew a cooling draught up over her blushing face. Then she fell back onto the pillow, a gesture of relaxation that parted her limbs slightly. ''Just ease your thigh up between mine?'' she begged. ''And hold it tight against me while I . . . oo-oh yess! God bless you, Charlotte darling, you are heaven-sent.''

She came in about half a minute and then, pushing my thigh away, she buried her face between my breasts in mock shame. ''Just a little one,'' she said, by way of excusing herself.

''And that's it?'' I asked. ''Twelve hours of happy copulation with the German army?''

''No!'' she giggled. ''It gets even better. After some weeks of happy copulation, as you call it, they get sudden orders for a night attack. There's only half an hour left – and they all want a last fling with me. They begin to draw cards but I tell them I have a better idea. I make one of them lie down on the bed, in full battle order but with his cock reaching for the ceiling. Then I lie on him – I'm completely nude, by the way – also facing the ceiling, and he rams his cock into my bumhole. Then the colonel gets on top of me – they're all in full battle order with their cocks out – such a lovely colour against the scarlet and blue. The colonel gets himself well and truly into the hole nature intended. Then I bend my limbs at the knee, drawing them up. Two of the others kneel beside me and lubricate the crook of my knees with lard." She frowned at my expression. "What's wrong?"

"Cocoa butter is best."

She laughed. "Cocoa butter it shall be. Anyway, now I've got four of them poking away at me. The fifth straddles me in front of the colonel and puts more cocoa butter between my bubbies and starts poking me between them . . ."

"Where does a high-born baroness learn such things?" I asked in amazement.

"From her high-born father's library — the secret one behind the panel with the painting of the Immaculate Conception! I've never done any of these things with any man, by the way — I hope you understand that. It's all imaginary. Anyway, where had I got to? Number five, poking happily away between my bubbies. Yes. Number six of course, is kneeling above my head and pushing his cock down into my mouth for me to lick and suck and bite."

"Six to go," I reminded her. "And not many orifices left to poke!"

She gave my nipple a little tweak. "Oh ye of little faith! It's probably not possible but anyway, two more lie down sort of slantwise, making an A-shape, crossing me where their cocks can poke up through my armpits, you see? More cocoa butter there, of course. And in the crooks of my elbows, so that two more can kneel beside me and thrust away in there. That's ten happy men."

She frowned and pretended to lose her

concentration. "Two to go. Now *how* did I manage to fit them in?" She thought about it briefly and then gave up. "Never mind. I *do* manage them somehow − you'll just have to take my word for it." Her giggle erupted into helpless laughter. "Your face! Wondering whether I'm serious or not! Anyway − that's my favourite-favourite daydream. And the best thing about it is that they all spout their sperm at me at once. My whole body's covered in it. And when they've gone, I just lie there, remembering all the wonderful, happy pokes we've had together, and rubbing their semen into me. They say it's good for you, don't they? That's why old maids who never get any are so crabby, you know. Now tell me your favourite daydream. I'll bet it's ten times more thrilling than mine."

I sighed happily. "I don't think it's half so good as yours. Also I'm a little afraid of telling you. These fancies reveal more of us than we might wish, you know."

"Why? What does mine reveal of me?"

"That you're a happy, cheerful, outgoing hedonist with a powerful sense of fun and adventure. Also that you know the big secret of life for a woman − never dedicate yourself body and soul to one man when there are ten thousand willing volunteers all waiting!"

She laughed and kissed me, and then told me I was only trying to delay telling her my daydream with all this flattery.

§

We rose and ate a simple supper of omelettes and cheese, helped down with liberal draughts of *Château Curé Bon la Madeleine*, my favourite claret of all. We laughed a lot, kissed a lot − while I tried to think of ways to censor my own favourite daydream. In the end I decided to be entirely honest with her, as I am now with you, dear reader, and for the same reason: If you deceive people, they will one day find you out; and then they will never trust you completely again.

"It is a very common daydream among women, I think," I began as our dressing gowns fell to the carpet and we slipped back between the sheets. "I mean — to be captured at sea, somewhere in the eastern Mediterranean, and to be sold into slavery in an oriental hareem."

"Oh, yes! That was my favourite at school — the caliph's most beloved concubine. Sorry."

"Well, mine is a variation of that. I get put ashore at Beyrouth . . ."

"Are you still a virgin?"

"Yes of course."

"And no one on the ship ravishes you! Gosh, doesn't that tell you you're being saved for something really big and important! Sorry."

"The pirate captain sells me to a slave trader, who has a caravanserai going up to Damascus the following day. And I'm taken in a palanquin, lying on silken cushions all the way, and heavy curtains to keep out the sun, because my skin is so milk-white and pure. And I have two handmaidens who rub my body with unguents and perfumes four times a day. Also they have to pluck every hair from under my arms and down on my belly and right between my legs."

"Every single one?"

"Only the finest down is allowed to remain. Then they have to rub healing salves into the flesh, which, of course, is tormented and made exquisitely sensitive by this treatment. And while they're working away on

124

my charms, they whisper to me all the secrets of the slave girls and how to please your master and avoid being whipped by him.''

"Whipped? Oh, I shouldn't like that."

I smiled grimly. "Just you wait! Anyway, when we arrive at the slave market all the pampering stops and I'm herded, naked with a dozen other naked young girls, into the Cage of the Virgins. We've been brought there from all corners of North Africa and the orient. I'm the only European girl there, though — which excites a lively interest among the wealthy men who have come to purchase us. There are Nubians with shiny jet-black skin and teeth like pearls. And nut-brown Moroccan girls with dancing eyes and smiles that would break any man's heart. And proud Spanish-Mauresque beauties with smouldering eyes and breasts like melons . . ."

"Yes-yes," Rosie exclaimed impatiently, before adding her by now customary, "Sorry."

"Anyway, when I get pushed up onto the dais . . ."

"Oh!" Her eyes were two saucers. "What must it be like, standing up there stark naked with a hundred men staring at you — and only one thought between them?"

"It's not like in the paintings. Not in my daydream. You know that one in the little back room at the Louvre? It's not like that. The men in my daydream are only interested in one thing, of course — our virginity. The auctioneer makes me turn my back on them and bend over and touch my toes, and then he forces my ankles even farther apart with the tip of his staff. And then everybody jostles forward to peer into my *concon*. And, of course, they can see every little fold down there because there's no bush to hide it."

She giggled. "You couldn't hide your candle under a . . . sorry!"

"The main thing is they crowd around me and assure themselves that no other man has been where they are now almost desperate to be themselves. And the auctioneer lets them caress the backs of my limbs and calves, to feel that my flesh is firm and supple."

"And make the bidding even more brisk. Sorry."

"However, the Grand Vizier of the Satrap of Damascus is down there buying for his master. So I get sold for the highest bid of the day — double that of any other girl — because, of course, it's unthinkable that the most powerful man in Syria should have an inferior concubine."

Rosie shivered and closed her eyes ecstatically. "Con-cu-bine!" she breathed. "Oh, I *adore* that word. Could you be an utter angel and bend your thigh once more in between mine, right up against my . . . oo-oh yess! Perfect."

"Here!" I protested. "Whose daydream is this, may I ask?"

She kissed my neck and ears fervently and whispered, "It's ours now, darling. And don't tell me you're not going to enjoy being ravished by my twelve Huns, too! Go on — sorry."

"Well, it takes two days to prepare me for the Great Satrap. During which time they anoint my body with spiced oils and perfumes, and draw patterns all over me with henna . . . And the handmaidens school me in all the oriental arts of pleasing a man as rich and powerful — and jaded — as my new master. And so at last the great moment arrives."

"What are you wearing?"

"If you'll give me half a chance! Actually, almost nothing — which is just as well, because it's baking hot even inside the palace. It's midday, which is when the Satrap always feels at his randiest. So all I have on is a fine gold chain around my waist, from which hangs a locket containing a little miniature carving of the Satrap — not of his face but of his erect tool, ivory white and fiery red, and hard as a brick. I have a thin blouse, or half a blouse, which finishes in frills around my shoulders and more frills just below my nipples. When I breathe in my nipples just become visible. And I'm also wearing those gauzy hareem trousers which are open right through the fork. Shall I go on, or wait till you've come? Yet again!"

"No, no! Go on — it's glorious! Golden, utterly golden!"

"So! I should explain that the etiquette for a slave girl is to enter the Satrap's bedchamber crawling on her belly and not daring to look at him. The floor is polished marble, and scrupulously clean — and beautifully cool, I may add. While they finished preparing my body they gave me an aphrodisiac to drink, and now it begins to take effect. Of course, as a virgin, I don't really understand what's happening to me. All I know is that I want to feel something . . . *anything* . . . inside me, filling me, rubbing me . . . My instructions are that when I've crawled to the foot of the bed I have to slip in under the cotton sheet, which is the Satrap's only covering. And then I've been told to kiss each inch of his flesh all the way up, from his toes to his lips — and taking especial care to pamper and indulge . . . you know what! It's like a great tentpole holding up the sheet over us."

"Oo-oo-ah!" She panted desperately and

abandoned herself to the toils of yet another seizure of delight. "Go on go on!" she urged. "Sorry."

"In fact, I manage the pampering and indulgence part so well he becomes quite desperate to possess me. So he just drags me by the hair — on my head, of course — the only bit they didn't pluck. He drags me up to the top of the bed and, thrusting my thighs rudely apart with his great muscular thews, he simply rams himself into me without any finesse. Of course, I am bitterly disappointed and lose all my desire at once."

I felt Rosie tapping my arm. "Just a minute, Charlotte, this is supposed to be . . ."

"I know what you're going to say. But believe me, they are like that — oriental men. They think only of their own pleasure and they treat their women just like bits of furniture."

"But it's a *daydream*, Charlotte. It doesn't have to be realistic."

"Just wait, will you? This isn't the bit I enjoy. That comes later. This is the bit I have to endure — in order to enjoy what comes later. When I'm pleasuring myself I want it to last an hour or more."

She put her lips to my ear and whispered, "Sorry."

"Well, since this part displeases you so much, I'll hasten the telling of it. To begin with, the Satrap is so delighted with me that he sends all his other concubines and wives to . . . I don't know. His *other* palace, let's say. And he just sports with me night and day, though he never pleases me nor even seems to realize that a woman can be pleased. But bit by bit his demands become more and more impossible to satisfy, and he gets angrier and angrier, and I get more and more desperate to gratify him. Eventually he loses patience with me altogether and has me tied up to a rafter while two eunuchs ply their wicked whips on my naked and defenceless flesh. My screams and the violence of my wriggling excite him so much that he rushes in and ravishes me before I've received more than half a dozen cuts. Then he tells me triumphantly that he's discovered the missing element at last: my screams of torment and the sight of my derrière as it wriggles and squirms to avoid the vicious sting of the eunuchs' lashes.''

I reached for her wrist and felt Rosie's pulse; her heart was going about double the normal rate. ''Don't,'' she pleaded. ''I don't even want to admit it excites me.''

''It's only a daydream,'' I teased. ''Anyway, it soon gets better. Day after day he ties me up to that odious rafter and calls his eunuchs in with their scorpion scourges. Then as I scream and shiver with shame and shock and rage he tears my flimsy clothing off me and rams his great ugly pizzle in and out of me. But what I don't know is that his son, Raschid, has been watching my torment and has planned a way to abduct me and carry me to safety.''

''He's a handsome devil, I'll wager!''

''He's Apollo, Heathcliff, and Lord Byron all rolled into one, with eyes as dark as jet and filled with all the glittering mystery of the desert and lips you only have to see to know what was lacking in every kiss you ever received from lesser mortals . . .''

''Go on − go on!''

''He drugs his evil father and the entire corps of eunuchs, and then he spirits me away at dead of night, both of us mounted on his valiant, milk-white steed. Not a word passes between us, but only because his arms around me have made all words superfluous. All night we ride, far out into the Syrian desert, through mountains and valleys, past oases and ruined cities until at last, with dawn breaking over Eden, we come to the most beautiful ruined city of all. Have you seen the engravings of Petra? That ruined city carved out of the living rock? 'Rose red city, half as old as time . . .' Well, I've borrowed that as the backdrop to this bit of the daydream. He takes me to the Old Nymphæum, deep in the rock, and . . .''

"What's a Nymphæum? Sorry."

"It's where the weary legions, in Roman days, could always be sure of finding a willing young nymph — at least, that's what it is in *my* daydream. And, of course, the ghosts of all who ever found true ecstasy within that fantastic cave-palace still haunt the place, waiting for new lovers to come and make use of it. And when they feel the heat of the desire that courses through our bodies, they unite with us for one of the truly great orgies of history. All the girls who ever spread their limbs for a lusty man there unite in me; and all the lusty men who ever crossed that threshold, pulsating with erotic hunger for a woman, coalesce in Raschid. And so, together there for seven days and seven nights, we explore the heights and plumb the depths of carnal attainment.''

"How?'' she asked. "What d'you actually do? I want to know everything, and I promise not to interrupt even once."

I laughed. "I don't imagine us doing actual things together. I get enough of that in my work, I suppose. Believe me, there's nothing more actual than carnal intercourse with a man who does not arouse you. If you're whirling your head off in that most divine of

130

jigs with him, you don't notice anything. But if you're just lying there, helping him to his pleasure but finding none of your own, you hear every little slap of his belly and groin, and every sticky crackle of juice as his tool slides in and out of you and every gurgle in his belly . . ."

"Yes, all right, darling — thank you! So if you don't imagine you and Raschid doing actual things together, what *do* you think of?"

"I think of my body stretched out against his . . . his kisses on my neck . . . his tongue in my ear . . . his hand round my breast . . . I think of every part of me fed with fire and ice and champagne. And I think of it going on and on and on for a whole week."

"But why a whole week? You can't imagine a whole week while you're lying there, fingering yourself."

"I don't know why. I think that was suggested to me by a gentleman who once whispered in my ear, 'I'm going to come back here and poke you, my little darling, every night this week,' just before he came. Then later he apologized and said he didn't mean it — it was just something he had to say to make himself come."

"You mean, he couldn't come unless he spoke those words?"

"That's what he told me. He said it went back to his schooldays, when he used to 'flog the bishop' — you know what that is?"

She giggled.

"He used to imagine himself poking a harlot. Isn't it sweet? He was only twelve at the time. I've never been able to see twelve-year-old boys in quite the same light ever since he told me this. Anyway, his dream-harlot was so wonderful to him he'd always end up whispering those words to her — 'I'm going to come back here and poke you, my little darling, every night this week.' And then he'd fill an old rag he kept to prevent soiled sheets from giving him away. Actually, it wasn't a rag, it was an old shift one of the maids had thrown away."

Rosie let out a silent whistle of amazement. "And they tell you all these secrets of theirs?"

"It's a funny thing, Rosie. In their heart of hearts they'd love to speak of such matters with their wives and sisters — share themselves properly, in the fullest sense, as ordinary mortals, full of funny ideas and little failings. But they can't. We harlots are the only women they treat as straightforward human beings — as beings equal to them in that most human sort of way. We're the only women they dare reveal themselves to, quite honestly and openly. Believe me, that's one of the great privileges of our profession."

She drew her knees up to her chin and hugged herself in an ecstasy of anticipation. "Don't delay, Charlotte, darling," she murmured. "Leave that horrid Numéro Douze place tonight and set us up in the Palais Royal just as soon as you can."

The delicate oyster folds of her labia were like two pale squiggles of paint in that dark delta a woman reveals when she sits in that position. I desperately wanted to lean down and kiss them with all the tenderness I knew. But she had just given me my orders and, as orders go, they suddenly seemed the very best.

So I rose, dressed, and hastened to obey.

§

When I returned to Numéro Douze I was about five hours late. To avoid instant dismissal any other girl would have needed ten top-quality excuses for such a flagrant breach of the rules; but La Marly could not dismiss me so easily. For one thing I was still too popular with the clientèle, and for another she did not dare risk the displeasure of those two most powerful men in my life, Bertie and M. de Cl—t. What she could do, however — and did with relish — was bawl me out in front of the other girls and the clients.

She called me every name under the sun, and when she saw how coolly I took it, she became more apoplectic still and started on the names too vile to show themselves by the light of the sun.

Two of the girls began to cry. I decided it was enough. "You, Madame Marly, are such an exceedingly vulgar old bawd, it is a great wonder to me that the distinguished owners and patrons of this fine House have tolerated you so long."

There is an unwritten rule among advocates that you never ask a witness a question if his or her answer might take you by surprise. It's a very basic and obvious rule; La Marly now broke it. "Vulgar, is it!" she exclaimed. "I'll give you vulgar, young madame! I suppose that's the purest blue blood that flows in *your* veins"

I smiled but said nothing — yet.

"Ha!" she exclaimed triumphantly. "Can't answer me, see!"

"For your information, Madame," I replied quietly — for by now you could have heard a pin falling through the air, never mind dropping — "my paternal grandfather is a duke in the Peerage of England and, though that venerable gentleman is still alive, my father sits in the House of Lords in his own right.'' (Which he did as a bishop, of course, but there was no need for excessive detail, I felt.)

There was a gasp all round and I knew that at one stroke, and a quite accidental stroke at that, I had found the answer to the snobbery which would have prevented me from opening the Maison ffrench, even with Venus, Aphrodite, *et al*. However, I also knew the French *gentilhomme* well enough by now to realize that, subtle and discerning though he maybe in all emotional matters, when it comes to hard fact you really have to bludgeon him about the head with it. So I persisted.

''Easily said!'' Marly sneered. ''But how are we to judge the truth of that. Anyone could throw out such claims.''

I smiled around at the now-swelling circle of gentlemen, all intensely absorbed in our quarrel as only Frenchmen can be. ''Such judgements are absurdly easy, Madame — among those of us who are brought up to make them as a matter of course. Only one not brought up in that way would dismiss them as impossible. I feel sure every gentleman in this room knows precisely what I mean.''

I thought she would start foaming at the mouth — that she, *she*, the Madame of the self-proclaimed ''finest'' House in Paris, should have to stand there and take this broadside from one of her own girls — and the one she detested above all others, at that. It rendered her speechless.

Nothing loth, I filled the silence for her. ''However, Madame, as you have impugned my honour and cast doubt on my veracity in front of so many, I now demand that you confirm openly, here and now, that

I was recommended to this House by — I name no names, but by a Prince of the blood royal, who is, moreover, the heir to one of the world's four great imperial thrones!'' I wafted my hand in her direction as I finished.

Three dozen pairs of eyes settled on La Marly; it was a challenge she could not possibly duck. But she did her damnedest. She pursed her lips so tight together I thought they would vanish into each other, and she gave the tightest, most reluctant little nod you ever saw. ''Get to work, Madame ffrench!'' she hissed.

I sighed. ''Madame La Marly, a delicacy you could not possibly understand makes it impossible for me to stay under your roof a minute longer than necessary. That same delicacy prevents me from claiming — or even touching — the money you owe me this month. It amounts, I believe, to five thousand four hundred and twenty-three francs.'' There was a gasp at that from the other girls, which I ignored. ''I direct that it should be sent to the Home for Infirm Prostitutes at St Sulpice. And you, M. Georges'' — I selected a gentleman I knew I could trust — ''may I ask you to accept the receipt from Madame on my behalf?''

He bowed amid cries of *Bravo!* and fervent applause.

And that is what I call ''bludgeoning them about the head with facts''! I could now start work on my House of Houses without a qualm.

⚜

When I left Numéro Douze the following morning, and for the very last time, I noticed a carriage waiting a little way up on the far side of the street. As my own cab set off, it began to follow me, keeping its distance all the way to Clifford's apartment off the Faubourg St Honoré. I was about to let myself in when the driver of the carriage brought me a note, an open note, saying that the occupant of the vehicle had a proposal to put to me, very greatly to my advantage.

I recognized him the moment I stepped into his equipage: M. Jacques Ferrand, one of the leading industrial magnates of the day. He was a regular customer at Numéro Douze and had, in fact, been present during my altercation with Marly the previous night. He referred to it at once and said it was the most magnificent thing of its kind he had ever witnessed.

I replied that I hoped he had not been forced to witness too many "things of its kind" because I myself had found it acutely embarrassing.

He said it showed what delicacy of character I possessed and asked what I proposed to do next.

I took my heart in my hands and told him – everything that Rosie and I had planned the previous afternoon and evening.

He laughed with delight and said, "That will be even more enjoyable!"

"More enjoyable than what?" I asked him.

"Well, Madame ffrench, I had been about to propose that you should become my mistress, but I think a lively young girl like you would soon grow restive with only one old fellow like me to look after. But a piquant little club like Les Amateuses is much more to your liking, I think – as, indeed, it is to mine. Perhaps I shall form a new gentlemen's club to . . . how may I phrase it? To *support* you! Yes – Les Amateurs des Amateuses, we shall call it. Ha!"

He was mightily pleased with his wit – but then,

so was I. I did, however, point out that, since Les Amateuses were so very exclusive . . . I let the rest hang.

But he knew what I meant well enough. He assured me that the exclusivity of the Amateuses would be matched by equally high criteria among the Amateurs. Blood-lines and breeding would be matched by money. "Most of us own racing stables," he pointed out. "It is an equation we are already used to making! Oh, and by the way, I know the very man for you to see about an apartment in the Palais Royal."

And thus began a time as happy as my eighteen months at Numéro Douze had been miserable. I actually took two apartments at the Palais Royal. One for myself and my three dearest friends, Sapphire, Cynthia, and Gisela — who, of course, I immediately recalled from their noble work as spies among the lupanars of Paris. They had seen and heard enough, I thought, and so I put them to work on the detailed planning of the conversions we would soon be starting out at Bougival.

Clifford, too — surprisingly — had had his fill (or perhaps I mean emptying!) of the light-heeled girls of those same lupanars. When I told him of his new rôle as "taster" and, if necessary, teacher of Les Amateuses, he was as happy as a skylark — and *up* twice as often!

And, as I say, I was happy, too. For the first time in my life I was truly the mistress of my own destiny. The reader may be puzzled at that since, when I was widowed at the age of seventeen, I was left an inheritance large enough to keep me in style if I lived another hundred years. But it isn't just a matter of money, you see; it's a matter of knowing what you want in life and then pursuing it. What I wanted in life was not love so much as lovers — many of them and none of those deep and bitter emotional entanglements that ruin so many of my sisters' lives. To achieve that was not a simple matter of publicizing my availability and waiting for the knocks at the door. It required certain skills and a profound understanding of those desires that would drive men to my door to satisfy *my* desires.

And all that I had now acquired. *Now* I could put my money to work and, like the good and faithful steward, multiply it into the bargain. My time was now almost evenly divided between the Palais Royal and the Château Bougival.

§

The Maison ffrench opened for business on New Year's Day, 1888. It was bitterly cold and overcast, I remember, the sort of day on which all sensible people either stay in bed or go back to it as soon as possible, preferably with something to keep them warm — an ideal day, therefore, on which to open a House like ours. We had oil flambeaux burning merrily on each side of the drive, dispelling the gloom; there were thirty of them, symbolic of our thirty pretty girls, all on fire with thoughts of the carnal joys to come. Carriages bearing the crests of the noblest families in France rolled up that symbolic *chemin de joie* in a steady cavalcade. And as their occupants drew near the old château they saw every window awash with the warm, seductive light of candles. One old duke told me later that, the moment he saw it, he fell to his knees and uttered the most heartfelt prayer of his life — to be allowed to live at least one more day. (Between you and me, I believe it proved so successful he now repeats it daily, for he is still, as the new century dawns, one of our most faithful patrons.)

Inside we had two small orchestras, who played their hearts out on Strauss, Offenbach, and light, gay music of every kind. The champagne flowed as if we had our own spring of the stuff. In England — indeed, in almost any other country in the world — the occasion would have been made grisly by the bluff, coy heartiness of men too embarrassed to confront their own animal natures. But the French have never had any difficulty in that regard, so it all passed off with wit, aplomb, and a great deal of knowing laughter. Our luncheon was one of those superb French meals that goes on and on for ever. There was a witty speech from dear, enigmatic M. de Cl—t, which neatly achieved the impossible by balancing his well-publicized hatred of brothels with his private delight in possessing an establishment of his own at last, if only in partnership. Then, with a canny glance at me, he assured the glittering assembly he intended to be no more than a *sleeping* partner! Upon which he stretched his hand toward me, as if inviting me to a gavotte, and led me through the cheering throng to the Grand Staircase. It was one of the proudest and happiest moments of my life; he took me to the most sumptuous boudoir of all, our *Boudoir du Roi* and there we inaugurated our new trade in the most lively and agreeable fashion. It was the moment when his château became my House.

It amazes me to say it, and perhaps I shouldn't, but thanks to all our planning — Clifford, de Cl—t, Sapphire, Cynthia, Gisela, and I — we hit the bullseye from the very first go. Almost anything I can say about the Maison ffrench in those early times (apart from the special brouhaha of our first few nights) is just as true today.

Our first clients, as I've already indicated, had the choice of thirty splendid fillies between the ages of eighteen and thirty-two — precisely the number we have today. On that special day, of course, they were all "clean, sweet, and ready for service," all thirty of them — and well and truly served they were, too, for we had almost four hundred gentlemen to satisfy! But after a couple of days, when things had begun to settle, we were down to the regular twenty or so "on" and ten or so "off."

We quickly reverted to the normal pattern in Houses of Pleasure, where a girl works for twenty-one days without a break and then takes seven days off. As the second week dawned, I instituted our rule that no girl should entertain more than four lovers a day. Later I modified it to apply on only four days of the seven-day week; the other three days she could pleasure as many as she pleased. The girls, who at first objected bitterly to this restriction, soon realized that it enabled them to devote so much time and care to each client's pleasure that, notwithstanding our minimum fee of *fr*125 [*around £350 in modern money*], they were earning almost as much again in *bonnes bouches*. Those who took advantage of my concession and pleasured as many lovers as they wished found they earned perhaps only half as much again for more than twice the traffic; worse, because they did not have time to pleasure their lovers so thoroughly, their patrons soon noticed the difference between them and the girls who spread the gentleman's relish only four times a day. The greedy ones soon became the gentlemen's second choice. After that, they began to limit their encounters voluntarily on their "unlimited" days; and now few girls at the Maison ffrench ever willingly pleasure more than six gentlemen a day.

In an average day, from our second week forth, the girls who were "on" took just over a hundred men up the stairs for a glimpse and taste of paradise; and that is still the typical pattern of our business now. About sixty of those eager lovers desire no more than simple, straightforward pleasure with a pretty girl writhing and sighing beneath them; the rest want something more piquant. For them we have our *chambres des spécialités*; they are all to the left when you reach the head of the stairs − the boudoirs all being to the right. The precise *spécialités* are changed from month to month, of course, as fashion and satiety dictate; but the general character of the rooms to the left of the stairhead never varies. No matter what fantasy a man may conceive (as long as it's not dangerous or illegal) the Maison ffrench can almost certainly supply it in one form or another.

It is the greatest possible tribute to the talents of my dear friends and partners. It testifies to their power of observation, to their understanding of that overwhelming lust which drives men in their thousands to come knocking at those portals of bliss which are our fortunes, to their sheer capacity for hard work (much of it horizontal!), and, not least, to their skill at cooperating with one another and with me in seeing our great enterprise established.

There was, however, one great difference between the Maison ffrench in our inaugural week and the House you will find today: We had no Amateuses to grace the splendid occasion of our opening night. But that was sheer cowardice on my part. I had hoped – justifiably, as you have seen – to attract a large, aristocratic clientèle; the last thing I wanted was for any of them to recognize his own wife among the girls in the salon, or even the wife of a friend. I needed time to see how I could manage the two businesses from the same premises – which I was determined to do. In fact, it was Rosie de C. who provided the answer. She had separated from her husband by then and was quite free to attend the opening. Even so, she did not parade in the salon; instead, she relied upon me to steer gentlemen of the Amateurs Club up to her boudoir. When dawn broke the following morning I was shocked to learn that she was then entertaining her *fifteenth* lover of the night – and was as fresh and hearty as any professional!

However, she persuaded me that the way to manage Les Amateuses was to establish them in a wing of the château and to steer the gentlemen to them. And that is still how we manage the business today. The gentlemen are given to understand that the ladies who work in that wing are the wives of the struggling but ambitious bourgeoisie – men in the professions whose income does not rise to match their outgoings (so their wives must, as the old saying has it, "be like the squirrels and cover their backs with their tails."). It is explained to these patrons that such ladies lack the skill of the ones in the main salon and, moreover, cannot be requested to do quite so many interesting things . . . and so forth. Well, the reader can easily imagine the sort of yarns we have to spin so as to mask the true situation. We have to explain to a gentleman why he will be able to make no choice of all the ladies there — for, indeed, *they* will survey *him* through an ivory grille and only those who absolutely do not recognize him will come forward. We also have to make him feel excited by this novel arrangement, which is all to his advantage when compared with the ultimate and unlimited raptures available to him in more skilled arms next door. Impossible, you might think; in fact, nothing is easier!

It never ceases to amaze me, but there are men, large numbers of men, to whom the thought of illicitly enjoying another man's wife is irresistible — especially if, through simple misfortune, the poor lady has been forced to swallow her shame and present herself at the Maison ffrench for the pleasure and delectation of any man with means enough to purchase her. Money is power, after all, and, for a man, there can be no more titillating way of playing his power than by forcing a timid woman to take off her clothes and open her reluctant thighs to his pleasure.

Of course, our Amateuses are no such thing! They are a group of healthy, high-spirited, high-born, bawdy young females intent on having as good a time as any man. They simply purvey a different form of that *Grande Illusion* which whips all those hordes of pitiable gentlemen to our boudoirs, month after month, year after year. And so there in the west wing, to this very night, you will find them still — anything from six to a dozen noble young ladies, randy as rabbits, happily pretending to be uncomfortable with their fate, happily "allowing" their lovers to coax from them those sighs of ecstasy they are determined to utter, come what may! But they are a quite separate enterprise within my House, managed entirely by Rosie.

As to my House itself, *the* Maison ffrench, I believe the best way of describing it and of answering all those questions which these slight memoirs of mine are designed to lay to rest is to reprint verbatim my famous little booklet — the one I place in the hands of all serious applicants for a horizontal position here.

A YOUNG GIRL'S GUIDE *to the* MAISON ffRENCH

by

Charlotte   ffrench

❧⚶☙

Being a Brief Description of our
Honourable Place in the Great Scheme of
Life;   our *High Standards* of Service;
our Methods of Working   the
Arrangement of our *Special Chambers* and
Boudoirs;   and, in short, everything a
youthful and pretty Aspirant to the
Oldest Profession needs to know in order to
lead a Richly Varied, Enjoyable, and
Prosperous Life beneath our roof.

Printed   privately   in   Paris

I know what most penny-a-line scribblers would have you believe. You must be expecting this little booklet to begin along lines something like these:

"So here you are, young maid, about to enter the oldest profession in the world — wondering whether or not to take that fateful plunge, and wishing there were some way to merely *try* it first, as a reluctant bather might dip no more than a toe into the water.

"Alas, sweet nymph, there is no such way for you. In the eyes of that respectable world to which you presently belong, 'dipping a toe,' as it were, is the same as 'taking the plunge.' Both represent a move from the absolute purity of 'The Angel in the Home' to the absolute corruption of 'The Fallen Woman.' Heavens, you could not dare whisper the merest germ of the dizzy ideas that are now swirling in your mind, not even to your closest friend, for you would at once gain the reputation of a girl polluted and defiled beyond redemption! No, my dear, it is not like other choices in life — something you may try and give over again if it turns out not to your liking; it is a step into an abyss from which there is no possible way out."

And so on . . . and on and on . . .

Poppycock, I say! Those of us who actually live in that so-called abyss know otherwise. I could name you at least a dozen titled ladies, all from this demimonde, whose aristocratic husbands were well aware of their profession when they went down on their knees and begged – yes, begged – the ladies' hands in marriage; I could name you a hundred eminently respectable wives among the bourgeoisie whose path to matrimony was similar. I do not claim that the life of every harlot is the primrose highway to a virtuous marriage; but it is not the absolute bar that society would have you believe, either. You wish me to put a figure on it? Very well. I should guess that, of every hundred girls who enter the upper levels of the profession – the levels at which we operate in the Maison ffrench – some eighty will leave it within ten years for a marriage that is happier and more successful (because more honest) than most; a further fifteen will be just as contented in their well-endowed spinsterhood; and no more than five will be left to furnish examples for the moralist's pen.

Let me turn next to some rather less encouraging news: The world is teeming with pretty young girls who are desperate to shed every last stitch of their clothing, every last scruple of their morality, every last ounce of their virtue, every last iota of their modesty, and spread their thighs as wide as the Straits of Gibraltar – to let any buccaneer with gold enough go raise his jolly roger in that open c.

Yet perhaps, after all, that is not so discouraging; it is always nice for a woman to know she is one of a large crowd of her sisters. We may like being singled out for our beauty, perhaps, but in most other things we prefer to belong together. How large is that crowd, you may wonder? Let us suppose (to make the figures easy) that you come from a town of one hundred thousand souls; fifty thousand women; twenty thousand of nubile or bedworthy age. Of those twenty thousand some four hundred will earn their keep entirely by the sale of their bodies to men; a further thousand will use the same means to supplement their inadequate earnings as lacemakers, laundry girls, scullery maids, and factory hands. Every week, just under thirty of them leave our noble profession — very few of them in a box headed for a pauper's grave, most into a successful and happy marriage.

It takes very little skill at juggling sums to realize that, in your little town of a mere hundred thousand souls four fresh souls each day make the decision you are now contemplating. For every girl who takes the plunge there are perhaps fifty who contemplate it and say, "Not today — but tomorrow, perhaps." You therefore share your doubts with at least two hundred others *at this very moment!*

And, naturally, if you live in Paris, sharing it with nearly two and a half *million* souls, then you are one of five thousand girls who are, even as you read these words, "thinking it over." If you today make the decision to cross that Rubicon, you stand shoulder-to-shoulder with a hundred others of your fair sex who today will make that same wonderful journey! And that is only in Paris. In Europe as a whole, that fateful river has seven hundred thousand potentially ruin'd maids standing hesitantly on its farther bank, again I stress *at this very moment*; and they are watching as many as fourteen thousand of their sisters taking the plunge into those waters for the first time in their lives. Today, tomorrow, and every day. When they reach the farther bank, they will join the full-time members of our noble profession, the most ancient

149

known to civilization; they number, in Europe alone, something like one and a half million. And there are a further three and a half million occasional female labourers in our sacred vineyards.

Consider just one of those dizzying figures: fourteen thousand new postulants every single day of the year! If this be the path to perdition it must mean that a like number, "used up" as it were by the traffic they have to endure, are cast upon the everlasting fires of Gehenna every single day as well. Can you bring yourself to believe that? Fourteen thousand lively females, most of them healthy, well-paid, well-fed, well-dressed and with a tidy sum put by, are cast out as human scrap each day? If you can, then ours — the most realistic, the least sentimental of all professions — is not the profession for you, my dear!

So, having — I hope — dispelled your doubts as to the loneliness and isolation of our profession, let me turn to the questions that truly ought to be buzzing like bees in your mind.

There are two extreme sorts of women, one absolutely born to this way of life, the other so unsuited to it that she ought to contemplate anything else — thieving, the religious life . . . even marriage — rather than enter our noble sisterhood. Which sort are you? That is what you should first decide, or, rather, which sort are you closest to being? For most women find themselves somewhere on the scale between those two extremes.

Ask yourself are you happy to be a woman? Do you like inhabiting your body? When you see men's eyes exploring your charms, do you relish a certain sense of power over them? Take off your clothes and survey yourself in the looking glass. Do you find a pleasing wholeness and harmony in the arrangement of soft parts and hard parts, of swellings and dimples? Do you believe (immodest though it may seem) that any man who enjoyed The Favour of you should consider himself one of the luckiest men alive?

And what of your temperament? Are you robust and outgoing? Do you enjoy social occasions at which you meet a great many people, and do you talk brightly, if superficially, with most of them? If, in the execution of some pet project, you are rebuffed or thwarted, do you mope a little then swiftly recover and move forward to whatever is next in mind? Think of the worst blow that ever befell you − a tragic loss, a deeply wounding insult, a vicious and unmerited punishment − something of that sort: Did you outwardly recover from it within days, or a week or two at most? No matter if you inwardly smarted still, did you put on a brave face to the world and continue with your life?

Enough! You see here a paragon of a woman, happy to be herself, in love with the gift of her sex, and proof against all the normal knocks and reverses of life. If you can answer an honest yes to all those questions, I pledge that you and the life you are contemplating are *made* for each other! You may begin at once and without a qualm.

Or do you resent being born a woman at all? Do you hate your muscular inferiority to men? Does the sight and fragrance of your person make you want to curl up in embarrassment? When men's eyes admire you, do you wish your chest was quite hollow and that your hips did not swell out in that degrading way? When you see men eyeing women across the ballroom floor, do you think of farmers prodding livestock into

151

the auction ring? Do you blush at the smallest reprimand? If a friend rejects you or if you overhear some cutting truth about yourself, do you rush to your room and weep your eyes dry into your pillow, remaining inconsolable for hours on end?

If you can answer yes to three or more of these questions, you should consider anything other than the life of the *horizontale*. The worst reason for entering this noble profession is the belief that you are so worthless anyway that you "might as well do it, since there's nothing much to lose." Harlotry to a woman is like champagne to a man; if he is sad, champagne will make him sadder yet; if happy, it will heighten every moment of his pleasure. Likewise, if a woman is full of jaded and unfavourable opinions of herself, harlotry will make them worse; if she is robust and confident, it will be the crowning of her life and character.

Few women are either the paragon or the drab I have painted. You must imagine a scale between those two extremes and place yourself somewhere upon it with all the honesty at your command; and if you are nearer the drab than the paragon, think again. It is a well-paid life but not an easy one. You will need considerable reserves of both temper and temperament to survive its worst episodes.

Here are other poor reasons for taking up The Life:

You have had a bruising experience with one or more men. The idea of marriage now repels you. You are bitter and angry. You say to yourself, "Very well, if *that's* all men want of me, I'll give it 'em — but my, won't I just make 'em pay for it!"

You have been left penniless and friendless in the world. You have tried several regular trades but none pays enough to keep body and soul together. You detest the idea of selling The Favour to strange men but can see no other way forward.

You are bored to death with society in a provincial town.

You want a life of unending gaiety and mindless indulgence.

You are addicted to the bottle and cannot pay for your addiction.

A certain very handsome young cavalry officer (at least, you *think* he's a cavalry officer) has put the idea into your head, perhaps to pay off a debt that will otherwise drive him into exile. He promises it will secure his love for you forever.

And here, for contrast, are a few excellent reasons:

You have granted The Favour to a number of men and were left feeling pretty cool about the whole business. It's not that you dislike the poor fellows — indeed, they are amusing and excellent company. But you cannot understand what all the fuss was about once your clothes came off. However, if they had given you a hundred francs each time, you'd gladly have helped them believe they'd lit the ultimate fire in your belly!

You have granted The Favour to a number of men, enough times to know that no one man would be able to keep you happy in that region. Also you suspect you are not "of the marrying kind." The thought of tying your fortunes, security, emotions, hopes . . . your every part and affection to just one man for the rest of your life brings on a fit of shivering. You are not so foolish as to suppose you will find bliss in the arms of every man who takes you to bed, but it will happen often enough to keep up your interest in life;

and as for the rest . . . well, the money will help make them acceptable.

You have a goal in life. By the time you are forty, you want to be the proprietress of your own small business — a private hotel in Deauville, say, or a riding manège at Fontainebleau. At the moment your only asset is that holey of holeys between your thighs, for the momentary occupation of which men seem willing to pay the most absurd gratuities. You wish to capitalize on it while it still has value to them.

You feel it is your destiny. When you first heard, in sniggerings and whispers among the girls at school, of "fallen angels, ladies of the town, doves with broken wings . . ." and all the other tasteless euphemisms for the noble name of harlot, it awakened something profound within you. And the more you thought about it, the more clearly you realized that, if you died without experiencing The Life, you would die unfulfilled.

Of all the reasons I have given in favour of becoming a harlot, this last is the only one that should induce you to make the choice at once and give it no second thought; all the rest require careful consideration — even if (being a woman after all) you have already made up your mind.

§

If, having read so far, you are still determined on working at the Maison ffrench, you may return for a second interview without further appointment. It will be a practical interview, conducted between the sheets — not by me but by my dear friend Clifford K—n, scion of the English nobility and one of the finest connoisseurs of female flesh in France. But be warned, I shall question you, too, and I shall expect you to have read the rest of this little book − whether or not you are an experienced harlot or are merely contemplating that thrilling first step. I shall quiz you closely, not only upon its contents but concerning your motives in entering the profession and your attitude to men, to other women, and to life in general.

To avoid disappointment, you should understand, too, that I see at least sixty applicants for each vacant place in my establishment. Rejection is *probably* all that awaits you here. It is not, however, the end of the world. It is not even the end of this particular road. It may simply mean that I believe you would be far more suited to work in some other establishment, and I shall send you there at once, and with my recommendation; more than half the girls I turn away go on to other Houses in that fashion − and many of the girls who work here were sent on to me in the same way by other Madames.

Nonetheless, I do engage at least one new girl each week − or some seventy-five each year. So, assuming you will be one of them, let us turn our attention to my House and the ideas on which it was founded.

§

Every House of Pleasure I ever worked in had a list of rules. In some places they were simply handed out to each girl as she joined and she was expected to read them at her own pace and leisure; in others they were read aloud daily, over the breakfast table − a few rules at a time, rather like the lesson for the day in a convent. I realize, of course, that no community such as ours can exist without rules of some kind, and yet every time I sit down to formulate them, I find myself reaching for phrases like "on the other hand" . . . "however" . . . "except, of course, when" . . . and so on. Almost every rule, I discover, must be tempered both to the girl and to the situation. So I have abandoned any attempt to make such a rigid formulary.

There are no rules at the Maison ffrench!

In their place we have something much harder: We have *expectations* – and high expectations at that. What follows, then is a guide to those expectations. I have chosen to address it to our most typical applicant: a young girl in her late 'teens or early twenties who has made a deliberate choice of this noble profession but whose mind may already have been corrupted – by earlier sojourns in less worthy Houses, or by an unfortunate association with an unworthy man, or by the quite scandalous hypocrisy that surrounds our craft in this age of sickening humbug.

For your sake, therefore, my dear young nymph, you had better either be, or force yourself to be, quite green in the matter of carnal commerce. Let me refashion you, step by step, into the grandest of *grandes horizontales*: the ideal Maison ffrench woman.

The Attitude of a Girl at the Maison ffrench

First, I expect a girl who works here to be affirmative in all her attitudes: to herself, to her person, to her colleagues, to me, to the *Maison* itself (by which I mean everything from its furnishings to its day-to-day routines) – and above all I expect the most positive attitude to those gentlemen whose cravings and purses make our privileged way of life possible . . . *Messieurs les Clients*.

Let me begin with them. The first thing you must establish in your own mind is what sort of professional you intend to be — how much of your own true self you will invest in your art. We are not the only profession to confront such a perplexity. Consider the doctor, who daily faces on behalf of his patients the great issues of life and death, of hope and heartache. Ask *him* how much of his inner self he allows to tangle with these moments of great emotion.

"None whatsoever," says Dr A. "If I allowed myself to become embroiled in my patients' emotions, it would get in the way of proper doctoring. I need to keep up a cool, detached spirit if I am to do my best for them. (Mind you — *they* will never know it, for I pretend to share their tribulations to the smallest degree.)"

But Dr B. may answer this argument with its contrary. "I worry about each patient as if he were my own flesh and blood," says he. "Would I do less for Madame So-and-so's sick child than for my own little daughter? Of course not! How then can I *feel* less? Besides, it's important for the patient to know how deeply I care, and that is something I could never simulate."

Dr C. may take the middle ground: "Sometimes I put all of myself into it, sometimes none; sometimes a little bit, sometimes a lot. I make no great distinction between my personal and my professional life in that particular regard. If my patient is the sort of person I'd warm to on a social occasion, then I warm to him or her as a patient, too. And for such an individual I'd naturally feel more *personally* anxious than for one

157

I cordially detest. But I treat both to the uttermost limit of my skill; my sentiments don't affect my professional engagement at all. (Mind you, neither the patient I like nor the one I detest would be aware of my personal feelings. Outwardly I treat them all as if they were the only suffering creature in the world!)"

So, as far as the patient is concerned, our three doctors all behave identically; they are all as tender and sympathetic as can be.

But inwardly — within themselves — they could hardly be more different. And which of them is right?

What an absurd question! They are *all* right — provided they have arrived at these attitudes after some thought and careful experiment. The young doctor starting out in his first practice may feel that Dr B. has the right attitude; later, after several blunders made in the heat of his emotion, he may feel that Dr A. is more prudent; later still, when his rigid detachment has perhaps cost him a patient or two, he may relax and adopt the mid-course of Dr C. Yet there are plenty of doctors A. and B. — and they are none the worse as healers for it. It is all a matter of natural inclination. The only doctor we can say for certain to be wrong is the one who adopts an attitude that runs counter to his own nature.

And it is precisely the same for a girl who enters our equally noble and caring profession. Let no one tell you it is wrong (or unhealthy, or sinful, or rustic) to enjoy a client as you would a lover. Let no one tell you it is wrong (or unhealthy, etc) to be inwardly aloof while you mimic the ultimate passion for his flattery. Let no one tell you to take these things as they happen, neither seeking nor avoiding what must inevitably overwhelm you from time to time. But let you take stock of your own temperament and disposition; know yourself for what you are − and decide for yourself what course you will take.

My own thoughts upon the subject (which may be quite unsuited to you) are these: Every week you work at the Maison ffrench you will spend between forty and fifty hours helping your gentlemen partners to that rapture they find between your legs; you will be doing things that, in other circumstances, would be highly pleasurable to you, too. *If* you can experience that pleasure with at least some of them, *without* diminishing theirs . . . well, it does help relieve the boredom that goes with the endless repetition of essentially the same act, day after day.

The Duties of a Girl at the Maison ffrench

There is a natural progression among houses of pleasure, rather like that which the wine-growers of this most wine-blessèd country have lately devised − the system of *vins paysans, artisans, bourgeois*, and *classés*:

In the cheapest sort of House − the "*Maison paysan*," as it were, for seamen and heavy labourers (or for semen and heavy labour, as someone once joked to me) − a girl's only duty is to lie on her back with her legs open, to keep her *vagin* well greased with cocoa butter, and to wash out her clients' discharges between times. She works naked or in no more than her stockings. There is no Parade − each client buys one or more coupons and is assigned to the first girl who becomes available. The coupon costs five francs [*half a crown − or about £8 in 1990s money*] of which the House takes three. The working day is fifteen hours long and a girl may *do* a hundred or more clients in

159

that time, each one occupying her time (and person) for no more than five or six minutes. The girl's only skill is to make her client spend as swiftly as possible.

In a "*Maison artisan*," for mechanics and small tradespeople, the coupon costs between ten and fifteen francs and it buys up to fifteen minutes with a girl. There may or may not be a Parade in the salon. Each girl will wear a few skimpy clothes, which it is her client's pleasure to remove. The only orifice of her body that is available to him is the one Nature intended for the Act. The only positions such Houses allow are standing or lying, face to face. Nothing goes on in such places that could not equally well occur between the most respectable married couple. A man who wanted to play the game of *soixante-neuf* would be thrown out on his ear. A girl in such a House may do fifty or more clients in a fifteen-hour day; apart from making a client spend quickly, she also needs to smile every so often.

In a "*Maison petit-bourgeois*," for retail tradesmen, schoolteachers, and lower civil servants, the coupon costs between twenty and thirty francs and buys the girl's services for up to twenty-five minutes. There will certainly be a Parade of all the available girls, who will be fully dressed, even if somewhat daringly. The girl's skills will include a modicum of preliminary embraces, kisses, and so on. A few more positions are permitted in these establishments. The client may bend the girl forward over a chair or bed, for instance, or ask her to sit astride him and do most of the work; but still he may enter no more than her natural orifice. She will smile often, taking apparent pleasure herself from the encounter — repeating the performance anything up to thirty times in her fifteen-hour working day.

A "*Maison grand-bourgeois*," for wholesale tradesmen, young officers, and *fonctionnaires*, is the first that a girl from the Maison ffrench might dimly recognize. Monsieur's choice begins not with one parade but with two. The girls — a dozen or more — are first called down from an upstairs waiting room to a back salon. Monsieur, with the Madame of the House at his side, watches them through half-silvered mirrors as they descend and makes a "short-list" of four or five. Madame calls the lucky few to the front salon where he makes his final choice of one or more of them; this is the first House where anything other than a solo congress is permitted. Some houses of this class permit anal coupling; almost all of them encourage oral pleasures — and charge the clients dearly for the privilege. The standard fare, however, permits the gentleman to light the *flambeau d'amour* with one partner in no more than half a dozen fairly elementary positions and to occupy her time and person for little more than half an hour. The fee for this is thirty to forty francs and the extras are steep; the game of *soixante-neuf*, for instance, carried to its final conclusion, is thirty francs again. In most of these houses the client settles with the Madame and gives the girl "ten francs for some perfume, mademoiselle," if she is pleasing to him. The working day is, again, around fifteen hours and she will satisfy a dozen or more men in that time.

So finally we arrive at the "*Maisons classées*," for aristocrats, plutocrats, politicians . . . the cream of society. Like the *vins classés*, such establishments could be divided into fifth, fourth, third . . . etcetera classes — all the way up to *grand classé*. And, just as that grand class in white wines contains only Château d'Yquem, so among houses of pleasure it contains only the Maison ffrench!

This brief survey does not even pretend to cover all possible houses. God forbid! Where would one put an establishment like that strange bastille at the end of the Rue de la Huchette, where every girl is a chimæra, a hippogriff, a wyvern, a freak! Or, again, what of that extraordinary establishment at Sceaux where the youngest "girl" is eighty!? Or the "convent" at Vincennes, where . . . but no! It is enough to realize that, where the mating urge is concerned, the diversity of the male appetite is boundless — matched only by the ingenuity and resourcefulness of our own noble profession in meeting their demands.

All I am concerned to do here is to show that there is a natural progression among houses of pleasure, from the roughest and cheapest all the way up to the Maison ffrench. As we move up that ladder, what do we see?

Most obviously, the basic fee charged in each establishment rises — from five francs to, in our case, *fr*125. The number of services included in this charge increases in proportion, together with the time during which the gentleman may enjoy them. What, then, may a patron of the Maison ffrench expect for his *fr*125?

■ He may take you to any of the de-luxe boudoirs to your right at the head of the stair.

■ He may undress you at his absolute leisure and explore any part of your person with his eyes, hands, fingers, lips, and tongue — and request you to do the same for him.

■ He may insert any part of himself (tongue, finger, *baton d'amour* . . .) into any part of you (hand,

162

elbow, mouth, *vagin, tire-lire*, or the "dairyland vale" between your breasts). But he cannot require you to do the same to him without extra payment.

■ He may enjoy you in any position that is not painful (to you) or dangerous (to either of you). This amounts to twenty-five positions, all of which are illustrated in the Blue Book in the Salon. (Some girls have taken this to mean that once a client has "used up" one of those positions, he may not return to it. That is not so. He may go back and forth through the list as often as he wishes.)

■ He may spend his semen no more than twice during any one session with you. The longest a session may last is ninety minutes, though few clients choose this "model session" and even fewer spin it out so long. For, just as no gentleman would dream of finishing every last morsel on his plate, so, you will find, few of them will "use up" a girl to the last permissible minute.

That, then, is what our patrons may reasonably expect for their *fr*125 − of which *fr*50 is yours [*around £140 today*]. To provide it, however, will probably be the least important aspect of your work as a professional at the Maison ffrench; like a first-class waiter, you must talk the gourmet up from the simple wholesome *table d'hôtesse* to the more exquisite and rarer (and costlier) *spécialités de la maison! − à la carte!*

Like all the other lackeys of the rich, the powerful, the cultivated, we are not really selling those things we are *apparently* offering by way of trade. The *couturier* does not really sell beautiful gowns to his distinguished lady clients, he sells them an impossible dream of beauty itself − a dream that would still be far-fetched if his client were Helen of Troy; the rag merchant who sells tenth-hand garments down on the quays near the Île de la Cité — *he* sells clothes. The *chef de rang* who discusses the evening's menu for half an hour each day with his gourmet master is not talking about how to make bellies feel comfortably full; he is offering a glimpse of the banqueting halls of the gods — ambrosia and nectar. The pie seller at the corner of Place Madeleine — *he* is the one who sells mere food.

And what if the gown does not transform madame into Helen of Troy, and the meal only comes close to being ambrosia and nectar? No matter, it is still a beautiful gown and the food was the best in Paris that night . . . and there is a tomorrow. And tomorrow . . .

And it is the same with us *horizontales* at the Maison ffrench. The tarts in all those lesser houses — they sell a snug, warm, slippery hole with hair round it. But we, who *seem* to do the same, are actually the purveyors of an impossible dream — a carnal paradise, eternal youth and potency, a hareem of girls infinitely available and supremely skilled. And what if we are not Venus and Aphrodite — we are still the best in all Paris! And we have done nothing to kill the promise of tomorrow. And tomorrow . . .!

There are dull and tedious moments in the practice of every profession, including ours. You will find it helpful, at such times, to remember the distinction I have drawn between the pie seller and the *chef de rang*. Be proud that you can draw the same line between yourself and ten thousand lesser practitioners of our art.

But it is no easy line to maintain. If you have never worked in a House of Pleasure before, or only at inferior establishments, even your minimum earnings of *fr*50 for each congress will sound like a fortune. Believe me, I have never met a girl who, after a month or so, did not feel she earned every last sou of it. (But that is because those who did *not* earn every last sou were turned away before the probationary month was up!) It *is* hard work — far harder than "doing" a hundred men a day. And for that reason we have this rather strange rule, which is, to the best of my knowledge, unique among the houses of pleasure in France: No girl at the Maison ffrench may have amorous congress with more than four gentlemen in a day! However, since all rules are made to be broken, girls are permitted to work as many hours as they wish and take in their stride as many lovers as they can manage on three days a week; interestingly enough, few of our girls avail themselves of this exception after the first few months — most settle voluntarily for at most six lovers on those days when they have licence to break my rule. (I must add that, between mid-April and the end of May, when the sap of spring rises with a flooding of lust that drives men almost insane, my regular limit of four is raised to six in any case.)

Oh, how we have been mocked for this moderation! Girls and Madames from other houses sneer that we are not true professionals; they say we are delicate little blossoms who could not stand the heat and traffic of what they think is the "real" world. Pay them no heed. They are jealous, of course. Ask them if, in an entire year on their backs, they could muster four men who would pay anything up to two thousand francs for their Favour! While they are scratching their heads, tell them you manage it every day! Tell them you earn fifteen hundred or more each week [*over £4,500 today*] from your "mere" twenty partners.

In fact, this rule, which has regulated the traffic at the Maison ffrench from the moment I opened for business, is the very secret of our success and popularity. When word of it first spread, the gentlemen and aristocracy of France were scandalized. They flocked out here to Vaucresson to assert their ancient *droit de seignieur*. Oh, what a caterwauling there was! What oaths and protestations! What threats and bribes and promises! Each valiant chevalier was determined to return to Paris boasting that he was the one who talked some sense into "that idiotic Englishwoman".

But men are not fools; they are just slaves of fashion. Those who came to jeer soon realized (as you, I trust, have already done) that a girl who is limited by the rule of the House to a *partie* of no more than four encounters a day — with some of the richest and most pleasure-loving men in the world — must deploy her charms and skills *to the very utmost* if she wishes to enhance her professional income. The astuter among our clientèle realized that no girl at the Maison ffrench would ever see her man-of-the-moment as just one more blur among twenty or thirty who had already occupied her that day. No wonder, they tell each other, that the girls in *this* House are always fresh, bright, willing, cheerful, and infinitely ready to please their partners!

"Oh, the adorable little minxes!" I heard one say quite recently. "Every time I visit this House I am determined I shall pay no more than Madame ffrench's most basic fee. After all, what more could a reasonable man desire than to pass ninety minutes with one of the most delectable young females in Paris and get two shots out of his locker with her skilled assistance? But

dash it if those adorable little fillies don't always talk
me up into a delicious romp that costs me twice as
much and leaves me for dead! But I tell you, I can't
resist 'em!''

That is the witchcraft you will learn and deploy here
at the Maison ffrench. Which brings me conveniently
to my next topic:

Daily Arrangements at the Maison ffrench

During my time of servitude in other houses of
pleasure, certain conclusions were powerfully forced
upon me. Some of those houses tried to control us girls
with elaborate systems of fines, whippings, and sundry
punishments; others used the granting and withholding
of food. The only product of such regimes is a House
of resentful and rebellious girls who will desert to
better establishments at the most damaging moment.
But I have known good houses, too, and from them
both — good and bad — I have derived this simple
precept: *The best way to keep a girl in any House of
Pleasure is to keep her happy!* And the best way to
keep her happy is to ensure that she is well fed,
comfortably housed, and — above all — able to earn
plenty of money. I have known girls from the lowest
sort of establishment, where they had to "do" more
than a hundred clients a day, who would not leave and
go to much higher-class houses where they might do
only a fifth of that number. Why? Because the House
of their choice was warm, and set a good table, and
enabled them to earn up to *fr*300 a day with tips and
extras; in the "better" House, by contrast, the food
was poor, the discipline harsh, and the *fr*350 they
might expect to earn was often curtailed by fines and
stoppages at the whim of the Madame.

There are no fines, no stoppages, no whippings, and no punitive diets at the Maison ffrench!

That is not to say a girl may behave just as she pleases. We do, as you will soon learn, have a system of fair trial and fair punishment; but, rather than commence this section on behaviour on such a negative note, let me describe how *you* (a good and sweet young nymph, to be sure!) *ought* to behave.

You will be scrupulously clean in your person, having a hot bath after work each day, and possibly upon arising, too. In your nightly bath you will wash your *concon* with care and make liberal use of the douche to remove the last proofs of the happiness you brought into the world that day. (Naïve English gentlewomen on their first visit to France may believe that bidets are for washing babies in; we, however, know they are for washing them *out!* Actually, very few girls in our profession become *enceinte*, despite the valiant efforts of so many thousands of men to bring us into that condition!)

In the morning, you will not wash between your thighs at all, whatever attention you may lavish upon the rest of your person; many of our patrons enjoy the fragrance and flavour of our intimate parts, provided the scent has not coarsened into odour, nor the flavour into a gamey rankness. Six to eight hours is ideal.

Before your morning bath (if you take one) you will put on gymnastic costume and join the other girls and me in some gentle exercises, or, in fine weather, in a jogtrot around our secluded garden. You may object that some of the "exercises" in which you engaged the previous night were far from gentle and that you hardly need more calisthenics now! But ask any physician with a practice among girls of our profession and he will tell you that the delicate and shapely bones of the female hip-girdle are not intended to support the passionate weight of a heavy man and his vigorous thrusts for several hours each day. Our morning dances are, therefore, expressly intended to counteract the damage we might easily sustain in our horizontal occupation.

Then you will take a light breakfast and, perhaps, a morning bath, after which you will attend to your toilette. A masseuse, two manicurists, and two coiffeurs attend the Maison ffrench every morning except Sunday. Their fees are reasonable and their skill unsurpassed, so you will have no excuse for slovenly hands and unkempt hair. Also each morning we have the services of three seamstresses, employed by the House to repair working costumes damaged in the heat of the ardent moment; they, too, will attend to your private wardrobe at a most reasonable charge.

What you do next with your time will depend on whether you are working the "long" day or the "short" day or one of the in-between days. The long day begins at noon and finishes between nine of the evening and midnight (or at whatever hour you please if this be one of your three "unlimited" days of the week). The short day begins at nine in the evening and finishes between three and four next morning. I will deal with the in-between days in a moment. But first, why do we need these "days" of varying length?

We try to keep a "stable" of twenty-one fillies at the Maison ffrench, falling to sixteen in July and August, when Paris is dead, and rising to twenty-five in the spring, when male Paris is very much alive! Since it is almost unheard of for one of our girls not to serve her daily quota, it follows that we gratify at least eighty-four gentlemen each day. In fact, the number is usually just over a hundred.

How convenient it would be if those gentlemen would only consult among themselves and report to us for their pleasures at intervals of precisely 10 minutes and 34 seconds! Unfortunately, more than five dozen of them (I deal here in averages) arrive during the six hours before midnight, whereas in the six hours after midday, when we open the gates of pleasure, a mere couple of dozen come seeking their relief. A further twenty or so turn up between midnight and three.

Each of them has a right to expect at least five girls among whom to make his choice, and preferably seven or eight in the evening hours. Long experience has shown us that we can meet their expectations in the following manner:

■ At noon, eight girls (the first *cotillon*) go into the salon to begin the long day; most of them will be on one of their days of unlimited choice.

■ At 4 pm, three more girls (the second *cotillon*) will join them; their day will end between 2 am and 3 am the following morning. Half the girls in the house are now in business.

■ At 7 pm, three more girls (third *cotillon*) enter, making fourteen in all.

■ At 8 pm, another five (fourth *cotillon*) go into the salon.

■ And finally, at 9 pm the remaining two (last *cotillon*) fill out the complement — though by then one or two of the girls who went on at noon may have completed their *partie* for the day.

That, however, is the arrangement for an ideal

world; in practice we may face a sudden flush of gentlemen who would bring all our nice calculations down in ruins. Therefore, whatever "*cotillon*" you may be assigned to on any given day, you will hold yourself in readiness from the time of the previous *cotillon* (unless, to be sure, you are in the first!). Girls are assigned to *cotillons* strictly by rota from day to day – fifth to first, first to second, second to third, and so on. On any given day, you may swap with any other who is agreeable, provided only that you tell me or whoever may be managing the House on that day. The rota for the following day, however, will be drawn up as if you had not made such a change; for instance, if you were down for a short day and exchanged to oblige a friend on the long day, you will still be assigned to the long day yourself on the day after your swap.

After twenty-one such working days, you will be free for an entire week – for obvious feminine reasons.

So, now that you know how and when you and your daily *partie* of gentlemen will get together, let us turn to your intimate behaviour when you take them upstairs – alone at last!

The Etiquette of the Maison ffrench

I have already dealt with the matter of your dress when presenting yourself for company in the salon. No one will mistake you for a wife of the bourgeoisie; but no one should take you for a common *putain*, either. Model your appearance upon the *demimondaines* whose pictures adorn the pages of *La Vie Parisienne* and other journals of fashion; dress with a demure panache by day and a stimulating décolletage by night

— forever trespassing upon, but never beyond, the bounds of delicacy.

And think of our salon as the drawing room of a fairly *bohème* hostess of the haute monde — one who, while she permits nothing indelicate, will not frown at a certain flirtatiousness . . . a few languorous glances . . . and so forth. Nonetheless, in our salon as in hers, the gentleman will always provide the lead. If he prove nervous or bashful, you may encourage him with a modest smile; but such tricks as wetting your lips with a suggestively lingering motion of your tongue . . . or parting them in a silent gasp of rapture . . . or fluttering your eyelashes like a pinioned dove . . . or smoothing your dress in such a way as to throw your bosom or hips or derrière into prominence . . . or any such conspicuous advertisement of your charms is to be deplored.

Similarly, you should show no encouragement to any gentleman whom you know to be an habitué of one of the other girls if she is likely to become available within the next ten to fifteen minutes. Such "poaching" creates much bad blood between girls and can spoil the whole atmosphere of the House.

So, let us assume you have sat in the salon for some brief while, conversing amicably with the gentlemen, when one of them indicates his ardent desire to take you upstairs. (We have no formal parades of female flesh at the Maison ffrench.) Now, indeed, your behaviour may grow a little more frank. I do not mean lewd, but you may allow your bosom to heave with pleasurable anticipation of his embraces, and your eyes may sparkle as your imagination kindles with thoughts of pleasures in store. The impression we seek to create at the Maison ffrench is that you and the gentleman have just made an assignation, so there is no booking-in at the Madame's office, no issuing of towels and soap, and all the other formalities by which houses of a lower class regulate their traffic. But make no doubt that the name of your partner and the time of your ascent of the central staircase will be carefully noted!

If your partner is an habitué of yours, you will need no guidance from me; but if he is new to the House, or even just new to you, this is your chance to broaden his mind and show him how, for a few hundred francs more, he could experience raptures undreamed of – or, more likely, *only* dreamed of. In short, this is your chance to deploy your professional skills to the full. If he is completely new to the House then I, or whoever maybe deputizing for me, will already have told him of our minimum fee and all the delightful services he may expect for it. That recital will finish with words to this effect: "That is our initiatory service here at the Maison ffrench, Monsieur. We do, however, provide much more incandescent and licentious pleasures – which most gentlemen of refinement prefer. However, the girl you select will tell you all about them!"

If all he knows of our noble profession is the sort of thing that goes on in inferior houses, he will by now be wondering what more you could possibly offer. It is for you to build on that curiosity, which (you should not need telling) is better done by suggestiveness than by outright exposition.

At the head of the stairs, for instance, a turn to the right takes you to the corridor off which lie our fourteen ordinary boudoirs, or *chambres privées*. On no account should you show him first to one of them! By the standards of other houses they are so luxurious, so suggestive of the sensual delights that await him, that his impatience will carry him forward at once. Say instead, "Would you care to see some of our more interesting and *curious* rooms, m'sieu?"

To your left, then, are the following rooms (or rooms like them — nothing remains the same for long at the Maison ffrench!):

■ **The Pasha's Hareem** This is a replica of one of the rooms at the famous French Hareem in Constantinople. [*For a complete description of that magnificent institution see my edition of* A Victorian Lover of Women, *uniform with this present book — FR*] Draw his attention to the silken couch, the *chaise longue*, the belly stools, the innumerable cushions . . . and say: "Many of our gentlemen like to bring two or three girls up here. The room is especially furnished to increase his enjoyment of such numbers." Let his imagination work on that before you add, with a seductive tremor and an intimate lowering of your voice: "It's one of the favourite rooms among us girls, too."

■ **The Governess's Room** Be utterly frank about this; tell him directly you enter: "This room is dedicated to those gentlemen who like either to whip or be whipped by young women before they enjoy them in the more conventional fashion." He will either say no thank you or you will see his eyes light up at the prospect. Nine men out of ten will say no thank you. Of the remainder, the vast majority are of the passive kind — they desire to be whipped before they enjoy their cruel mistress. If your partner prove to be of this persuasion, you will deal with him; I shall explain this part of the business to you in person. If he is of the rarer breed who like to hurt a girl before enjoying her, you may still be able to earn the considerable fee we ask for this service − without suffering actual pain yourself. Say, "Well, m'sieu, if you wish to *play* at giving me pain, I'll be happy to oblige you. Here, as you see, we have an Iron Maiden with spikes of rubber . . . thumbscrews that twist and screech convincingly without actually tightening . . . and a cat-o-nine-tails that, for all its ferocious appearance, does little more than tickle . . ." And so forth; go on showing him our range until he either waves the offer aside or takes you up with glee. Some men need time to make this decision, especially if they have never attempted such a thing before, so do not hasten him to it.

Again, most of those gentlemen who enjoy hurting young girls will accept this offer; but there will always be the odd one for whom the pain must be genuine or it yields no pleasure. To such men you say regretfully: "That is not part of *my* service, m'sieu. But if you will be so good as to return tomorrow, Madame ffrench will find you a pretty young female who will be eager to oblige you. She has stereos of them, nude and in chains, in her office and you may make your choice at once."

Do not be tempted, as one poor girl was, to soften your refusal by saying, "I should love to oblige you, sir, but to ask you to compensate me for my loss of earnings over the weeks it would take for my wounds to heal would be altogether too much." The suggestion that the gentleman might be too mean, or too poor, to pay for his pleasures goaded this particular specimen into offering her ten thousand francs to submit to his tortures. And, having already said she would *love* to oblige him, she had no choice but to accept. On that occasion I waived my legitimate share of her fee (which, let me say, is something I have never done before or since!), yet even so she said she would not endure such an ordeal again, not for a hundred thousand. So be warned! These men are perilous to be near. Even those of them who choose the simulated torture will be required to pay for two girls, one of whom must be unchained at all times and will never be out of the other's presence.

But most gentlemen, as I said at the outset, will pass on from the Governess's Room as soon as you make your opening remark, especially if this is their first visit to the Maison ffrench. However, the idea of pain in association with erotic pleasure holds a peculiar fascination for many gentlemen; and once you have implanted the idea that they might enjoy a realistic charade of it, their minds will mull over the notion between times. So do not be surprised if, on their second visit, they ask again for a tour of the rooms to the left of the stairs. Ten to one they will, this time, make a more leisurely tour of that particular chamber and its specialities! It may, however, require several visits more before they finally take the plunge.

■ **The Servant's Garret** Tell him: "This is for gentlemen who have the happiest memories of their first seduction by a buxom serving wench or upstairs maid. We have innumerable liveries and uniforms to suit all classes of servant girl, as you see." Rifle your fingers through them suggestively. "And if the gentleman will give us specific directions as to how the affair is to go – whether we are to be coy or forward, for instance, and what degree of resistance we are to offer before surrendering our Jewel — why then we do our best to oblige.''

Even gentlemen who never got within ten yards of securing that particular Jewel will leap at the chance to relive what all men have achieved in phantasy!

■ **The Railway Carriage** This is one of the triumphs of the new Electric Age that is now upon us — a compete replica of a first-class railway carriage on the Dieppe—Paris line. Say: "Now this is very popular with all the gentlemen. I don't suppose there's a man born who hasn't sat on a train opposite a pretty girl and thought to himself, 'Ah me . . . if only . . .' The chance to make it all come true at last is just what the doctor ordered." Invite him to sit in the seat. Switch on the motors. Let him see the cycloramic landscape rush past and feel the realistic swaying of the whole compartment as the dee-dah-dee-dah of the wheels upon the iron rails rings in his ears. Seat yourself opposite him, eyes downcast, and look demure. This is the one that seduces them when all the others fail!

■ **The Magical Room** To our more imaginative patrons this is the most intriguing room of all. Except for a simple bed, a carpet, some cushions, a chair, two mirrors, and a fireplace, it is bare. There are no pictures on the walls and the decorations are minimal. "What the devil?" is the characteristic response to it. Reply: "This is for those gentlemen who find that the opulence of the other rooms impedes the flow of their imagination. This is the room where their dreams have scope. If you have such a dream, m'sieu, I will help you make it come true — in here." Of course, he will press you to explain what sort of dreams, and how do you make them come true? Return the subject deftly to him: "Surely you have some dream, sir? Some favourite little drama involving a girl? Or two girls . . . or more? Something you re-enact in your mind to while away a moment of ennui?" You will be quite safe there, for all men have such phantasies.

He will be most unlikely to blurt it out at once, though; instead he will press you for more detail . . . beg you will give him an example. Reply: "Why, only last week, sir — you will hardly credit it — but I was blind as a mole. Truly! And then a certain kindly old gentleman brought me to this room and gave me some medicinal root to suck, which only a gentleman could give, and filled me with such copious draughts of his elixir that my sight was restored to me at once!"

Do not be surprised if many gentlemen ask you to re-enact this particular phantasy with them at once! It is an old favourite and was probably enacted in the lupanars of Ancient Greece and Rome. Later, they may ask you to furnish others (which I will supply if your own imagination fails). Only after they have acquired confidence in you, through several such meetings, are they likely to tell you the phantasy that is truly personal to them. If you laugh (no matter how funny it may be) or show signs of disgust (no matter how nauseating it is) you will be asked to leave the Maison ffrench. To show a shallow or negative emotion in the face of a gentleman's deepest desires is, perhaps, our one unforgivable sin.

To prepare you for that shock (and I am the first to concede what a shock the desires of men can often seem), here are some of the more common requests they may blurt out when they have summoned the courage:

"I wish you to command me to put on the costume of a lady's maid and make me comb your hair." (Which he will then do for anything up to an hour — often without any open sign of arousal or the traditional celebrations of masculine satisfaction!)

"You are to go on all fours like a bitch and let me sniff and lick your hind quarters, also push my tongue into your *bienséant*." (Again, a performance that can be maintained for an eternity and without frank excitement on the gentleman's part.)

"Let me festoon your nakedness with jewels, mam'selle, then lay my head in your lap and sleep while you stroke my hair." (Yet another performance that may leave you as bewildered as he will be satisfied.)

"You are to tie me with ropes, mistress, and lock me in a box and sit on it until I bang the side." (One gentleman lay thus for three hours, and paid over *fr*600 for the privilege — so you see what I mean about keeping a straight face! Boxes and other stage properties necessary to the phantasy can be provided at a moment's notice. We are by now familiar with all these oddities of the masculine urge.)

"I want you to squat naked over my face and *faire comme la vache qui pisse*" . . . or "shower me with gold" — or some such euphemism. (Do not attempt to gratify this phantasy without first getting a rubber sheet from me. If you want to know why, look at the stain on the ceiling over my private staircase, which no amount of distempering seems able to efface.)

"I'm a naughty boy and you're my older cousin, come to stay, and you're sitting eating dinner, and I'm hiding under the table, and I get under your skirts, and at first you struggle to fight me off — without arousing the suspicions of the other diners, of course — and then, slowly, you begin to find it pleasurable, and you let me do anything I want and you encourage me with your fingers and show me what to do, until at last you throw all caution to the winds and join me on the carpet for a wild old frolic!'' (Many of them will be even more detailed than this in their instructions. The more detailed they are, the more comical, too — so be prepared not to laugh as he hands you something that resembles the script of a four-act play to perform!)

''Take off all your clothes and put a paper bag over your head. Then walk around the room and allow me to watch you.'' Be cautious when any man you do not know asks you to mask your eyes. Do not let him tie the bag but keep the mouth of it open enough to allow you to see his feet if he should approach — and do not hesitate to whip the bag off if he does. Usually, however, such men desire merely to play with themselves and fetch themselves off and they don't want you to watch — so don't be too alarmed, either.

''Let me shoot my wad into your mouth and then don't swallow it but kiss me on the lips and let it all run back into my mouth.'' (I'm sorry if I have just made you sick, but it's better for you to prepare for such things now than to have them take you by surprise when they happen — as happen they will. Remember, it is a matter of Professional Pride at the Maison ffrench that we do not judge the tastes and whims of our dear patrons, we simply cater to them — to the limits of our ability and of their purses. As you will be privileged to encounter the very best in manliness during the time you work here, so you will also,

180

occasionally, be obliged to serve the very worst. Do *that* to the best of your ability and your character will be enlarged, your pride in yourself will be justified.)

It is no exaggeration to say that the Magical Room is the absolute heart of our business here. Its very existence is the most powerful magnet to those cultured, wealthy, and worldly wise gentlemen who form our clientèle, even if they never make use of it themselves. You should realize that, even for the oriental pasha with a thousand lascivious maidens at his exclusive bidding, the finest carnal pleasures still take place in the head. Everything we do with our partners, and everything they do to us, is really just phantasy; the fact that we have a special room for phantasy's special varieties is merely the cream that tops the most luscious of fruits!

■ **The Needlewoman's Garret**   This you should approach with some caution, for every word you say about it will be the stark truth — and few things are more dangerous in a House of Pleasure than that! Say, as if you are talking about *other* gentlemen, but not, of course, the one to whom you are showing the room: "Many of the gentlemen who visit this house find themselves almost daily in contact with pretty young girls in the most wretched poverty — as landlord, perhaps, or employer . . . government inspector . . . that sort of thing. The temptation to relieve her poverty in the most obvious way is almost overwhelming. Yet their scruples restrain them — for what true gentleman likes to think of himself as the ruin of an honest and virtuous maid? So here they can bring one of us, suitably disguised, to this replica of her wretched garret and re-enact what their noble natures forbid them in daily life to do.'' Then yield up a little sigh at the ineffable sadness of everything. Then give a bright little smile and add, ''Mind you some gentlemen just choose it because it's a jolly sort of a lark, don't you know!'' One way or the other, it hardly ever fails.

If you succeed with it, do not, as with the servant-girl's seduction, ask him what degree of resistance and modesty he wishes you to evince. Resist him as fiercely and piteously as you feel you dare. But remember this: *All* gentlemen believe that *all* ladies spend most of the time pining for their *concons* to be stretched by that magnificent organ of theirs; the more vehemently we protest it is not so, the more certain they feel that it is. So, even as you defend your honour with the utmost vigour, take care, too, to show a languishing eyelid, a bosom heaving with frustrated longing; say *no!* with your hands and tongue and *yes!* with everything else.

■ **The Condemned Cell** Every year, in Paris alone, up to a dozen young girls are sent to the guillotine, most for infanticide or the murder of their masters. Many honest gentleman will tell you how profoundly each such execution affects their sympathies: ''Such a waste!'' they say and they dream of bribing their way into her cell on the young victim's final night and making it one of such ecstasy for her that she'll go out to her death singing. Here, as in our other specialized rooms, you will be pushing at an open door.

■ **The Nun's Cell** In fact, this should be called 'The Postulant's Cell,'' for men find the situation of the postulant, who is still poised, as it were, between a life with men and a life without, much more poignant than that of the nun, for whom the decision is irrevocable. This is the "Such a waste!" emotion in a different disguise. You, as the postulant (or nun, if that is his wish) will find his embraces so enjoyable that you will renounce your vows, provisional or absolute, and dedicate yourself to the life of the senses from that moment on.

■ **The Morgue** Yet another variation on the "Such a waste!" emotion. You are a beautiful young girl — so beautiful, indeed, that the angels wanted you among them at once, before Cruel Life laid the lineaments of care upon your alabaster brow . . . et cetera. Any cause of death will do as long as it wasn't infectious; gentlemen's phantasies are strangely susceptible to deflation in such minute particulars. I once made the mistake of telling a patron that the sweet young thing had died of consumption (thinking it a romantic disease, since it had carried off so many good poets). The poor man had to get dressed and leave — even though he knew full well that the girl was alive and healthy and was merely feigning death!

There, then, you have a brief resumé of the rooms to your left at the head of the stairs. They are always undergoing slight modification as fashion changes or as our habitués demand some new novelty; but, since there is, in reality, nothing new under the sun they will be of the same general character as those I have described above — which is enough, I trust, to enable you to grasp our purpose.

Consider this:

The actual business of carnal gratification can be got over with in fifty thrusts and four squirts — a matter of a few minutes, as the females who work in the very cheapest houses will inform you. All else is phantasy, even what we call our straightforward service in the *chambres privées* to the right of the stairhead. What takes place in the particular rooms I have described above is a further refinement of that same act of fantasy — allowing it to crystallize, if you will, into some particular form with a compulsive strength of its own.

The point I wish to make is this: Do not imagine that *Phantasy* lies all to the left of the stairs and that what happens in the "ordinary" rooms is "ordinary business." It is *all* a magnificent *coup de théâtre*.

⁋

Now I shall assume he is one of those gentleman who needs a week or so to mull over the possibilities of our *chambres aux fantasies* So, despite your best efforts to seduce him into tasting the delights of even one of them, he says, "I think I will, after all, mam'selle, take you to your *chambre privée*." On no account show the slightest chagrin or disappointment. Be ready with an excited little skip and an impulsive hug. Allow him to understand that your greatest joy lies in yielding to his caress and opening yourself to his embrace. You may, however, cast a brief glance of longing at the Pasha's Hareem as you pass it on the return journey; it has the desired effect on about one gentleman in every eight.

But not, I will assume, on this present stick-in-the-mud. All he wants is an hour of straightforward carnal pleasure in the lap of luxury (which, at this moment, for him, is the same as saying your lap!). How do you fill an entire hour in such a way that he will be desperate to return when his purse and potency are restored?

In one way the gentlemen who choose "straightforward" pleasure are the most difficult of all, both to gratify in the flesh and to deal with in cold print like this. For hardly any two in a row are alike; they range from the best to the worst. The best are experienced, worldly-wise darlings who understand every inch of a woman's anatomy, her passions and sensations . . . who know instinctively the uttermost of which she is capable. An hour with them will fly by in minutes and you need have no worry as to how to fill it. The worst are sour old misogynists who detest that same female anatomy precisely because it holds them in such slavery. Remember that (and pity them for it) when they curse you for a clumsy, unfeeling mule, as they paw you roughly this way and that, as they use and abuse you like the commonest drab. It is themselves they hate, not you. But each five minutes with them will drag like an hour.

For this little handbook, however, I shall take as my example a gentleman of middling difficulty. Gérard, let us call him. At first you were delighted that his choice fell upon you, for he is young and good-looking with a strong, manly frame; his breath is sweet and his shy little smile quite engaging − just the sort of partner you dreamed of when you first began to wonder about taking up our noble calling!

However, when you bring him to the head of the stairs and lead him on the tour of our *chambres des spécialités*, you begin to have second thoughts. He dithers at each one. He seems in a daze. He swallows often though his mouth is dry. He laughs nervously at nothing. You keep catching his eye upon you but he looks away at once and cannot meet your gaze. His courage and panache were, it seems, exhausted by the very act of choosing you. The prospect of an hour with this pathetic specimen begins to pall — and the door is not yet closed behind you!

But stop and think. Put yourself in his shoes. See yourself through his eyes. He is obviously not the most experienced fellow in Paris. Perhaps he *once* got his hand inside a maidservant's bodice, *once* took a *midinette* into a cab. Perhaps the cocotte laughed at him. What a miserable list of battle honours to trail into your sumptuous boudoir!

And how does he see you? Why, you are the past-mistress of all carnal pleasures. Your body has known the caresses of the most skilled voluptuaries of Europe. It would take a man, indeed, to awaken in you those sensual passions every man desires to see burning in the woman he possesses — a far better man than he. Perhaps you will laugh at him, too!

Remember our golden rule — all the best carnal pleasures occur in the mind. They are phantasies. But this poor fellow's mind is so choked with terrors his phantasy has no scope. Give it him, then. Throw our usual practice to the wind (again, you see why I speak of the impossibility of "rules") and lead him directly to the bed. There make him lie down beside you — but not too close — rather like two chaste lovers in the Bois; you lie near him on your back while he leans on one elbow and gazes down upon you. If he had a stalk of grass, he'd start to tickle you with it.

Go straight for his greatest fear — that he will prove inadequate. Give a little sigh and say you were overwhelmed with joy when he chose you. Startled (perhaps even a little disbelieving), he will certainly ask why. Tell him: "That awful voluptuary the Chevalier de . . ., well, never mind names — the Chevalier often arrives at this time and usually makes straight for me."

Now look at him, slightly afraid, as if you've only just realized what you've said — or at least implied. Reach up an apologetic hand, quite spontaneously, and caress his cheek. Bite your lip like a naughty little girl. Say, "I'm sorry, my love. I didn't mean to imply that . . . you know . . . I'm not saying he's a man who demands my utmost while with you I can take life easy."

The thought may not even have crossed his mind, but now you've put it there he's bound to ask what the devil you did mean, then.

"I only meant we'll have a nice, *natural* time together, just doing all those lovely, wonderful, happy things that boys and girls were meant to do in each other's arms, hein? Don't tell me *your* palette's already jaded, *too?*"

There! A mere two or three sentences — but see what they have achieved! First you brought his fear into the open. Then you put yourself in the wrong (so that even if he thought you high and mighty, you've brought yourself down for him). Then you suggested he might harbour an unworthy suspicion — a suggestion he will now be eager to dispel. And now you have pushed into the limelight the seductive nuances of all the "lovely, wonderful, happy things" you and he might do together.

While he is still swallowing hard at the thought of them, press on with: "Tell me your favourite, or shall I tell you mine?"

Whichever way he answers, I think you will now be under starter's orders at least.

(To be sure, it may not go at all like that. Do not make the mistake of supposing you must fit every encounter into some such dramatic script as this. All I'm concerned to show you is that you must be alert to your partners with all your senses and all your sympathies; if they are difficult, you must be able to divine the cause of it and so steer them into those pleasant capers for which they have paid.)

If he now takes you up on your suggestion, ". . . shall I tell you mine?", you must have an answer prepared. Here, for the absolute *ingénue*, is one possibility:

"Well, first you understand, m'sieu, we have all the time in the world here at the Maison ffrench. There's no need on your part, nor desire on mine" – produce a roguish smile at that – "to *come* to a hasty conclusion. So I like a man to undress me slowly, really taking his time to savour each new delight as he gently lays it bare. I love him to explore me with his eyes – oh, how I *melt* to see naked adoration and burning desire swell and burgeon in men's eyes! And then I like him to continue his admiration of me with the very tips of his fingers." Wriggle a little with pleasure; breathe in to thrust out your bosoms. "When his fingernails lightly rake me here" – delicately inert a finger into your décolletage and let him *imagine* you touching your nipple – "or when the soft pad of his finger finds that exquisitely sensitive little rosebud of joy we keep secret down here," – lay a hand briefly, vaguely, in your lap and allow his imagination to do the rest – then a little shiver of passion will be enough to complete the thought.

"And then his hands . . . all his fingers exploring and caressing me! And then his tongue! Oh, the feel of a manly tongue as it delves and probes in my *centre de délices*. . . I tell you, it can drive me to distraction even before we have truly begun. Then I am overwhelmed with the feeling that I *must* see him — or see that one part of him which *stands* at the centre of every girl's dreams! How my fingers shiver as they fumble at the cruel buttons that keep me from my *proud* warrior! How my heart turns somersaults of dizzy ecstasy at the first glimpses of that pearly pink hero!"

"No matter how large?" he asks. "Nor how small?" And there he addresses his real fear, of course.

You give a tinkling laugh and say, "Men! Will we ever be able to understand you? All you think of is size! Give me your finger. No, no — come on. I'm not going to bite! Just give it here. That's right."

With another roguish smile you put it in your mouth and encircle it completely between your tongue and palate. His eyes bulge, his breath grows short, he breaks out in a sweat. You release his finger and ask, "Now, did my mouth touch you on this side? And on this? And this? And this?" To each, of course, he answers yes. "And," you conclude, "d'you think I am made any different down there? So what has size to do with it? *Touch* is all."

By now he is drooling to begin. You have filled his imagination with so many images of your charms, your ardour, and your utter availability to him, that his passions have overcome whatever scruple or fear might once have held him back.

But don't stop there. While he is doing his best to recall Scene One of your favourite drama, you supply him with the material for Scene Two:

189

"And then, I love to take his *joujou* into my mouth and see him nearly pass out with pleasure at all the cunning little tricks I know. And believe me, my darling m'sieu, I know every millimetre of that priceless and revered organ. There are tingles and tremors and thrills hidden away inside that vibrant flesh that only I can unlock . . ." Et cetera. (You may also call it his *bondon des filles* or *M. la Pine* . . . I have a list of acceptable euphemisms, which you may study in my office.) You continue to embroider the notion until he starts turning purple. Then you speak of the complementary activity on his part.

"The most amazing thing of all," you murmur as he continues with the fondlings and explorations of Scene One, "is that men who have never been especially competent at pleasuring a girl in that manner, suddenly find within themselves the aptitude and craft of the most practised sybarite. And what a pretty return it is for the efforts I have made, to feel my lover feasting on my *porte de paradis* and teasing my delicate *bouton de plaisir* with all the voluptuous tenderness of a true Casanova! And what delight it brings him then, when I return to my oral homage while he continues his!"

And thus you have set forth Scene Two, into whose motions he duly progresses. All this while, garment by garment, you are completing his déshabille. Your chance to tutor him further is now somewhat limited, since at both the beginning and end of the previous scene your mouth and tongue are otherwise engaged. In any case, you have now not only broken the ice but have melted it quite away! You are approaching the stage where your body, using no more than subtle twists and graceful insinuations can coax him through the rest of the drama. However, now that we have aroused his manhood and got it, all rampant and eager, into the light of day – or at least of the boudoir – let us consider its wants and ways.

From your very first encounter with this amazing organ you should study it with care. That limp appendix, smaller than your thumb, can swell to something like a small flagpole in a matter of moments. Its pale pink head, cool and wrinkled, can turn fiery red, its tender skin stretched almost to bursting with the importunity of its letch. When your (even more superior) organ has defeated it and tamed its ardour, you will think it a lamentable, laughable little tail; but when your beauty provokes it to stand and throb with its need for you, it can seem awe-inspiring indeed – and not a little alarming, too.

Do not expect me to describe it to you, this gristle, this belly ruffian, this girlraker . . . staff of life, baguette, boudon, saucisson, ramrod, lance . . . it has as many names as it has forms, and as many forms as there are noses for the human face. Here is one, short, dark, wrinkled, with his dear pink head only half peeping out of his foreskin collar – and too great in his girth for you to close your fingers round him. Here is another, thin as a finger, long as a hand, with his head all taut and scarlet, ready to burst, you'd think. Here is a third, who tapers like a parsnip and is as uneven in his surface as that same vegetable – a gnarled old warrior of who knows how many hundred such encounters as this (and yet, after a year in this fine profession of ours, you will match him ten for one). Now a fourth, the very opposite to the previous; for you can get thumb and little finger to meet around his root at the belly end, but thumb and long lauder between them cannot touch round the fiery helmet that caps this wondrous lance — and how importunately he throbs and swells do you but try! A fifth is the nearest thing to a banana you ever saw, with a curve on him that you think will split your c— into the shape of its initial letter!

A sixth curves to an equal degree but away to left or right. Some girls will try to tell you these are men who enjoy frequent pleasuring at their own hand and that the radius of the curve is the length of their forearms. But it is not so; for, right-handed or left, their *flageolets* curve to left or right indifferently — and many a man who "flogs the bishop," as they call it, has a horn that is ramrod straight.

The seventh my favourite, is also, alas, the rarest — though perhaps that is all to the good or many a night I should have been worn to a frazzle, for rare indeed is the possessor of such a tickletail who did not carry me with him to the promised land. It is both long and thick but most important of all it has the shape of that old-fashioned ſ you see in books from the last century. Aiee! I grow moist and weak at the very contemplation of it! Be advised by me now: Give that happy gentleman, the possessor of such a ladies' delight, the finest hour of his life — without tapping his milt; then, when he has sworn to himself for the hundredth time that he will return for more as soon as his magazine is refilled, stretch yourself face down beneath him, place a pillow or one of our special stools beneath your belly, and let him rod you to the climax in that attitude. I promise you, if you have had a whole week of disappointing lovers, he will efface their very memory.

However, long or short, tapering or columnar,

smooth or gnarled, veteran or novice, curvilinear or straight, be sure you study it minutely; for the more intimately you know and understand this ardent lance of the flesh male, the more it will repay you in pleasure given, pleasure taken, and money earned. And when I say study it minutely, I mean at close quarters — fondle and caress it, kiss it, give it loving little licks with an artful tongue, engulf it in your mouth and let it luxuriate in the warm, supple bath it will find therein — and study its responses to each particular caress. You will discover that parts of it are no more alive to your stimulus than, say, his elbow or thumb; while other regions are so exquisitely sensitive that the merest touching of them — by a woman who knows what she's doing — is like a detonation in his sinews.

The "ordinary" parts are as follows: most of the upper surface (the surface that slaps his belly when you've inflamed his longing, or that faces you after you've mellowed it), and the same upper surface of its knob or head. On all this upper surface, from its root in his belly to its one baleful eye, only the groove or ridge that divides head from shaft is sensitive. But the underside — ah, the underside! It is all, as doctors say, "exquisite" in its power of sensation — especially the tube up which he will finally pour into you the tribute of his rapture; so, too, is the flesh immediately above and below the "helmet" on that nether surface.

Understand that this splendid organ is far more important to a man than our secret cavity is to us women. For, though our pleasures may be centred on that region of our bellies, they fill every corner of our being. Every cell in our bodies, from the soles of our feet to the crown of our head, partakes in that magnificent riot of our female flesh when it is held in the grip of tumescence. For a man it is all centred in the knob of his wand. Perhaps no single nerve of ours will ever experience an ecstasy as intense as the lucky few that are gathered in the fibre serving that favoured region of the male; we compensate by going on fire all over.

The difference is especially important for a harlot to understand. No man will thank you for kissing his neck at the moment of triumph, or running your nails lightly through his hair, or raking them up and down his spine, and so forth — all actions that would make a woman spin more ecstatically yet. But if you can turn your *centre de délices* into a milkmaid's hand, squeezing in time with his ejaculations (in fact, a half a second ahead of them, releasing the pressure at the moment of his anointing surge), he will account you a passed mistress of the carnal arts and swear you gave him pleasures that only sorcery can explain.

I will add here that some men, a bare majority, perhaps, are as tender and susceptible about their nipples as any woman; with such men, a gentle stimulus applied to those unimpressive adornments is as good as the milkmaid's hand, both at the supreme moment and in the episodes leading up to it.

However, we still have the best part of an hour to go before we get to *that!*

So, while he is giving you your "pretty return," you sigh out some such words as: "Oh, how wonderfully you move your tongue, my lamb! You make me tremble with longing to feel your manhood lodged where he has now earned every right to enter." (Never use a direct or vulgar phrase where an oblique allusion will do. Vulgar phrases stifle the *imagination*; oblique ones fertilize it.)

Later, when you feel him growing sated with the delights of *soixante-neuf*, you rise suddenly and, as the nymph may tease the satyr in the forest glade, you tease him with offers and escapes. But, as the nymph at last gets the satyr just where she wants him, so you, finally, come to the *chaise longue* or one of the well-padded chairs, where you bend over and offer him your beautiful derrière in a mischievous invitation that is as unambiguous as it is irresistible.

Callow lover that he is, he rushes upon you and prepares to thrust importunately within, threatening to bring the whole enterprise to a conclusion both swift and unsatisfying. If you are so foolish (or relieved) as to permit it, be warned − he will not return again for the sake of so brief a romp.

Therefore you murmur, "No, no, my dear. Not so hasty now! See what a warm and welcoming smile I have, just for you! Never mind that it runs up and down rather than side to side, it's a smile nonetheless, and it's just for you to explore. Give your *poignard* his head, then. Let him wander and graze there at his will."

Thus he spreads your juices up and down and makes his later entry all the easier on you. Perhaps he lacks the courage to go all the way up to that other hole, your *chute de rein* or *Madame Gingin*, as some call it − which, though kindly Nature may not have intended it for the purpose, she nonetheless left it happily close by! Alas, shy M. Gérard does not get Madame Gingin nicely juiced up for you, so you wriggle and squirm, apparently to increase your own pleasure, but also, and quite artlessly, offering him a joy he had not yet envisaged.

From now on the two most useful words in any

language are, *Ooh* and *Ah!* Or *O-o-oh!* and *Hah!* Or *Oo-o-oo-h* and *Aaaaaaah!* Or . . . but in this House we sell their variants by the gross! With the help of no more than a dozen or two, together with other sighs and lascivious wriggles and writhings, you encourage him to mount you and remount you and mount you yet again, in all the positions we offer in our *table d'hôte* – or perhaps we should say it *d'hôtesse!*

When he has poked you well and truly in that first position, bending over the chair or *chaise longue*, you straighten with a sigh and guide his hands to your breasts, or down to your belly and to the smile that still grins wide below. You squirm side-on to him, lifting one foot to the seat of the chair. A minute or two of gentle rodding in this position will suffice. Then at last you face him, belly to belly, where you can wriggle against him, kiss his neck and cheeks and lips, caress his nipples, throw your legs about him. And you *ooh* and *aah* with rapture all the time.

Next you seat him on the chair and, bending forward, backing yourself toward him, you let him hold wide your nether lips while you close the softest, sweetest grip in all the world around his *flèche d'amour*. Little poking is possible in this position but you compensate for it with the ecstatic writhings and wrigglings of your hips – and, to be sure, the gasps of rapture that never cease to pour from you.

It is the same when you turn sideways on to him, still sitting in his lap; and again when you straddle him and stretch yourself up to let him feast on your breasts. Now your cries of joy border on delirium.

When your pleasure-sated frame can take no more, you rise again and lead him, trancelike, to the bed. He is in a trance, too, by now; he has never known a girl so frank and unashamed in her enjoyment of these pleasures with him. Nor one so inventive. Nor one so willing to extend his thrills. Nor one so knowing where his deepest pleasures are seated.

And he hasn't experienced the half of it yet!

At the bedside you perhaps tease him a little. You fall to your knees in an attitude of prayer. What's this? He stands aghast. Then a little wriggle of your hips, a sinuous ripple of invitation curves your spine, a suppressed giggle gives the game away – and he's eagerly at you again, dropping to his knees behind you and thwacking the backs of your thighs with his yard of eager gristle. You sigh again as you skilfully open up to let him in. And so you restore that sweet solemnity between you as he pokes away with gusto.

If you have been observant on your visits to the zoo (in those seconds before your parents hurried you on), you will have noticed that the position you and your lover have now adopted is the one used for the carnal act by almost every animal that lives. That must explain why men are so astonishingly prone to shoot their wad, all unawares, in this particular pose. It is also true that our *canals d'amour* are furnished with exciting corrugations and ridges on their forward surfaces, and the underside of the male priap is, as I said, acutely sensitive to such stimulation.

Therefore be especially on your guard for this; it is the same when he bends you standing over the bed resting your belly on a heap of pillows. You can use the fact to fetch him off if he is experiencing difficulty in the achievement. But if you sense the crisis is upon him and he has not yet had his money's worth, be ready to flip yourself over upon your back and spread yourself wide in that invitation no man can refuse. It is a curious fact that a man's letch for a woman can be inflamed to the very borders of reason by the sight of her stretched wide before him, with her well-rodded grotto gaping and pleading for his entry, yet it is a position in which he will find it difficult to rise swiftly to his crisis. You may take advantage of this fact with those men who shoot their bolts the minute you touch them. It is a distressing affliction, for them and for you, but they cannot help it, poor things; the moment they see half a naked breast, old rantipole down there throbs away like a demented snake and fills the air with flying gobbets of his starch.

The correct procedure in such a case is to chide him in a warm and friendly manner for being such a traitor, then lie with him and cuddle and caress him for ten minutes or so, and then bring him back to life once more. Usually your mouth is most effective at this sweet service. Then lie on your back with your thighs well spread and your ankles as far apart as comfortable and teach him to poke you with long, slow strokes, withdrawing moderately and pushing in again only as far as he can reach without clenching the muscles of his buttocks. Half a dozen encounters of that nature, spread over two or three weeks, can often cure such difficulties; indeed, I have known such men to be so thoroughly cured that their ability to postpone the ecstasy made a positive drudgery of the work.

A further word on that impetuous and passionate gristle which hoists his hungry monocle aloft at the very sight of your charms. Almost every girl who enters our noble profession falls sooner or later into the trap of hating that polyprogenitive wand. Some never get over their hatred; they turn into sour, embittered misanthropists, old before they are thirty. They do not hate this or that man's particular incarnation of it . . . indeed, the individual gentlemen themselves almost vanish in the face of this special sort of hatred while its target, the Phallus itself, acquires an independent life and character of an especially odious kind. A girl in this phase of her professional development comes to see the Phallus as a one-eyed monster of greed and craving. She forgets that the thirty or forty incarnations of Phallus she satisfies in a week are each of different ownership and provenance; she sees them as forty heads of one single hydra, a monster with a thousand more, all waiting their chance to go nosing into her tenderest and most private demesne. Indeed, if one of these modern "psychologists," who are all the rage nowadays, were to prove that the legend of the Hydra grew out of a young harlot's nightmares, I should find it a hundred times more convincing than many of the other theories those learned gentlemen have proved to their own satisfaction.

It is very natural, this feeling of hate toward the Phallus. Imagine — you have spent an exhausting hour in your boudoir, on the rug, on the *chaise longue*, in bed, and in a dozen less obvious positions, taming the raging letch of one of those rampant hydra heads. Out he goes, limp and feeble, yielding victory at last to that conqueror of all Phalli, the Grotto of Power between your thighs. And then — hey presto! — there he is again in yet another guise, head high, scarlet and throbbing for more. And after him another, and after him another . . . until you realize he will never be satisfied. Then, indeed, Phallus becomes a tyrant of infinite whim and unsleeping avarice; and the girl who abandons herself to this mood becomes his slave of slaves.

199

Fortunately there are at least two cures for the condition. And the sooner you apply them, the quicker you will enter into the correct feelings toward the men in your life, which are pity, compassion, and tenderness. The first cure is to realize that Phallus does not exist! You created him so as to exclude the individual men behind each individual hydra head. Refocus your attention and efforts on those men rather than on that importunate column they waggle at you like a birthday present, and you are halfway rescued.

The second — if you absolutely cannot forget that tyrant rod — is to realize how much greater is its tyranny over *him*, the poor man who owns it — or, rather, is *owned by it!* Imagine yourself a man; it is something a good professional harlot should do fairly often. It is morning. You have just awoken. Are you married? Did your wife grant you the Conjugal Favour last night? No matter. What's past is past. The grand dinner you devoured last night has not spoiled your appetite for breakfast. Forgo breakfast and by tonight you will be ravenous again. And it is the same with that dreaded monster of carnal appetite down there between your legs.

Don't think of female flesh now!

Ach, too late! One brief image flashed before your mind — a postage stamp in a gale. In that flickering moment you saw a mossy cleft with its lips gently parted to reveal a pale flower, a pursed grotto . . . or perhaps it was not even that. Perhaps it was a nipple as large as an old gold louis, all swollen and warm, begging your gentlest caress. Or a mischievous, provoking eye. Or a tongue lingering on a moistened lip. It is enough! Wham! Like a sudden squall in a slack mainsail, the Old Tyrant down there is gorged on blood and throbbing for exercise. (You think this far-fetched? Let me simply list for you some of the stimuli that gentlemen, happy and relaxed after an enjoyable frolic between my thighs, have confessed to me: a dog barking on a summer's eve; a newsboy crying up a murder; the rustle of silk from the pew behind in church; a woman's shoe discarded in the gutter; a leaping horse; a clashing wave — all of these and more have driven at least one man of my, admittedly vast, acquaintance to a letch so overpowering that hardly a woman under eighty was safe in his company. Men can be roused by *anything!*)

So there you are, lying in bed, with that importunate serpent staring mutely up at you through his one baleful eye. He cannot speak but you cannot doubt his question: *When?*

You groan inwardly. Was last night not enough to be going on with?

When?

Does he, this implacable serpent, think you're made of money?

When?

Does he suppose you guard your health merely so that he may squander it?

When?

You sigh. Tonight.

Where? With whom?

Does it matter?

The serpent smiles. *No, it doesn't matter. The more the merrier.*

And so that monstrous reservoir of lecherous desire starts to fill again. Night falls and you are a trembling wreck, an abject slave to that importunate bludgeon which parts the darkness before you, seeking some vessel into which it can discharge its intolerable accumulation.

So there! That is surely real tyranny? Rejoice you are a woman!

If you ever consider that same serpent to be a tyrant over *you* in its insatiable longing for union with your flesh, just imagine what it must be like to be glued in a permanent, indissoluble union with it! Imagine it plaguing you night and day to squander your purse and health in its unending pursuit of the Hairy Oracle! And believe me when I say I pity the poor men who are so driven to seek us out, and I ache with my sorrow for their helpless addiction to that brief aphrodisiac moment they enjoy within our bellies.

And if some of them hate us, is it any wonder? For we — not all women, but harlots like us — we live in reality a life to which they may aspire only in the most absurd kind of phantasy; even worse, they have to pay us for it!

Poor, poor creatures!

§

Enough of that! What you have read so far in the pages of this little handbook to our noble profession should enable you to carry off your first few dozen encounters with some panache and as much pride as is proper for a beginner to feel. But harlotry is above all an art — that is to say, it is a blend of science and magic. And at the level at which we at the Maison ffrench practise our profession, it is a fine art of the very highest order. When you are a passed mistress of our guild, you will be a sorceress who can conjure magic and mystery out of a commonplace nothing.

You will take the mundane lechery of ordinary men and raise it to a yearning that belongs among the celestial spheres; you will take the leaden gift of his lust and transmute it into pure twenty-four carat gold.

How?

Ah, if I could tell you that, I could make a Rembrandt of every scribbler for *La Vie Parisienne*!

All I can do is give you a number of hints that may shorten your journeying days, the days of your apprenticeship. I once asked a great French painter — his name would be known in every household in Europe — how he learned his art. His reply: "As to my art, chère Madame, I cannot tell you that, any more than you could tell me how you learned yours! But I *can* tell you how I acquired the skill that supports it. Quite simply, I adopted a favourite painter from the first moment I took a brush between my fingers. I changed him quite often, to be sure. In the beginning he was called Titian. Then Raphael. Then Rubens. Then El Greco. But, whatever his name, I was never without him for the first ten years of my professional life."

Profound words, dear beginner! They apply to all the arts, and above all to ours. Your way to the very top of our profession will be hastened beyond measure if you can acquire "a favourite harlot" to emulate while you learn. Her name can change as often as the moon, but while you have some ideal pinned up, as it were, in your heart, you will surely forge ahead.

"But how can I do that?" I hear you say.

Well, assuredly not by reading the memoirs of the great courtesans. They are all marred by pandering to the prejudices of gentlemen (who are assumed to be the only readers) and by ritual homage to prudery. You know the sort of thing: "I burn with shame to confess it now but . . ." and then follows ten pages of drooling over some impossibly voluptuous encounter. "Burn with shame," indeed! (I make one exception, here: *Fanny Hill*, by John Cleland, which has been the sole "manual" of carnal education for the gentlemen of Europe for the past two centuries; but that is a work of art disguised as autobiography. Read it, little nymph, and you will profit from every line.)

But your right-down regular way of acquiring a suitable heroine will be found every day in our salons at the Maison ffrench. Girls who are good at their work enjoy talking about it, too. Listen to them and you will assuredly not lack for profitable examples. And here, as a further aide to your progress, is a brief *catalogue raisonnée* of four of the finest harlots who have worked here over the years. And, for contrast, I also give you one upon whom no girl should try to model herself.

§§

Delphine Vaucher was far and away the most extraordinary girl I ever knew. When I tell you that in all the two years she worked at the Maison ffrench she never once put in an appearance downstairs in the salon, rarely worked past ten in the evening (until her last months here), regularly entertained up to a dozen gentlemen each day, hardly ever spent longer than twenty minutes with any of them, was never taken by them into any of our *chambres des specialités*, rarely took off any of her clothing or that of her lovers, you will understand why I call her extraordinary!

When she first applied at our door, I did not even interview her. She was turned away without so much as a hearing for she looked no more than twelve years old and stood little over four feet even in her shoes. But she was a strong and determined young lady and wrote me a letter that induced me to see her at least. She said she was, in fact, twenty-two years old and had a son of three; she brought a certificate of her own birth, her school records, and several other proofs of her claim — not to mention her little three-year-old himself, an angel called Paul who became the favourite of us all.

At least I was convinced of her true age, despite the plain evidence of my eyes, which still informed me she could not possibly be more than thirteen; even so, I was not sure that the Maison ffrench was right for her. You must understand that every week I am approached by at least one gentleman with a request to procure for him a girl of twelve or less. I think I could buy half Paris with the fees I might have earned for such vile pandering. But I have always refused even to consider it, and my reasons are these:

I have never believed that the service we offer is a simple barter of an available hole for available coin. The very basis of our business is that no encounter between man and woman under our roof is limited to the mere *commerce*. One cannot deny that commerce lies at its very core, but that is not its limit. There is no house rule, no custom, and no compunction within the girls themselves to exclude tenderness, affection, genuine desire, even a sort of fleeting love on occasion. How often such emotions are added to the basic commercial transaction, is neither here nor there — and in any case it varies enormously from girl to girl, and even from day to day with the same girl. But doesn't that prove my point? There could be no such variation if the transaction were strictly limited to the mere commercial engagement; the fact that it is open to every possible emotion, too, *is* at the very heart of our service here.

Now how can one ask a girl of twelve to open herself to the emotions of a woman twice her age! It is absurd. I confess I even have doubts at taking in girls of eighteen, which is my present lower limit. Despite the fact that I was barely that age when first I started to spread the Gentlemen's Relish, I have known few other eighteen-year-olds who were sufficiently in command of their own erotic natures to benefit emotionally, as I believe I did, from such casual and frequent liaisons. If I accept such youngsters, it is only because I know they would fare worse in other houses, where no one would give a hoot about their feelings and their own private adventures in erotic self-discovery — which is, in my view, the greatest adventure open to any girl. Here, at least, we try to guide our younger sisters and help them develop a fully rounded individuality.

However, Delphine was undoubtedly twenty-two and very much in command of herself, so how could I refuse her? And it would at least stop certain gentlemen from badgering me to employ a girl at the lower end of the legally permitted age. [*The legal age of consent at that time was ten!*]

Normally I would never allow a girl to determine how the House that bears my name will conduct its business; but in Delphine's case I had to permit her to frame her own rules. None of our gentlemen, of course, had the faintest inkling that she was anything other than a sweet young flower of twelve. She brought with her a nanny for her little boy, who lodged in Delphine's own little cottage in the grounds. The story she put out was that the woman was her aunt — Tante Agate; Delphine was available for men's pleasure *"seulement dans la présence de sa tante."* To be sure, Tante Agate did not actually sit in the room with the amorous pair, but in an adjoining anteroom with the door left discreetly ajar.

Now let me tell you why Delphine Vaucher was such a superb artist. I can say it in one word: thoroughness! At ten o'clock of an evening, like any little girl of twelve, she could no longer keep her eyes open. She worked every day from two in the afternoon to ten at night, and I placed no restriction on the number of gentlemen she might pleasure in that period. Never mind that at four in the morning, when we close for the night, she was up and about again, ranting and laughing with the rest — at ten each night she would yawn and slump and giggle and show her knobbly, girlish knees and elbows . . . It was such a perfect imitation of the real thing that my heart sometimes sank into my boots for fear that I had, after all, been lured into what I would regard as a crime.

Two or three mornings every week you would see her standing outside the playground of the *Ecole des Jeunes Filles* at Ville d'Avray, watching the girls of her pretended age, studying their walk, how they shook their hair, their laughter, their games . . . soaking it all in, never believing her performance was at last perfect. Thoroughness!

And every single day she would sit naked before a looking glass and spread her thighs wide while she directed Tante Agate as to which of her pubic hairs should be plucked; she permitted herself to bear no more than two dozen, sparsely scattered and singed short — just as in a girl when she first begins to develop the divine moss that half hides, half reveals her portals of enchantment. The old woman would rub her finger and thumb in resin, to stop them slipping on the moist hairs, and pluck with a hasty twitch that caused no pain or swelling to her tender mistress's most tender parts. Thoroughness!

And then little Delphine would go to bed for an hour or so while she rubbed one fingerful of lotion after another into those same tender parts, keeping the skin there young and supple and as virginal in appearance as when she truly had been twelve. You would never believe those succulent and amorous little lips had yielded to the importunate thrust of even one lusty male. I never saw a *concon* that looked as if it had endured less traffic; yet she engulfed ten or more eager gentlemen inside that pale and delicate little bower every day. Thoroughness!

During that hour of gentle massage she induced in her own flesh a dozen or more of those transports of rapture that can overwhelm any professional girl when she least expects it. It would, of course, have been quite out of character for one of such apparently tender years to have given herself over to such abandon with any gentleman. So she charged all her desires in that way before the first of them came panting and trembling into her maidenly boudoir. Thoroughness!

And with each gentleman who visited himself upon her in that excited condition, she somehow managed the impossible. They knew, of course, that she was a harlot, a twelve-year-old harlot, but a harlot nonetheless, working in the best-patronized House in Paris. They knew that what they were about to do with her, she would do with many others that same day, just as she had done it with hundreds before them. (In fact, it was many *thousands*, but they never suspected that!) And yet she somehow managed to make them believe she had been at it no more than a week or two – a month at most – and that it was still a curious sort of novelty to her.

I used the privilege of the spyholes that allow me to supervise what goes on in all our boudoirs and *chambres des spécialitès* (did I warn you of that? Well I have done so now), and was always amazed to see how she managed the business.

She had a careless, artless gift of arousing desire in men. She made shrewd use of her high cheekbones, her big, moist, soulful eyes, and her graceful hips, which were just beginning to swell out as they do in a girl on the first threshold of womanhood. Her usual costume was that of a wee lassie who has not quite finished dressing herself, namely: a simple linen bodice that unbuttoned down the front, a very slender corset of the kind that little girls wear to flatter themselves rather than from necessity, several petticoats of a light, frothy tulle, and white lisle stockings held with plain garters just above her knees. Beneath the petticoats were flimsy cotton drawers that provided a generous opening for excited hands and venturesome fingers; it ran from her sweet little navel right through her fork and all the way up to the small of her back – and a deliciously *small* small it was, too! Her long, loose hair was caught in ribbons behind each ear, from which it fell in dizzy ringlets to well beneath her shoulder blades. The whole effect was of a girl who had arisen from her bed some ten minutes earlier and was still engaged in her morning toilette – which was, of course, perfectly calculated to drive her gentlemen callers into a frenzy of erotic excitement.

A gentleman would naturally seat himself soon after entering her room, if only to bring his head down to the level of hers. No sooner had he done so than little Delphine, clad — or half-clad, as I have described her — would slip herself shyly onto his lap. She conveyed the suggestion that this was what Tante Agate had told her to do; often she had a little lollipop in her hand, which she would go on innocently sucking in a manner that never failed to send the man into a fit of trembling. Then, the moment he touched his own trouser buttons to ease a pressure that was no doubt growing intolerable, she appeared to recollect some further instruction and hastened to complete the task for him — which she did most nimbly. One, two, three, and she would have his *flageolet* waving in the open air. Then she would charm it out with her deft little fingers and handle it as if it were a slightly naughty plaything — suggesting it was still a bit of a novelty to her. How gingerly she would explore its parts! How delicately her fingertips would tease its most sensitive regions! And how delightful was her girlish little giggle when he showed his pleasure at her apparently unintentional skill!

At that moment nine gentlemen out of ten would slip their hands under her petticoats to explore the petite and delectable furrow, coyly hidden between her birdlike thighs. She would permit them free rein for a minute or two, giving out the occasional slight gasp of happiness at his skill, then she would proudly throw up her clothing and show off her dainty jewel, flaunting it like a badge of pride. You can easily imagine the effect this had on most men! The sweet disorder of her clothing, the careless revelation of her most intimate treasure — which they were now certain they had bought too cheap (even at two hundred francs, which was her minimum fee) — the blatant invitation to stop its exquisite little gape with something more substantial than a finger. How could they refuse it!

They didn't, of course. At the slightest encouraging signs she would lift the thigh nearer him, wriggle her tiny little bottom, and engulf him into her. She took care always to keep a good handful of his rampant pego in her hot little fist, only allowing its upper three or four inches inside her. This latter caution was not strictly necessary, but it was part of her performance. After the birth of young Paul her *vagin* was quite large enough to cope with the most well-endowed gentleman, both in length and girth. However, in keeping with her masquerade, she would give out a little cry of pain if anyone fed her the full length of his manhood — unless, of course, he were one of those naturally small fellows with a *piccolo* that could not possibly hurt her. I often waited at my spyhole for that moment when an impassioned lover forgot himself and gave her a good hard prod; how I used to chuckle at the way she made him blush and apologize and promise not to do it again. Yet she rewarded them well for their courtesy, for the very next thrust — or half-thrust — would fetch from her lips a strange little cry, half-surprise, half-rapture, suggesting she was astonished to discover she could find some pleasure in it too. There was even a hint that this rapture was something no previous gentleman had ever been able to elicit.

In this position, of course, it was she who controlled the whole affair. She had more ways of wriggling her naughty little bottom and squeezing with that choice little *concon* than any two other girls put together. She was, as I say, phenomenal, and it was a rare lover indeed who was not almost lifting her off his pego on a veritable fountain of joy before a quarter of an hour was past — and never a complaint at the brevity of the encounter. Many's the gentleman who confessed to me on his way out that it had been the most intense and torrid experience he had ever enjoyed with a girl of any age. And they had not even taken off their trousers or so much as unbuttoned her bodice!

In time, of course, the simple business with her sitting on her lover's lap would no longer satisfy an experienced roué; they insisted on getting properly undressed and taking her into bed. There she revealed a new technique.

Because of her tiny body and delicate bones, she almost always lay on top of her gentlemen. Again she controlled their escalation toward the grand climax with exquisite judgement. She would allow them to caress and (if they were short enough) to suckle her tiny little breasts, which were almost all nipple; for she had nipples as big as any other woman her age. If they insisted on lying upon her, she, once again, would insist on clamping her diminutive fist around the base of their pegos to stop them thrusting in too hard — and most especially if they wanted to mount her from behind. Such gentlemen rarely went fifteen minutes with her — which would be cause for dismissal in any other girl at the Maison ffrench. But Delphine's lovers never complained; and she confessed to me that she used her fingers to help them to paradise. Even the men she rode from on top went only twenty minutes or so, because the muscles of her *vagin* were as good as those of any hand. And again there was never a complaint. They all came back for more. After a few weeks she (or Tante Agate, who pretended to handle all the money) could write her appointment book a month or more in advance.

In time, of course, even a naked encounter between the sheets was not enough for some of them. And that was where poor young Delphine made her only serious mistake. Old Chevalier de S—y importuned her for weeks to grant him the Favour the whole night through. Eventually she told him it would cost him three thousand francs, thinking that would put a stop to his pestering. He paid up without a qualm. After that, of course, she could not refuse other gentlemen who got to hear of it. She raised her price yet again, to four thousand francs, and still she was booked up weeks ahead. Now she could no longer work during the days; so, in Maison ffrench terms, she went from the ridiculous (a dozen men a day) to the sublime (a single lover each night). And she was making twice as much as before.

But it did not suit her at all. She could maintain a little-girl masquerade with any one lover for up to half an hour; after that she needed a change of audience. Her succession of single, all-night lovers soon wore her to a frazzle. After less than two months I took pity on her and sent her to a House I knew of in Milan, where she could resume her former act and — this time — refuse all offers of an all-night encounter.

You may think that so singular a harlot could have little to teach her sisters in this House, but she had. I encouraged several of our girls to watch her in action. Of course, no other girl could pretend to be as young as twelve; you would need Delphine's preternaturally juvenile looks to carry off such a deception. But many of the other girls saw ways to shave a year or three off their actual ages — and they registered a greatly improved satisfaction among their lovers as a result.

Delphine became, as it were, one of their heroines for a season. They did not slavishly copy her; no good artist will stoop to that. But they took from her what they saw would help them in their own artistic development — and that is something all artists, even the greatest, have done in their day.

§

Sheba Lejonkrona, a young Swedish harlot, was another heroine of our early days. She looked like . . . well, I was about to write that she looked like a queen, but, in fact, she didn't. Study her picture in my office and you will see a fairly standard sort of beauty — a long-legged, slender girl with large, firm breasts and a classically cool sort of face. She was blessed with the most intelligent blue-grey eyes and sensuous lips. Though she did not look like a queen, she certainly acted like one and convinced many of our gentlemen that she was, indeed, of high aristocratic lineage; even dukes and former butlers and people like that, who have a good nose for such things, were quite convinced of it.

How she came to us was something of a mystery. She brought with her a letter of recommendation from the King of Denmark, yet would not explain how she came by it. She made several close friends among the other girls while she was here yet never once spoke of her past. She told me she wished to earn a million francs and then leave the profession for ever. Of course, I've heard *that* tale a thousand times, yet somehow I believed it of Sheba. I told her she could make it much more quickly as a *grande horizontale*, for which she had all the physical charms and social graces; but she would not hear of it. She said she would be too exposed to recognition in that situation whereas here at the Maison ffrench she could remain more anonymous.

Few girls I have known valued anonymity more. She would not even tell me whether or not she had worked professionally before. She was adamant in her refusal to say even a word about her past, yet most courteous, too. She maintained that the king's letter ought to be enough to secure her a trial week, after which, if she did not give satisfaction, she would understand perfectly and leave. With some anxiety I took her on, but I need not have worried.

She was popular from the very first night — something that I, who watched her closely, found hard to understand, for she never seemed to *do* anything! She did not encourage her lovers to take her to any of our *chambres des spécialités* — perhaps because she offered such wonderful *spécialités* of her own; or, rather, one particular *spécialité*. She was, as I said, tall and willowy, with the most graceful walk you ever saw — every inch a queen. Gentlemen told me that to follow her upstairs, or just to walk closely behind her along a corridor, was enough to bring them to the point of crisis, and yet there was never the slightest hint of lewdness or indelicate provocation in her movements. She never grew excited, never gave any sign of an unruly passion. Every motion was part of one long choreography of alluringly sensual movements, each flowing into the next, creating an effect on her lovers that was almost hypnotic.

When she was naked – and she always peeled right down to her beautiful skin – she would stretch out on the bed, or the bearskin rug, or wherever her lover desired to mount her, *close her eyes*, and, lifting her gorgeously curved derrière toward him in a slow, sensual provocation, she would give out a happy little sigh as if her entire day were just about to reach the pinnacle of enchantment. In a way she turned the tables on her lovers and challenged them to give her the sort of pleasure they had paid to take from her. Some of her partners, a few, resented this, but, being well attuned to the moods of men, she would swiftly change her attitude, become as sprightly as a wood nymph, and make it up to them in measure. Yet a surprising number were intrigued by the challenge and, mounting her from behind – almost always it was from behind – would set about pleasing her as hard as they could.

Did she actually enjoy a single one of those encounters? I watched her dozens of times and was never sure. She appeared to, of course; but even if it was all mere technique, then it was still a most extraordinary bit of theatre. Most girls when they experience (or pretend to experience) a climax go rather wild; they cry out, shake their head, clench their eyes, gasp in the last extremity, clutch their lover tight, squeeze him hard, wriggle their bottoms, and in general behave as if they're on the verge of fainting or even of expiring altogether. Not so Sheba.

She hardly opened her eyes from the moment her lover took up her unspoken challenge (no, I mean her *wordless* challenge, for her body could *speak* volumes in the way it moved). But she never clenched her eyelids tight, either. An air of seraphic calm descended about her, in which, of course, the slightest disturbance became significant. After her lover had been doing his best for a few minutes she would emit a long "oo-oo-ooh" of a sigh, a mere breathing out, as she stretched luxuriously and arched her back so as to wriggle herself into an even deeper penetration.

And that, really, was all she ever did. Her sighs, which remained well spaced, grew deeper and deeper, her lecherous writhings became slower and slower, the arch of her back more and more bowed until her slender, naked body was curved like that of Valentin le Désossé, the elastic man at the Moulin Rouge. Other girls might suggest that their lovers were lifting them to the very pinnacles of erotic delight; Sheba, by her very stillness and the unbearable tension in her body, suggested the very opposite – that they were taking her into the darkest depths of that profoundest mystery of the human condition: the female *orgia*.

One gentleman, who never so much as looked at another of our girls while Sheba worked at the Maison ffrench, took her to bed twice every week for more than a year. "D'you know, Madame ffrench," he said to me after she had left us, "I never got the *physical* satisfaction with Sheba that I get with most other girls. In fact, usually after leaving her I would return to Paris and pick up a cocotte just to gratify that rather shallow need." He gave a little laugh and repeated the word in a kind of surprise. "Shallow! I should never have called it that before I knew Sheba. But she made me feel she was sharing some deep sort of mystery about herself with me. She made it seem far more important than mere physical satisfaction – and so it was, of course."

"And what was it, exactly, Monsieur?" I asked.

"That's just it." He gave a resigned smile. "I don't know. I knew it just for a few seconds while I was with her. I would see it so clearly — like the ultimate secret of life. And then the knowledge would pass from me. And so I would keep coming back to find it again. You know what the Greeks called 'seeing the Great God Pan'? Well, that was it. That was the glimpse Sheba used to give me."

§

Céleste Batim was the Maison ffrench girl whom no one should emulate. She was, without doubt, one of the most flawlessly beautiful women I ever saw. When she first applied for a position here I thought it one of the luckiest days of my life. Like many girls of the Norman race she had raven black hair and pale blue eyes. She was twenty-one and had three years' experience in our Great profession — which makes what happened all the more inexplicable. Her complexion was flawless, her figure divine, her temperament jolly and outgoing, and she was, as may be imagined, extremely popular with the gentlemen. For the first few months I could find no fault with her at all.

At around that time there was a fiery young member of the Chamber of Deputies called Pierre Carre; he is quite forgotten now but at that time he was the talk of Paris — a most striking person with hypnotic eyes and a manner that compelled attention and respect. He addressed many public meetings on his pet subjects — patriotism, France, the glories of yesterday, the glories that would return if his policies were adopted. One notable feature of those meetings was the extraordinary number of women who attended them, and the near-hysteria with which they applauded every other word he uttered.

Céleste attended one of his lectures and couldn't stop talking about him for days after — so much so that I felt impelled (if only out of curiosity) to attend his next meeting and see this New Adonis for myself. He didn't deceive me! I saw his trick very early on — indeed, I'm astonished the whole world hadn't been up in arms about it ever since he came to notoriety. Put crudely, he performed certain movements during his speech, usually at the most emotional and impassioned moments of his rhetoric — movements that hinted at the Carnal Act. Of course, he did not blatantly move his hips back and forth; the motion was slight and subtle but, to my eyes, quite unmistakable. And when he reached the climax of his oration, he pushed his fork forward like a man straining to pack every last millimetre of his cracksman into a girl's belly, and raised his hands high above his head, unfurling them in a gesture that clearly (again to my eyes) mimed the action of a fountain bursting into life. And the women went wild!

Did they realize what he was doing to them? If so, it was the most extraordinary mass collusion I ever witnessed. If they did not, then I tremble for our entire sex that can be so blatantly manipulated into feelings and actions quite contrary to our own true interests. If I had needed proof that my fears were all too real, I had not long to wait.

The very next week Céleste came running into my office and slammed the door behind her, panting as if she had run half a mile and blushing like a bride. "He's here, Madame! He's actually come here to the Maison ffrench!"

From her behaviour over the past weeks I needed no two guesses.

"Carre?" I asked.

She nodded wide-eyed, and gulped strenuously. "And he's chosen *me*."

"Then what on earth are you doing in here?" I asked crossly. "What must he think of you? Why aren't you with him?"

"Oh, I couldn't, Madame! I'm going to him at once. Please forgive me, but I needed time to gather my wits."

"But what have you told him?"

"I told him you were at his last meeting and would never forgive me if I did not tell you at once that he was here."

She was such a treasure that I easily overlooked this quite severe breach of etiquette — for once a gentleman has chosen a nymph at the Maison ffrench, she is his and the rest of the world ceases to exist for her until his appetite is quite sated. "Go on with you," I chided. "And never let it happen again."

I thought all was well and no harm done when, after two hours with her, he sent down the maid to say he would be staying all night.

My misgivings began the following morning when Céleste came down for a late luncheon — the very picture of a young girl head over heels in love. And so, indeed, it proved to be. She did not go entirely to pieces. She was experienced and professional enough to go on giving the same splendid service to all comers; but she simply went to pieces on those nights — and they soon became weekly affairs — when Carre came a-visiting. Once he almost chose another girl but he caught sight of Céleste's expression and pretended he was only teasing.

I tried talking to Céleste about it, to warn her that the stupidest thing a harlot can do is to fall in love with a client.

(The next most stupid thing is to believe that because a gentleman is relaxed and friend*ly* with her, he feels the slightest degree of friend*ship* for her. I know one girl who had been intimate with a certain advocate for years. He had taken her away on holiday and passed her off as his wife; he had shared all his family affairs with her, canvassed her opinion on gifts for his wife and children . . . in short, behaved as if he was her staunchest friend in the world. Then came the day when she needed legal help − not behind the scenes but in open court. She asked him to represent her, fully expecting him to accept the brief and to add that he would, naturally, charge her no fee. In fact, her request was the last communication that ever took place between them! That's clients for you! They're lovely fellows as long as they pay up, get up, do their best to please you, and leave in good order.)

But poor Céleste would hear none of it. She agreed with me about every other client in the world but Carre was different. Carre genuinely loved her and she thought the world of him. As soon as he could manage it, he would come and take her from the Maison ffrench and put a wedding ring round her finger. It was, of course, a situation I could not allow to persist. I hated doing it to the poor girl but she left me no choice.

One evening, when Carre visited the Maison ffrench and, as always, chose Céleste, I waylaid them at the foot of the stairs. I told her to go on up and prepare herself, and I asked him if he would very kindly come to my office for a moment or two. As soon as he closed the door behind him I taxed him with all this talk of wedding bells. He smirked and, raising his voice, said it was quite true. He plainly thought that Céleste could overhear us. I assured him there was no fear of that — and even opened the door and invited him see for himself that I spoke the truth. (But I did not tell him that my office — like many of the smaller rooms on that floor — is a mere box constructed inside what used to be the grand stateroom. So an astute girl like Céleste could easily conceal herself near the opening where the unglazed window of my "box" coincided with the original glazed window of the stateroom. She could conceal herself there and overhear every word. I suspected that was precisely what she was doing; I surely hoped so.)

"Tell me, Monsieur," I said, flattering him for all I was worth with my eyes, "why do you come here to my House?"

"Because it is the best in the world, Madame," he responded easily.

"But look at the ladies who flock to your meetings. I saw them myself only last month. There were dozens of them there who would have laid themselves down beneath you and spread their thighs as wide as you'd wish. They were desperate to go to bed with you. Or don't you realize that?"

"Of course I realize it," he exclaimed indignantly. "But nothing would induce me to stain their purity in that way."

I offered up a silent thanksgiving to whatever angel was my (or perhaps Céleste's) guardian that night, for now I knew I had him. "Stain their purity?" I echoed in disbelief. "But *they* are the ones who are willing to throw all notions of purity to the winds."

"Exactly so, Madame," he responded glacially. "They are weak vessels, like all women, but *they* are still pure. It is therefore my duty as a gentleman, as a Frenchman, as a man of high honour, to protect them from their natural womanly frailty."

"But they would tell you that the honour would be all on their side. They would consider it the greatest honour ever done to them – to be permitted to grace your bed for a single night."

"They may be frail, Madame ffrench, they may let their hearts rule their heads, but still they are the women of France! They *are* La Belle France! Their honour and purity are the sacred trust of every Frenchman with the slightest sense of the destiny of . . ."

Whenever I hear the word *destiny* on the lips of any Frenchman I know it is time to interrupt. "And my girls here, Monsieur Carre? Are they not women of France? Especially Céleste – is she not the very flower of French womanhood?"

"How can you say such a thing?" he shouted at me.

"You only have to look at her."

He visibly fought for mastery of himself and so successfully that I thought he would deny me the final nail in his coffin, the one that would clinch it shut for ever. But then he said it. Drawing himself up to his full, majestic height, he spoke these words: "It is quite clear, Madame ffrench, that your long association with your corrupt and degenerate trade has quite perverted whatever virtues and principles you may once have possessed. You are incapable of drawing even the most obvious moral distinctions. For your information, then, Céleste is a *putain* — beautiful and vivacious I grant you, but a foul *putain* nonetheless. To speak of her in the same breath as those fragrant flowers of French womanhood is a blasphemy.''

I rang a secret bell I keep for just such occasions as this.

''And all your talk of a wedding?'' I asked.

His lips curled in a sneer. ''Women whose very trade is a deception cannot complain if the trick is practised upon them, Madame!''

Pete, my big and beautifully ugly doorkeeper with an impeccable sense of timing, entered as he spoke. ''Monsieur Carre has changed his mind,'' I said coldly. ''Please send for his carriage. Oh, and Pete — he tells me he will never come here again.''

''I said no such thing,'' Carre exploded rashly.

''Pardon me, Monsieur, but I believe you did. Do you imagine you would ever be admitted here again — after what you have just said?''

''But what about Céleste?'' he whined.

I raised my voice a little and said, ''Yes, that is a difficulty. I must somehow persuade her that a little disappointment now is far preferable to the much greater one you were preparing for her.''

''Lord,'' he said contemptuously as he left, ''you *do* give yourself airs! You speak as if she still had a heart. *Putains* like that have no feelings at all.''

After he had gone I gave Céleste time to extricate herself from her hiding place. Five minutes later she was going upstairs on the arms of a gentleman whom we all knew to be the dullest creature imaginable; she was laughing with gay abandon and I think the sharpest eyed person in the world could have stared into her eyes and never guessed how her heart was breaking.

She never mentioned M. Carre again and she became once more the very model of a Maison ffrench girl. Perhaps I was wrong when I advised you not to emulate her. So instead I shall say that if you are so reckless and irresponsible as to fall in love with a client, be sure to follow Céleste to the end of that particular road.

⸿

Bubbles Velasquez, the fourth of my heroines, was, as her surname suggests, Spanish. She was dark in her hair and skin as it is possible for a white woman to be without having a touch of the tarbrush somewhere in her family. The traditional notion of those dark, Iberian beauties is of proud, temperamental women with flashing eyes and strong passions; but Bubbles, as her other name implies, was not remotely of that type. Her eyes flashed, all right, but with perpetual merriment; she could hardly complete a sentence without erupting into laughter. Everything to her was the most wonderful, most amusing game ever thought of.

She was of medium height, with lustrous jet-black hair down to her shoulder blades, wavy rather than curly, and with a blue-black sheen to it as if her own share of romantic moonlight followed her around permanently. She had a slim but muscular body that made artists wonder which tool to take out − their pencil or the one they grew up with. Her fine, dark skin made everything look sleek and well rounded, yet there was no fat on her. You could count every one of her ribs, which made her breasts look especially seductive, being ample, firm, and high, with nipples that seemed permanently swollen in desire. Her lower limbs, too, were slender and did not quite meet in her fork, so there was always a little delta of light beneath her dark delta of Venus. The oyster folds that guarded her Gates of Paradise were especially luscious and plump; and she plucked them free of moss so that their shape showed clearly in that divine clink of light I mentioned. She knew a thousand ways of provoking her lovers with glimpses of that ultimate enchantment, and she would bubble over with naughty mirth at every little sensuous movement she made.

I studied her often, too, and encouraged other girls to do the same. There was one invariable little action she performed with each and every lover (I hesitate to cal it a trick for she made it seem so natural). At the moment when his proud baton first nosed up between those beauteous lips into her centre of bliss, she would give out a delighted little cry of, "Ooh!" as if no one had ever before done that to her in quite such a scrumptious way — followed, to be sure, by the inevitable, and now thoroughly salacious, giggle.

She provoked men to suggest outrageous things to her, impossible positions, unsustainable flights of erotic phantasy. And when, inevitably, the enterprise foundered in a collapsed heap of limbs, she would laugh until the tears ran.

On the hottest summer days, the gentlemen's clubs of Paris relax their rule that members must wear waistcoats and cravats. Our equivalent relaxation at the Maison ffrench is that the gardens are no longer out of bounds to loving couples — and it is entirely thanks to Bubbles. She was upstairs one very hot day with a portly lover who looked in danger of entering the permanent form of paradise before he found its temporary equivalent between her thighs. She hit upon a desperate expedient and, throwing dressing gowns over herself and him, led him out into the shrubbery, where it was shady and the breezes cool. There, against a conveniently sloping branch of the ancient thuja by the waterfall, she brought him to his own cascade of rapture soon enough. And so every day in that long, hot summer, alfresco encounters became the rule rather than the exception.

I accepted it rather reluctantly at the beginning for it seemed indecorous to me; but I noticed that the incidence of quarrelling and backbiting among the girls fell away markedly during those weeks. Now we can hardly wait for the temperature to rise sufficiently to make such delightful encounters possible.

Again, to show you her sense of fun, I remember how Bubbles once took out a rather clumsy gentleman to the arbour by the goldfish pool, where there is a large rope hammock hooked to the rafters. They were lying in its embrace, with him pegging away at her like a threshing engine, when somehow he managed to get the rope off the hooks, dropping both of them to the floor. Fortunately there were plenty of cushions beneath them. Bubbles, of course, gave out a great scream, which quickly turned to delighted laughter as the man continued to peg away at her. We in the salon, hearing only the scream, came rushing out – gentlemen and girls together – to see what was afoot, only to be confronted by the sight of this couple, in flagrante, enmeshed in what looked like a fisherman's net, and with dear Bubbles almost in hysterics.

But I must not give the impression that Bubbles was all froth and frivolity. Like all good harlots she had a very tough streak in her character. I shall never forget one night when she showed it to the very best advantage. It occurred some months after she joined the Maison ffrench, by which time her effervescent character was well established. Three young Austrian officers turned up around ten o'clock; none of them had visited the Maison ffrench before. They were high-spirited, boisterous, perhaps a little tipsy — but certainly not drunk or they would never have been allowed in. However, they all decided they wanted Bubbles and would not take any substitute. I was spreading the relish for a gentleman upstairs, or I should have nipped the whole business in the bud. By the time I became free again they were about to strip to their jackets and duel for her with their sabres — not to the death, of course, but certainly till first blood.

Bubbles took me to one side and quickly put a certain plan to me. It required my connivance in a lie of the kind we do not usually stoop to, but exceptional circumstances demand exceptional remedies. So, trusting her instincts, I acquiesced. I called the three young fellows into my sanctum and explained the situation to them. Donna Velasquez (!), I said, was the high-born daughter of an immensely wealthy Spanish grandee of ancient lineage. She had been seduced and then abandoned by her lover, whereupon her proud father had cast her out. Her lover, having no means to support her, had brought her to me. I and the other girls had taught her what we could but this was her first night in the salon. She had only just come down, ready to take her first customer up to bed with her. "And what does she find?" I concluded. "Why, three lusty young blades ready to fight a duel over her. Gentlemen, you have frightened her to death!"

It was comical to see how their contrition fought

with their lust, which my tale had stoked to a raging
fever in each of them; and, of course, each was now
more determined than ever to have her, no matter what
the cost. Ah, those beautiful words, no matter what
the cost. They are music to a harlot's ear!

"Fortunately," I added, softening my tone, "she
has also taken something of liking to all three of you
and wishes you to be the first lovers to start her off
in this very different life. So what she proposes is that
you hire three of our boudoirs for the entire night and
she will slip into your beds in turn, passing from one
to the other all night long. If you will do this, she will
take no other lovers than you — all the night."

They could not wait to get out their purses! But the
initial sticking point remained — to whom should fall
the high honour of initiating her into The Life? It was
solved with the aid of a deck of cards. I do not
remember the young fellows' names, if, indeed, I ever
knew them, but I shall call them Athos, Porthos, and
d'Artagnan, after a time-hallowed custom vis-à-vis
military lovers in the big-number Houses of Paris.

D'Artagnan won. He was the shortest and youngest
of the three, being about twenty-one years old. He was
also the least handsome, having little but his youth and
figure to commend him; but he was ugly-interesting
rather than ugly-repellent. Athos, the oldest, in his
mid-twenties, and far and away the most handsome,
was to be next. Porthos, a decent, nondescript
youngster, was last. D'Artagnan left in half swoon to
claim his prize.

I then had an inspiration of my own. It so happened
that Clifford was due to try out a new applicant that
evening, a lovely young lady from Périgord called
Arlette. She had long, wavy flaxen hair, bright blue

eyes, large, sensuous lips, a slender figure, and full, firm breasts. She seemed a fine recruit to the Maison ffrench in every way, but there was something about her that disturbed me — those large lips, perhaps, which suggested a wanton vulgarity that would not do at all. So I told Athos and Porthos that, for an extra three hundred francs (on top, that is, of the thousand each had already paid for his boudoir and the favours of the Donna Velasquez), I could arrange a delightful exhibition to stimulate their imaginations and while away the hour or so that now awaited Athos. To Porthos I promised yet other delights to relieve his further hour of torment.

Clifford was very happy with the arrangement; he always did love an audience. I then ran to see how my proud Iberian beauty would manage the business with d'Artagnan. Bubbles, who had passed many a vigil watching little Delphine at work, now adapted her pranks and wiles to the character of a young Spanish girl of tempestuous desires and no experience. It was uncanny to watch her in the role, especially when I knew her as a fun-loving little hedonist to whom everything was deliciously naughty and nothing came as a surprise.

She undressed d'Artagnan with the absorption of a little girl playing with her dolls. He was very pleased to leave it all to her, half-lying back in a voluminous chair, hands linked behind his head, gazing down at the solemn young wench with amused affection. When she drew off his trousers it freed a slumbering giant of an organ, which held his shirt aloft like the centre-pole of a circus tent. She gave out a little Delphine-like *ooh!* of delight and begged with her eyes for permission to uncover it entirely, which he conveyed with eager nods.

The sight of her dark, nimble fingers plucking daintily at his shirt buttons and drawing the taut linen further and yet further aside almost gave him a fit; I could see his hands twitching to join hers and make short work of what she was turning into a fearful tease. But at last it was there, fat, sleek, and magnificent, fully eight inches long and thick as a girl's wrist; as it emerged into the candlelight it stretched to its full majesty and the hot, scarlet knob burst from its foreskin and hammered at the air to the throbbing of his heart.

"Oh! Oh! Oh!" The young Spanish girl had never seen anything so sublime and arousing in all her days.

Gingerly she touched it and gave out a long, deep sigh. By some magic her untutored fingers found precisely those places where their gentle caress sent thunder and lightning through his veins and he had to snatch the prize from her grasp before she brought it all to a premature conclusion.

Full of remorse she reached forward and kissed it. Jokingly he began to beat her about the face with it, using it as a play truncheon. She chuckled and tried to give it little nips with her teeth. And, to make a proper no-hands game of it, she clasped her fingers together behind her back. This had the effect of revealing to his astonished eyes almost all of those deliciously firm but fulsome breasts whose ripeness was already one of the toasts of fashionable Paris . . .

And so it went on for just over an hour. Childlike in her sense of wonder, artless in her use of her charms, she led young d'Artagnan to seduce her into the splendours of that most ancient dance of all. After each new thrill she stared at him in a trapped and helpless kind of awe, implying not only that she had

231

never guessed such pleasures were possible but also that it wouldn't take many more of them to drop her in a swoon of passion.

At last he was exhausted. She, by contrast, now gave the impression of getting into her second wind. "More?" she begged.

He groaned and told her to go to Athos.

"Oh yes!" she exclaimed, as if she had forgotten all about him — another new toy to unpack and play this delightful game with.

Poor Athos was so randy by the time she came to him that his cracksman was about ready to shatter with its brittleness. "Oh!" she exclaimed naively. "It's as good as d'Artagnan's was at the beginning. He's done such thrilling things to me with it, I can't even begin to tell you — but now it won't go at all."

Athos *rose* to the challenge and, to give him his due, stayed in a fair old state of excitement for the next hour, too, while she made one more fantastic discovery after another. At last, when it lay lank and limp between his exhausted thighs, she flung herself on top of him, wriggling like an eel, and begged him to make it stand once more.

"Go to Porthos," he moaned. "For pity's sake go!"

"Oh yes!" she exclaimed, as if she had forgotten all about him — yet another new toy to unpack and play this even-more-delightful game with.

"Oh Captain Porthos!" she sighed as she slipped between his sheets. "This is the happiest night of my life. No wonder they go to such astonishing lengths to keep such blissful knowledge from us unmarried girls. I tell you, if I had known such thrills were possible, I would have come to Madame ffrench when I was twelve!"

"I thought we might do this," he murmured, showing her some photographs in an album I had left for his comfort.

"Oh, I've just been doing that," she said in a disappointed tone.

"Or this?" He flipped a couple of pages.

"Oh yes!" she brightened. "Let's! Captain d'Artagnan was superb at that."

"What about this, then?" His tolerance was growing thinner with each word.

She looked at it critically and said, "I can't remember which of them I did that with, but I know I did it with one of them."

"I don't give a brass kopec what you did with either of those . . ."

He got no further because she was on him like a kitten, stopping his lips with kisses and rubbing her nakedness all over his. "Silly darling," she cajoled. "I'm only teasing. Surely you know what I really want to do?"

"What?" he asked, breaking back into a broad smile once more.

"This!" she cried, snatching up the album — closed — and sandwiching it between them. "Everything that's in it! Everything a man and a girl can *possibly* do together! I want to feel it all, know it all, have it all! I want you to make this night absolutely unforgettable for me!"

Porthos possessed more stamina than his colleagues and it was ninety minutes before Bubbles was free to put the second phase of her plan into operation.

She took a hasty bath, perfumed and powdered herself again, lubricated well all around Cupid's valley and love lane, and went back to d'Artagnan once more.

"Are you recovered enough for another round of these wonderful pleasures?" she asked.

He groaned.

"It's all right!" she assured him. "The other two said not to disturb you if you still weren't quite up to it yet. They're keen as mustard so I can easily come back to you later."

He groaned again but opened up his sheets to let her in.

Forty-five minutes later she went to Athos and said more or less the same — and got more or less the same response.

An hour later it was the turn of Porthos. "You know this wonderful sort of fire of happiness that spreads through my body," she told him. "Captain Athos says its proper name is *orgasm*. It's Ancient Greek, you know. And I can't seem to stop myself from having them. It's dreadful! I'm going to be dead with exhaustion before tomorrow comes."

It took poor Athos, already "dead with exhaustion," almost an hour before he rose to even one more orgasm.

Then another quick bath, more powder and perfume and cocoa butter, and back she went to d'Artagnan. "From this night on" she announced boldly, "I shall only grant my Favour to Austrians. Heavens, you are not men, you are gods! No wonder you've the richest and most powerful empire in the history of the world — and no wonder the emperor is so proud of you!"

Athos, Porthos, d'Artagnan, Athos, Porthos, d'Artagnan, Athos, Porthos, d'Artagnan, Athos . . . yes, Athos was the first to crack. By then Bubbles was half-way through her sixth round and the blear fingers of a terrible dawn were inching over the window sills of boudoirs that, for three lucky men, had changed from pleasure palaces into torture chambers during eight brief interminable hours.

"But you can, you can!" she cried like a spoilt and angry child. "I know you can!"

And down she went and sucked his pitiable little cracksman back to an exhausted, semi-turgid rod. The pain was almost intolerable — but so, as the poor fellow now discovered is the male imperative to serve any willing female who wriggles her derrière at him in an appropriately inviting manner. She did not stop wriggling her derrière at them in her deliciously inviting manner until each of them had begged her for mercy — and even then she made them gratify her insatiably voluptuous body one more time.

Two days later she collapsed in exhaustion; but during those two days she lived like a true conqueror, drunk on the fumes of victory. The three musketeers were carried to private rooms elsewhere in the house and did not stir for almost twenty-four hours. As they departed, they were heard boasting to each other how many times they got it up, how they'd almost killed the delicate Donna with the orgiastic pleasures they gave her, and how swiftly they'd be back to give her more.

In fact, that was the last we ever saw of them.

And the moral of the tale — as far as *you* are concerned, sweet nymph — is that, no matter how successful you are at establishing a particular professional character, you must, like dear Bubbles, be ready to drop it in the twinkling of an eye when something quite different is called for.

§

Véronique Delacourt was a sweet little gazelle, shy yet not timid, modest yet not shrinking. She came to us straight from her convent school, a virgin, a simple girl from a small country town in the Midi. Her mother had died when she was fourteen and her father remarried soon after. She and her stepmother fell out and she was sent away into the care of her late mother's sister, who (though no one in the family, nor any of her friends and neighbours, knew it) had been a highly successful courtesan in Vienna between the ages of seventeen and forty; she had moreover put by a considerable fortune. The lesson was not lost on Véronique. The aunt coached her in all she knew and then brought her to me on her eighteenth birthday. I accepted her without a moment's hesitation − a decision that was fully justified the following week when we auctioned her maidenhead for over ten thousand francs. She stayed with us for two years and then, at the age of twenty, married an Austrian nobleman − one of the New Nobility, it is true, but still better than nothing.

Véronique had the most singular manner. She behaved as if she never lost the bloom of her innocence. I remember her first night down in the salon, after the lucrative (and, happily for her, most enjoyable) loss of her maidenhead. She was snapped up almost at once by a Colonel E—y, a rather brusque and fastidious customer; he was never rough or unkind to a girl but he had high expectations and kept her up to them to the last minute. He was hard work, but if you pleased him, he showed it and left you feeling you had really achieved something.

So, having doubts as to whether our shy little doe would be a match for him, I followed them up and watched. I need not have worried, of course; her wise old aunt had prepared her for everything. As she reached the foot of the stairs she turned back and glanced at the other girls with the most extraordinary expression — a smile that seemed to beg their understanding for her weakness, a smile that seemed to say, "I don't usually do naughty things like this!"

He took her to one of the most luxurious boudoirs on the first floor. Now the usual thing, on entering those rooms, is for the girl to go around the room turning up the lamps; gentlemen who have just bought an armful of beautiful and costly charms like to examine their beguilements and allure in the best possible light. But Véronique did no such thing. She just stood with her back against the wall, only a foot from the door, and smiled that same enigmatic, slightly naughty little smile.

The Colonel looked at her, slightly askance, and set off to turn up the lamps himself. He took no more than one pace before he felt her delicate little fingers plucking him by the sleeve.

"Eh?" he grunted testily, turning back to face her.

Still that smile, naughty, provocative . . . tense. She swallowed heavily and her bosom trembled; you would swear she was already in the grip of an amatory passion that nothing would shake, except for her own ultimate satisfaction.

"What's this?" he asked. I never heard him less crisp, less sure of himself; it was a most unusual blend of curiosity, delight, and alarm.

Briefly she fluttered her eyes at him; they gleamed almost supernaturally in that dim light. She looked away again as if the sight of him was too enthralling to bear. I never saw a girl convey more with less effort.

"What?" he repeated, and now his tone was almost solicitous, as if he were entreating her to tell him what she wanted and he'd do his best to serve her.

She moved an inch or two away from him, bringing her right breast into the lamplight. She swayed back into the dark of his shadow, nearer him than before, and raised those daintiest of fingers to a button on her chemise — not the top one but one between her breasts. She let her hand drop without opening it, as if she was now almost swooning with desire for him.

He would have been carved from stone not to take the hint. A moment later, like the shyest of student lovers, he slipped his hand inside her partly opened chemise and touched her breast. She emitted a small, strangled sigh and, breathing deeply in, braced herself against his hand and responded to its every caress with shy little movements of her own.

At first I thought it the most wonderful act I had ever witnessed, especially from one so new to the profession; but then I realized she was being herself — a reticent, even secretive, young girl, straight from a convent, making her first passionate experiments in the world of carnal adventure. And old E—y was so captivated by it that the colonel, the major, the captain . . . all fell away from him, leaving the raw young lieutenant to rediscover that fiery, beautiful, almost innocent ardour of his youth.

He enjoyed her Favour twice that evening, which he had never done before with another girl of the Maison ffrench. Usually he directed the whole thing like a military operation, keeping the girl busy at pleasuring him, this way and that, until, like a victory to crown a well-fought engagement, he came inside her in a mighty cannonade of liquid spasms, all the mightier for his masterly delay. But there he was that night, astonishing himself in an old-fashioned perpendicular jig like any fresh baccalaureate in a back-alley doorway — and adoring every minute of it. All ten minutes of it, in fact.

After that she sprang to life, more like a tigress than the timid gazelle he had led up here. She pressed her now naked body hard against him and bore him backward to the bed. There she entwined herself with him, wriggling and slithering over and under him, shivering with amatory passion, giving out little animal cries of delight, stretching herself in unbearable ecstasies, showering him with kisses, licks, and bites — in short, overwhelming him with a display of female lust the like of which he had never before witnessed.

My memory now leaps forward two long years, to her very last frolic with a lover in the Maison ffrench, the month before her marriage. It was almost an exact replica of that first. It must by then have been a mere performance, of course; after almost three thousand repetitions with more than a thousand lovers it could hardly have been otherwise. And yet you would have thought it the first time for her, all over again.

More than my other four heroines, Véronique exemplifies what I mean when I say that we at the Maison ffrench are selling something infinitely more promising and exciting than the mere availability of our bodies. We sell glimpses of the impossible, and for a fleeting moment we make them more real than anything the gentlemen are capable of feeling on the merely physical plane. The fact that those glimpses vanish again when the heat and the passion are done is all to our advantage. The mere sight of the Promised

Land is enough to make our lovers return and return again, to dance that everlasting jig of life between our all too fleshly thighs!

§

I have picked five heroines for your education; I could pick a further fifty — but these will do for present purposes. Gentlemen may think that all they require of a harlot is a complaisant body and an open c. — and if that is all she gives them, they go away satisfied (I do not say happy) and never know what they missed — until they meet one like Delphine, or Sheba, or Céleste, or Bubbles, or Véronique . . . or, let us hope, *you!* After that they are your slaves and addicts until the day of their dying.

Yes, yours! Profiting from these examples, you (who may not yet have traded your jewel for that ever-flowing gold) already know more than most of the gentlemen you will one day gratify so mightily and with such profit. You already know that they visit Houses like ours in search of something beyond mere bodily stimulation, mere physical relief. Deep within them is an unfulfilled need for something mystical, something magical, something that a woman who merely thinks of herself as an available hole can never provide.

Somewhere inside you, at the very heart of your being, is an ethereal quality, something essentially feminine and mysterious, which they will be privileged to awaken from its slumbers so that it may possess you. With Bubbles it was excitement, adventure, laughter. With Sheba it was an orgiastic power, awesome to behold. With Delphine it was something she merely hinted at — a young girl's first reluctant awakening to the magic of erotic dance. She managed to suggest that, although it frightened her a little — even repelled her, perhaps, with its very strangeness — nonetheless there was something about it that held her in a spell of fascination. Her lover had managed to give her the first small glimpse of the wonders that lay in wait for her in those forbidden games. With Véronique it was perhaps the most essentially feminine mystery of all — an astonishing blend of shyness and reticence with a carnal hunger that compelled her lovers to their utmost exertions in order to satisfy her.

I have obviously chosen extreme cases of what you might call our *genre*. But please understand that there is no compunction on you to choose any of them as your own particular model. You can adapt a little bit of each if you will, or set out to make your own discoveries. The vital thing for you to remember is that you must offer *something* of that *otherness* these four skilled girls so successfully represented. If you find you cannot do so, then, sadly, you do not belong at the Maison ffrench, no matter how pretty your looks nor how seductive your figure.

I will conclude by telling you another little "trade secret" that M. H—, my artist-friend, imparted to me. When I asked him if he still had heroes now that he was so famous himself, he held up his fingers and said, "These! Yes, Madame, these are all my heroes now. I used to look at the world with my eyes, analyze it with my brain and send messages to these ten little fellows, telling them how to wield the brush, mix the colours, and so on. But no more. That was when my art was all in my head. Now it's trickled down to my fingers themselves and resides there all the time. Often I just stand before my latest canvas and watch them with dumbfounded amazement as they work away before my very eyes. 'Where did you learn such tricks?' I ask them. But, of course, they cannot answer me.''

Rest assured, sweet nymph! The same will be true of *your* skills in your own very different art one day. You will lie in bed with your lover of the moment, watching your own body with dumbstruck amazement. You, too, will ask her where she learned such tricks; and, like M. H—'s fingers, she will be quite unable to tell you!

⚘

Conclusion

I hope my little ''anatomy'' of my House, our deals, our daily arrangements, and some of the more outstanding girls who have worked here has at last enabled you to decide what to do with *your* anatomy! Earlier versions of this booklet used to finish at this point with some remarks of general encouragement to the girl whose mind was only ninety-nine per cent made up. She, of course, would be one who had never before worked in our noble calling.

However, I am always striving to improve my advice (as I strive to improve every aspect of our delightful business). Some girls who sold their Jewel for the first time at the Maison ffrench have suggested that my text concentrates too much upon how an *individual* girl should behave with an *individual* client. I therefore fail to give a true impression of the sheer numbers involved – even with our limit of four clients a day on twelve of the twenty-one working days that kindly Dame Nature allows a girl each month. So here, on the principle of, ''Don't say later that I never warned you!'' , is an outline of what you may expect of *La Vie Horizontale* in general.

The typical girl at the Maison ffrench remains under our roof for about one year. She then progresses to other Houses, often in other lands. We maintain good connections with Houses of a similar high class in cities from Stockholm to San Francisco. Every week, I receive at least twenty letters from girls who used to work here, all of which add to my store of knowledge concerning this universal demimonde. From these continuing contacts, and from girls who, having worked their way around the gay capitals of Europe, return to their alma mater for a while, I can fairly confidently tell you that a girl who joins our profession at, say, eighteen, will probably leave it before she is thirty. A typical pattern for her life during those dozen well-paid years would be: Paris, Rome, Munich, Vienna, Prague, Berlin, London, New York, New Orleans, San Francisco, Lisbon, and Madrid — spending roughly a year at each House. In some countries, especially Italy and Spain, the Houses have arrangements with each other to move the girls around every three or four months; so a girl nominally working at a House in Rome, say, will do several months in Florence, Milan, and Naples, too.

During that time she will part her thighs, or some other desired orifice, for about twenty-five thousand clients. Her share of the fee will amount to about £17,850 sterling [*or about one and a quarter million in 1990s currency*!]. The most prudent girl I know managed to keep aside some £11,000. She was thirty years old then. She now lives in retirement in Shropshire, in England, where she rents a small country estate and indulges her passion for riding to hounds every day of the week during the season. Though she poses as a widow, everyone there knows how she made her money; but because she behaves impeccably now, gives to the right charities, supports the right causes, and is the pillar of her local parish, nobody has cut her. She is courted madly, gallantly, assiduously by half a dozen bachelors but tells them all she will never marry "again."

If you really wish to know what twenty-five thousand clients entails, let me pass on some astonishing statistics kindly supplied to me by an amiable but utterly insane Englishman who patronized the Maison ffrench a year or two ago. He claimed to have made a study of Houses of Pleasure all around the world, especially those of the superior kind. He told me that the typical encounter between a girl and her client in superior Houses lasts forty-six minutes and thirty-seven seconds; and during that time the most delicate few inches of flesh in her body will be parted by, on average, 463 in-and-out proddings of his male organ − at the climax of which that same organ will anoint her with an ecstatic libation of one centilitre of life's quickening fluid.

[*Charlotte gives no positive clue to the identity of this "amiable but utterly insane Englishman," but he can surely be none other than dear Walter who wrote his erotic memoirs as a counterblast to the rather mechanical pornography of* My Secret Life. *I recently published an edited version of this other Walter's memoirs under the title* A Victorian Lover of Women, *uniform with this present volume. Readers of that book will recall his statistical* tour de force *among the delectable young ladies of the French Hareem in Constantinople the coincidence of the figure 463 for the number of "penile thrusts" a working girl's vagina receives during each encounter with a client is too great to be explained as chance.* — FR]

So now, if you have stomach for it, you may work out precisely what awaits you if you decide to join us on the sunnier bank of the Rubicon. During the next ten years you will spend just over twenty thousand hours in intimate embrace with around twenty-five thousand gentlemen. In their rapture they will baptize you with enough of their juice to fill ten dozen magnums of champagne — despite which (though you may find it hard to believe) you stand a mere four-in-ten chance of being quickened with child. In their eagerness to taste that rapture between your thighs they will part with just under £45,000, of which almost £18,000 will be your share. You will have banked as much of it as your character and temperament allow.

In short, if you meet those criteria of aptitude, disposition and humour that I set out in the beginning of this little booklet, you will find the work both pleasant and character-forming. It will be pleasant in that you will meet hundreds of fine, interesting gentlemen who will talk to you with a candour and intimacy they would offer no other woman; they will include kings, princes, and aristocrats of every rank as well as prominent men in the world of government, industry, and high finance; men who control the destiny and fortunes of millions will lie at your feet and adore you. And it will be character-forming in that you will also meet thousands of dull men, and several dozen absolute rotters. And you will learn to take them all in your stride!

You will live well and dress well in the most glittering cities of the world. You will make deep and lasting friendships with dozens of women of all backgrounds and nations. You will join a female freemasonry that goes back to the dawn of civilization itself. And you will leave our Noble profession with sufficient competence to keep you in style for the rest of your days, whether you choose to marry or no. Can you, in your present situation in life, "choose to marry or no"?

Is it any wonder that we at the Maison ffrench must regretfully reject offers from dozens of bright, keen, pretty young girls each and every week?

Thus I end my modest little booklet. Thus, too, I cease my narrative and bid my Gentle Reader farewell. But, perhaps, if he (or she) has found stimulus to action in these pages . . . perhaps I should merely say, *Till we meet again!*

Sweet Fanny

The erotic education of a Regency maid

Faye Rossignol

'From the time I was sixteen until the age of thirty-two I "spread the gentlemen's relish" as the saying goes. In short, I was a Lady of Pleasure.'

Fanny, now the Comtesse de C———, looks back on a lifetime of pleasure, of experiment in the myriad Arts of Love. In letters to her granddaughter and namesake, she recounts the erotic education of a young girl at the hands of a mysterious Comte – whose philosophy of life carries hedonism to voluptuous extremes – and his partners in every kind of sin. There is little the young Fanny does not experience – and relate in exquisite detail to the recipient of her remarkably revealing memoirs.

FICTION/EROTICA   0 7472 3275 X

A selection of bestsellers
from Headline

FICTION

RINGS	Ruth Walker	£4.99 □
THERE IS A SEASON	Elizabeth Murphy	£4.99 □
THE COVENANT OF THE FLAME	David Morrell	£4.99 □
THE SUMMER OF THE DANES	Ellis Peters	£6.99 □
DIAMOND HARD	Andrew MacAllan	£4.99 □
FLOWERS IN THE BLOOD	Gay Courter	£4.99 □
A PRIDE OF SISTERS	Evelyn Hood	£4.99 □
A PROFESSIONAL WOMAN	Tessa Barclay	£4.99 □
ONE RAINY NIGHT	Richard Laymon	£4.99 □
SUMMER OF NIGHT	Dan Simmons	£4.99 □

NON-FICTION

MEMORIES OF GASCONY	Pierre Koffmann	£6.99 □
THE JOY OF SPORT		£4.99 □
THE UFO ENCYCLOPEDIA	John Spencer	£6.99 □

SCIENCE FICTION AND FANTASY

THE OTHER SINBAD	Craig Shaw Gardner	£4.50 □
OTHERSYDE	J Michael Straczynski	£4.99 □
THE BOY FROM THE BURREN	Sheila Gilluly	£4.99 □
FELIMID'S HOMECOMING: Bard V	Keith Taylor	£3.99 □

*All Headline books are available at your local bookshop or newsagent,
or can be ordered direct from the publisher. Just tick the titles you want
and fill in the form below. Prices and availability subject to change without
notice.*

Headline Book Publishing PLC, Cash Sales Department, PO Box 11,
Falmouth, Cornwall, TR10 9EN, England.

Please enclose a cheque or postal order to the value of the cover price
and allow the following for postage and packing:
UK & BFPO: £1.00 for the first book, 50p for the second book and 30p
for each additional book ordered up to a maximum charge of £3.00
OVERSEAS & EIRE: £2.00 for the first book, £1.00 for the second
book and 50p for each additional book.

Name ....

Address ....

....

....